DYING FALL

DYING FALL

Cynthia Harrod-Eagles

SEVERN
HOUSE

First world edition published in Great Britain in 2021 and the USA in 2022
by Severn House, an imprint of Canongate Books Ltd,
14 High Street, Edinburgh EH1 1TE.

Trade paperback edition first published in Great Britain and the USA in 2022
by Severn House, an imprint of Canongate Books Ltd.

severnhouse.com

British Library Cataloguing-in-Publication Data
A CIP catalogue record for this title is available from the British Library.

33614082773580

ISBN-13: 978-0-7278-5018-8 (cased)
ISBN-13: 978-1-4483-0731-9 (trade paper)
ISBN-13: 978-1-4483-0730-2 (e-book)

All Severn House titles are printed on acid-free paper.

Typeset by Palimpsest Book Production Ltd.,
Falkirk, Stirlingshire, Scotland.
Printed and bound in Great Britain by
TJ Books, Padstow, Cornwall.

To Tony, for tea, sympathy, and always being there.
I couldn't do it without you.

ONE

The Fault Is in Our Stairs

'I thought after all this time I'd know everywhere in Shepherd's Bush,' said Slider.

The crawling traffic stopped for a red light up ahead, and he inched up to the tail and halted obediently. The sun glanced ferociously off glass and metallic paint. The sky was gin-clear; the summer heat was bright and dry, unusually for London. A rash of sleevelessness had overcome the locals: who said only Americans had the right to bare arms? Shepherd's Bush Green was littered with sun worshippers, the men stripped to the waist – the glare off their blue-white bodies could have brought a plane down. Every café with an inch of pavement to call its own had put out chairs and tables. The coffee-sippers had that slightly stunned-herring look worn by a Londoner when it gets warm enough to sit outdoors. It happened so rarely.

'But I've never heard of Dunkirk House,' Slider went on.

'Neither have I,' said Atherton. Left elbow resting out of the window, he was looking for a house number, but Uxbridge Road was an ancient high road and almost nobody displayed their number on their frontage, commercial or domestic. 'They had that film on again last night.'

'What film?' Slider asked vaguely.

'*Dunkirk.*'

'Oh. I've seen that. Disappointing.'

'Why?'

'I thought it was going to be William Shatner's autobiography.'

'Ho ho. Please remember I'm your bag man, not your straight man,' said Atherton. The traffic began to move again. 'It must be somewhere hereabouts. We're nearly at Askew Road.'

Askew Road marked the boundary of their territory. Beyond that, it was Acton's ground.

'When I first came here,' Slider said, 'I thought it was A-*skew* Road – as in, not straight. Because it runs at a slant between Goldhawk and Uxbridge Road.'

Atherton snorted. 'I suppose you think Prime Minister Asquith was not very *squith*.'

'He was a Yorkshireman,' Slider gave back sturdily. 'They *pride* themselves on not being *squith*.'

Atherton pointed. 'There's our wheels. That must be it.'

Slider indicated and pulled over to the kerb to park behind the department's car: model, Ford Asbo; colour, Boring Blue. On the far side of the pavement there was a length of high brick wall – the usual Victorian stock brick of which ninety per cent of London was built, its original yellow darkened by a century of soot. Too high to see any building behind. It was an anonymous, unremarkable length of wall that the eye would never trouble the brain to notice, though you passed it every day.

There was a tall gate of vertical iron bars, but it had been boarded from the other side so that nothing could be seen through it. It was guarded by PC D'Arblay, trying to look as if he just happened to have come to rest there, like a fallen leaf. Happily there were no pedestrians around to pay undue attention to him – people didn't tend to walk along this side in this section of the Uxbridge Road, there being no shops – so no curious crowd had gathered.

D'Arblay looked startled as Slider got out of the car. He licked his lips nervously. 'I didn't expect them to send you, sir,' he said. A man who has woken the mighty behemoth of a murder investigation was bound to fear the consequences if he'd got it wrong.

'They sent me,' Atherton said.

'I just came along for the ride,' Slider explained. 'Nice day, fresh air, etcetera. Anonymous nine-nine-nine call, wasn't it?'

'Yes, sir. From a payphone.' The sun was almost vertical, and despite a short-sleeved shirt, and standing in the narrow strip of shade along the wall, he must have been uncomfortably hot.

'I didn't know there were any phone boxes left that still worked,' Slider said.

'It was one of those inside Westfields, sir. They have security guards walking about. So they don't get vandalized. Informant was a female, sir, and not a kid. The operator said it sounded like an elderly woman, so they took it seriously. Sergeant Paxman sent me round here just to be sure, and there was the body all right, at the foot of the stairs like the informant said. It looked at first glance like an accident, but it just didn't sit right with me, sir.' His bright blue eyes were steady, neither appealing nor defiant. He was standing by his judgement, and Slider liked that. A copper without a copper's instinct was a near liability. Anyway, he knew D'Arblay, and trusted him.

'All right, walk me in.'

The gate had no lock, just a simple thumb latch; behind it, the garden was an overgrown mess of weeds, long grass, brambles and flourishing buddleia, with a path from the gate to the front door. The house was not large for the size of the plot: a late-Victorian double-fronted villa, with bay windows and mock-Tudor woodwork on the gables.

'Five or six bedrooms, if I'm any judge,' said Slider. 'Plus the attics.'

'Doesn't look lived in,' said Atherton. 'No curtains at the upstairs windows.'

The ground floor windows had internal shutters that were closed. The windows were dirty, paint everywhere was peeling, and the stucco, which had once been painted white, was dingy grey. Squatting in its rampant garden, the place looked forlorn and abandoned, even on a bright, sunny day.

'So what's the story with this place?' Slider asked.

'I don't know anything about it, sir,' D'Arblay said, looking almost shamefaced. He prided himself on his local knowledge. He had been a community liaison officer before there was such a thing, back in the days when Community Policing was just known as Policing. 'I've never been to a call-out here. Never heard of any trouble connected with the address.'

The front door was the original Victorian one, panelled, with two narrow vertical lights of stained glass depicting stylized lilies with green leaves. In the centre of each was a small circle of clear glass, presumably so that the householder could see who was outside before opening the door. Above the door was a square stained-glass fanlight with a scenic design, a view of a castle on a high bank over a river. Amazingly, all the glass was intact.

'Was the front door closed like this?'

'Yes, sir.'

He had knocked and rung the bell, without response. 'Then I looked through the clear bit in the stained glass, and I saw a woman lying at the foot of the stairs. She wasn't moving at all. So I used a mica sheet to slip the lock.' Mica sheets were one of the many handy implements a well-tooled officer carried these days. 'There's a deadlock, as you can see, sir, but it wasn't engaged.'

Well, you wouldn't expect it to be if someone was inside.

'She's obviously been dead a while, sir. She's quite stiff. But I've called in for the police surgeon.' Even a corpse with its head detached had to be declared dead by a fully qualified expert in deadness; the copper on the spot couldn't assume it.

D'Arblay had put the door on the latch, and pushed it open now. Slider and Atherton gloved up.

The entrance hall was spacious in the Victorian way, high-ceilinged, with doors to the front-facing rooms on either side and a passage off to the left, presumably to the kitchen area. The stairs were straight ahead, nicely wide with turned balusters and handrail, and a decorative newel post topped with a large ball. The floor of the hall was covered with elderly linoleum – the sort with the parquet pattern that was popular in the fifties – while down the passage there were only bare floorboards. Up the stairs was a central carpet runner, with bare wood either side that had been varnished dark brown. The carpet was dark red with a vaguely Turkish pattern.

The air smelt dry and dusty, with none of the scents resident people create around them: food, laundry, cleaning, hygiene. The house was silent.

The woman was lying bunched up at the foot of the stairs, one knee drawn up, the foot of the other leg resting up on the lowest tread, one arm outflung, head turned to one side.

She looked in her thirties, slim, with short wavy hair. She was wearing new-looking, light-navy, cotton trousers, cut like jeans but obviously smarter and of a more expensive material than denim, and a blue-and-white striped shirt. She had on some kind of nylon foot-covering, probably pop socks, but no shoes. A glance up the stairs revealed two low-heeled black court shoes lying on different stairs halfway down. The gold chain of some sort of necklace gleamed at the back of her neck, and she wore a nice-looking watch on a leather strap. There was a gold and diamond ring, something like an eternity ring, on the middle finger of her left hand, but the ring finger was bare.

'You see, sir?' D'Arblay appealed. 'The way she's lying – it's too neat. I've seen people who've fallen downstairs. It's as if we're *meant* to think that's what happened.'

Yes, Slider thought. That foot resting up the stair, the outflung arm: it was . . . *artistic*. He crouched down to look more closely. There was a massive blow to the right side of the head, which had made a sticky mess, but it hadn't bled much, so death must have been almost instantaneous.

'That's the other thing, sir,' D'Arblay said. 'I couldn't see what she could have hit her head on – not that hard, at any rate.'

'Yes,' said Slider. A fall down stairs was usually a sliding, bumping process. People didn't do perfect swan-dives from the top of the flight. They tried to save themselves, which made for a messy tumble, with a good chance of broken bones and the possibility of a bang on the head against a baluster or a stair nosing. But a blow like this . . . And from the point of view of a person coming downstairs, the handrail was on the left, while the wound was on the right side. How would that have worked?

'I think your instincts are right,' Slider said. D'Arblay didn't exactly smile, but a tension went out of his face. 'And then there are her tights, stockings, whatever they are. Look at the heels,' Slider said. Each heel had a ragged hole in it.

'I didn't notice that,' D'Arblay said apologetically.

'That doesn't look like wear,' said Atherton. 'It looks like tear.'

'Exactly,' said Slider. 'If she was dragged by someone holding her under the armpits – the easiest way to move a corpse a short distance – the heels would drag along the floor.'

'Lino's smooth,' Atherton said. They all glanced towards the kitchen passage. 'But bare floorboards are always snaggy.'

Slider stood up. 'Where have you walked?' he asked D'Arblay.

'Nowhere, sir. Just from the door up to the body and back. As soon as I saw her, I didn't want to contaminate anything.'

'Good lad. Do we know who she is?'

'There's only her trouser pockets, sir, and you can see the back ones are empty. I haven't tried the front pockets, obviously, not wanting to move her. And I haven't seen a handbag,' said D'Arblay.

There was a small wooden table with barley-sugar legs just inside the door, the place where a person entering would naturally put down their bag or keys, but there was nothing on it but dust. The next most likely places were the kitchen and the bedroom.

'Atherton, just peep into the kitchen and the other downstairs rooms for a handbag. I'll look upstairs.'

Stepping carefully on the side of the stair, Slider went up, passing the abandoned shoes. They looked fairly new, and were well-polished. At the top, there was a hole in the carpet, just where a person about to come down might catch a toe and stumble forwards. It was obviously an old carpet, and might well be worn just in that place, but Slider, bending for a closer inspection, saw that the exposed under-fibres looked light-coloured and clean. As if someone had recently cut the hole on purpose, either to deliberately trip someone – or to add verisimilitude to an otherwise unconvincing narrative.

The runner continued left and right down the passageways, and it took no more than a glance at each door to see that only one room was furnished. It contained an old-fashioned iron bedstead, the bed made up with clean linen and neatly-tucked blankets, as if it hadn't been slept in yet. There was a bedside cabinet and reading lamp; a single-size wardrobe; a three-drawer chest with an adjustable mirror on it; and an upright wooden chair in the corner. There was no handbag in sight, and even from the door Slider could see the dust on various surfaces. There was no 'stuff' lying around. Whatever might be in the wardrobe and drawers, it was impossible to believe that the woman at the bottom of the stairs lived here. And if she didn't live here, where was her handbag?

He went back down, careful to step in the same places.

Atherton came prowling back from his tour of downstairs, tall and lean, always elegant. Atherton moved like a cat, except that he did not spray the furniture as he passed. Slider told him about the hole in the carpet. He raised his eyebrows significantly at Slider and beckoned him down to the kitchen.

There were blue-and-white lino tiles on the floor; in the middle of the room a kitchen table and four chairs. Under the window was a sink and draining-board; facing the door a work surface with cupboards over; at the end of them, a fridge and electric cooker. There was an electric kettle and a microwave on the worktop. Just about what you'd need for basic life support. And – as Slider pointed out for Atherton's benefit – the mains light over the cooker was glowing red. 'The electricity must still be connected.'

'That wasn't what I wanted to show you,' Atherton said. He squatted, pulling a biro from his inside pocket, and pointed.

Slider crouched too. A smear on the floor, and a couple of flecks on the door of the cupboard under the sink, of what could be blood.

'He whacked her here, dragged her out to the hall, and took away her bag to hide her identity,' said Atherton.

'If it's blood and not brown sauce,' Slider qualified. He looked back towards the door to the hall, and tilted his head this way and that for the light. 'Photography might find drag marks along the floor. That would clinch it.' He stood up. 'What's through there?'

There was a door on the far side of the kitchen. Beyond it was a small sitting room. There was a square of carpet on the floor, stained floorboards showing round the edge. There were a couple of saggy old armchairs, a scarred wooden coffee table decorated with an Olympic logo of mug rings. In one chimney alcove stood a vintage television with a casing of something that looked almost but not quite like wood. The other alcove was filled with a very home-made looking cupboard with shelves over, on which lay a scattering of dog-eared paperbacks and a metal ashtray in bright yellow with Double Diamond inscribed round the rim. The fireplace was boarded up, and on the tiled hearth stood a two-bar electric fire that Moses might have made toast at.

From the doorway, Atherton said in hushed and reverent tones, 'You could sell this whole room, exactly as is, to the Victoria and Albert Museum.'

'It's odd,' Slider mused.

'It is,' Atherton agreed. 'The two main reception rooms are unfurnished, but there's this little bolthole here, and an apparently functioning kitchen.'

'And all the bedrooms are empty, bar one, which has the minimum for a single person.'

'Almost as if there's a caretaker living here,' said Atherton.

'Maybe there is,' said Slider. 'It's an empty house that hasn't been vandalized.'

'I'd give a lot to look in the cupboards.'

'Can't, until SOCO has been. They won't like us faddling about on their territory.'

'You're calling it, then? There's enough here?'

'There's *something*,' Slider said. 'Whoever's living here, I can't believe it was that woman. She's too smart. And where are all her things? Where's her handbag?'

'Yes, the murderer, if any, made a mistake taking that away. Makes it look much less like an accident.'

Back in the hall, Slider stopped to look one more time at the body. Corpses never looked like people asleep, no matter what Victorian novels said. There was something infinitely pathetic about the huddle of flesh that needed the animating spirit to be a human being rather than a heap of trash. The sun shining through the stained glass made a pattern of colours over it, like a heartless joke. You lived inside your life as if it was permanent, getting up, going about your business, never thinking that the day you greeted with a yawn or a grumble might be the last of your measure, because it would be impossible to go on if you did.

Dying had not been on her list of Things To Do Today. *Who*

are you? he thought. Why had she come here, at whose behest? Who had wished her harm? Her clothes were good, her shoes were polished, she had well-kept hands. She was no great beauty, to fire male madness, but no gargoyle, either. Not victim material either way. She looked . . . ordinary. She had an ordinary face. 'God in his mercy lend her grace,' he muttered.

Atherton gave him a glance, mentally placing the quote. 'Well, she looks as if she lived with little joy or fear. She looks like a librarian.'

'Needlessly reductive. I'm sure librarians face both every day.' He turned to D'Arblay. 'I'm ready to back your judgement. Suspicious death at least, possibly homicide.' He liked the fact that D'Arblay wouldn't let himself look pleased. 'Get things moving, then you'd better go back out to the gate. The surgeon should be here any time.'

'He's here, sir,' said D'Arblay, jerking his head.

Through the open door, Slider saw Dr Gupta, the duty surgeon, approaching with the flinching steps of the indoor man who fears what might lie under flattened grass. You almost expected him to shake each foot as he lifted it, like a cat.

News never took long to travel. When they stepped back inside Shepherd's Bush nick, Paxman, the relief sergeant, imposed his mighty bulk between Slider and the door to the stairs in order to say, 'Dunkirk House? Suspicious death?'

Paxman was a mighty man, six foot two and built by the same firm that did Stonehenge. He looked as though he could pick up Atherton and snap him in two with his bare hands. Often he stared at Atherton as if he wanted to. Paxman belonged to some very forbidding evangelical sort of church, and didn't approve of hanky panky, whereas Atherton's whole life had been dedicated to as much hanky as he could possibly fit in, preferably with added panky. Paxman had a mighty stare – the stationary and ruminative gaze of a prize Hereford bull wondering which part of the puny human to stick its horn through.

'Woman apparently fallen down the stairs,' Slider said, offering a placatory minimum.

'Apparently?' Paxman queried.

'I have my doubts,' Slider said.

Paxman nodded his massive head. 'Dunkirk House, that's where that woman died – what? Twenty years back? Before your time. Went down as accidental death in the end, but some of us had our doubts about it.'

'You think it's a House of Death, then?' Atherton said whimsically. '"The curse has come upon me, cried the Lady of Shalott."'

Paxman gave Atherton a look that would have turned a lesser man to stone. 'If you want to know anything about it,' he said, evidently to Slider, 'give me the nod. It's called police intelligence – not that Bambi here would know what that was.'

Slider grabbed Atherton's arm with steely fingertips before he could make some retort on the subject of intelligence, and used the grip to hustle him away.

'A death in the same house twenty years ago?' Atherton complained when they were out of earshot.

'You're very irritable these days,' Slider said, heading upstairs. 'Not getting enough sleep?'

'Sleep is not the issue,' Atherton grunted.

Emily had finally left him. Her biological clock, she had said, stood at five to midnight, and she could spare no more time for him to bring himself round to the idea of marriage and children. She had put her flat on the market and gone back to New York, where a job offer had made the decision easier for her. Atherton had moved back full-time, with his cats, into his own house, a bijou artisan cottage in West Hampstead. Though he generally called it an artesian cottage because of the damp.

It was Joanna who, privately in bed, to Slider, had opined that Atherton's heart was broken. Slider saw no sign of it. If anything, he thought his bagman seemed slightly relieved to be unfettered again.

'But that's the worrying thing,' Joanna had said to him sternly. 'He's in denial.'

'Like the man who fell off the Cairo ferry-boat,' Slider added – intrigued, as always, at how readily and confidently women reeled out the psycho-bollocks.

'You can laugh,' Joanna said, 'but watch him, all the same. You can repress it, but it's bound to come out somewhere.'

So far it seemed to be coming out in a pattern of drinking wine and chasing women.

When Slider had mentioned his excesses to him – purely in the interests of departmental efficiency – Atherton had said, 'I'm thinking of chasing only wine-drinking women. Cuts out one process.'

'Wine and women, fair enough,' Slider had said. 'Let me know when you get on to the song, so I can bring earplugs.'

And that was all two men, good friends and long-time colleagues, needed to say to each other on the subject.

Detective Superintendent Porson, Slider's immediate superior, was not a happy bunny. 'This is the last thing we needed,' he said, as he paced up and down the strip of carpet in front of his window. The blinding sun outside showed up the streaky dust on the panes. A fly that had been beating its head against the glass all morning had been reduced to crawling along the windowsill, its engine worn down to a sputtering drone. 'We're supposed to be concentrating on Operation Foxglove.'

This was an inquiry into the use of young boys from the White City Estate in county lines drug running.

'Homicide trumps drugs,' Slider said.

'In your opinion. *If* it's homicide. You've taken a lot on yourself, calling out the circus on not much evidence.'

'It just didn't look right,' Slider said, aware of how feeble that sounded out in the open air. 'I've got a hunch.'

'You'll have a limp if it turns out to be nothing,' Porson barked. 'Mr Carpenter'll cut your legs off!'

Borough Commander 'Call Me Mike' Carpenter was not a copper's copper. The days when the police relied on instinct and conducted their own prosecutions were over before ever he joined the Met. He had come in straight from university. He was a child of budget spreadsheets, feasibility studies, quarterly crime targets, and the Proactive Intelligence-led Approach with added Stakeholder Engagement.

'And there's the budget. We can't afford an expensive investigation into san fairy ann,' Porson said.

'There's the blood in the kitchen—'

'If it turns out to be blood.'

'And no handbag.'

'If it's not in a cupboard.'

'Women don't tend to put their functioning handbag into a cupboard when they get home.' In fairness, Porson knew that was true, if not infallibly, and he only made an irritable movement of his head. The fly started wearily up the windowpane again, and Slider tried to wrench his attention away from it and defend himself. 'There's no sign of any personal possessions at all. It's all bare. I can't believe she was living there – and if she wasn't, what was she doing there? It makes foul play more likely.'

'There's no witnesses, no CCTV, you don't even know who she is,' Porson said. 'Even if it is homicide, you'll never bring it home.'

Slider knew the odds. 'But we have to try,' he said. It was only inwardly that he added, Or what are we for?

Porson sighed like a Pacific Class coming to rest at the buffers. 'Nothing I can do about it now, is there? It's a fat accomplice. But if you've got nothing by the end of the week I'll have to shut you down.'

'Yes, sir.'

Porson jerked his head towards the door. 'Better go and clear your desk while you've got a chance.'

The fly lost its grip and fell onto the windowsill, on its back, burbling feebly. Slider longed to rescue it, but Porson would have thought him potty. And in any case, modern office windows didn't open.

TWO

False Premises

Freddie Cameron, the forensic pathologist, was wearing a biscuit linen suit and a canary yellow bow tie, a look that only a man of enormous self-confidence could carry off. His brown shoes were so glossy you wanted to stroke them. 'What ho, Bill,' he said.

'I haven't seen you for . . . must be six months,' Slider returned. 'I thought you'd left us.'

'Sabbatical,' said Freddie. 'Edinburgh. They found a corner of a bench for me in my alma mater. I was feeling stale, needed to refresh my mind with some pure research. Sometimes you have to get back to basics to put the universe into perspective.'

'You were looking at the bigger picture?' Slider suggested. 'Through a microscope?'

'That's where perspective lies, old chum. The world in a drop of water, as the poet said. How's your new baby girl?'

'Flourishing, thanks.'

'What did you call her, in the end? I don't think I heard.'

It was a sore point. It turned out that there were no girls' names that went with 'Slider', except for Kate, and he had one of those already, from his first marriage. You couldn't have anything with an 's' sound, so that ruled out Sophie and Stephanie, which would have been Slider's pick. You couldn't have anything with an 'a' sound, which ruled out Joanna's choices of Olivia and Martha – and indeed ninety per cent of girls' names. 'It'd be easier to change your surname,' Joanna had told him tersely.

Slider's father had suggested Violet, but Violet Slider sounded like some kind of fancy hair ornament. Or a trendy cocktail. *Shoulda seen me on Sat'd'y – I got wasted on Violet Sliders!* Daughter Kate had liked Phoebe, but that just sounded comical. And when Dad's wife Lydia had suggested Vivienne, which qualified on most counts, a weary Joanna had said in frustration that she just didn't like it. Sorry.

In the end, after much trolling through books and scrolling through websites, the choice had come down to one name and was therefore no choice at all.

'Zoe,' said Slider.

'Oh, I like that,' said Freddie. 'Yes, that's very nice.'

'But it hardly matters,' Slider continued, 'because while we were still working on it, George decided to name her Teddy, and I'm rather afraid it's going to stick.'

'An enterprising lad, your George,' said Cameron.

'Naming the cat went to his head,' said Slider. 'He counts himself the authority now. He's started eyeing me thoughtfully. He's not sure "Daddy" really suits me.'

They were standing in the garden of Dunkirk House, and he glanced towards the door, where PC Gostyn stood guard, keeping the log. He was a bulky man, made bulkier by the fifteen-pound weight of the fully-kitted Metvest, and was sweating unbecomingly in the heat.

'What about our dead body?' Slider asked.

'I've had a look at the stairs,' Cameron said, 'and I can't see that head injury being caused by a tumble. It was a massive blow, and the profile of the wound has a square edge, untypical of anything she would have met on the way down. I would suggest something like a heavy spanner, wielded with force. Very little bleeding, so death was virtually instantaneous. Can't see any other injuries, but I'll confirm when I get her back to the works and stripped off. There may be bruises and so on. But there are no defence injuries to the hands, so if it was a homicidal attack I imagine she was taken by surprise. Lividity is consistent with her present position, so if she was moved it was soon after death. What else can I tell you?'

'Time of death?'

'Rigor is completely established, so it could be anything from twenty-four to thirty-two hours. Not later than yesterday morning.'

'Not much help.'

'I might be able to give you a better idea when it starts to pass off,' said Freddie kindly. 'Despite the heat outside, the temperature in the house is moderate and stable, so I would expect onset and passing off to be in the middle of the range.'

Slider said nothing, deep in thought, and Freddie looked around and said, 'Strange set-up, this. This big empty house, hidden away behind high walls.'

'And the victim doesn't match the house. What was she *doing* here?'

'Getting herself killed,' Freddie said.

You had to do it, but it didn't look as though house-to-house would achieve anything. Dunkirk House was on the corner of a small side-road, Askew Gardens, so there was no neighbour to the right. To the left, the first house on Uxbridge Road had been converted into a dentist's surgery, which would have been closed on a Sunday. The property was surrounded by the high wall on all sides, with more of the plot behind it than in front, so the next neighbour down Askew Gardens was separated by a high wall, a tangled garden, and the house itself from noticing anyone coming in or leaving by the front gate. Not to mention the well-known local custom of Minding Your Own Business, *orright*?

Slider disposed his troops, and went to meet Bob Bailey, the SOCO chief, at the door. Bailey was, in the opinion of most of the firm, a total tit, but as Crime Scene Manager and a civilian to boot, he wielded complete authority over access. He stood in the doorway, blocking Slider, while he leisurely removed his mask and mob cap, in order to deliver the fiat that Slider might now enter his domain.

'Your stains in the kitchen,' Bailey said as they walked along the passage. 'They are blood.' They had UV penlights now that could not only discover stains even when invisible to the naked eye, but could distinguish between blood and Daddies Sauce, and tell semen from superglue. 'Of course, you'll have to match it to the victim. I've bagged samples for you.'

In the kitchen, he used the light to point out the additional tiny flecks on the window above the sink and on the cupboard door over the work surface. 'Spatter marks,' he said. 'Looks as though she was standing by the sink when she was whacked. The smear on the floor would be where she fell down. Then' – he changed to a different penlight – 'you've got a mark *here* on the lino, looks like it was made by a rubber heel.'

'That could have been made at any time,' Slider mentioned.

Bailey gave him a boiled look, like a vicar hearing a fart during his sermon. He didn't like being interrupted. '*And*,' he went on, 'you can see, *there*, parallel smudges such as you might get from the heels of a body being dragged out. Also, you see here at the door, the gripper bar? Tiny shreds of nylon on two of the screw heads. Off her stockings, probably.' He displayed another evidence bag.

'I suppose her shoes were loose fitting and came off when he started to drag her,' Slider said.

'Could be,' Bailey allowed generously.

'All right if I look round generally now?'

'Be my guest. Everything's been dusted. Lots of finger-marks, probably too many to be useful. At least three different sets. Freshest in here and on the front door. I'll get the photos and everything over to you later today.'

'Did you dust the flush lever on the lavatory?' Slider asked. It was something that sometimes got missed.

'Both of 'em,' Bailey said. 'There's a bog through there, through the other side of the sitting room.'

'Servants' lavatory,' Slider said. At the time this house was built they would certainly have had a couple of servants, a cook-housekeeper and a maid, minimum. The kitchen and the attached sitting room would have been their domain and the lavatory for their use was a normal adjunct.

'If you say so,' Bailey said loftily. 'Water's still on, by the way,' he added, reminded by the subject. 'Water and electricity. Queer set-up. Doesn't look as if anyone lives here, but they could if they wanted.'

He went away and left Slider to explore. The fridge was plugged in and switched on, but there was nothing in it except a small tub of butter-substitute, a carton of longlife milk, and a sealed pack of the sort of orange processed cheese slices that nothing short of a direct nuclear strike would degrade. All were unopened and none actually needed to be refrigerated. In the freezer section was a small sliced loaf. In the cupboards over the work surface there was a collection of tins – baked beans, corned beef, soup, Irish stew and the like. There was a tub of instant mashed potato, and several of Pot Noodles. An unopened pack of Weetabix. A jar of instant coffee, a jar of something white that turned out to be sugar, a jar of Marmite. A bottle of orange squash, the sort you dilute with water.

Strange, Slider thought. You could arrive here at any time of the day and prepare yourself a very basic meal suitable to the occasion. It reminded him of those Alpine huts stocked with the bare minimum to sustain life for someone who stumbled in out of a blizzard. The expiry dates on the tins and tubs were well ahead, suggesting the stock had been placed – or renewed – within, say, the last year. He thought of the smartly-dressed, middle-aged woman lying at the foot of the stairs and failed to imagine her regaling herself on Dinty Moore Beef Stew or a marge 'n' Dairylea sandwich.

'All washed down with orange squash,' he said aloud. 'Who drinks orange squash? Only children.'

'Sorry, guv?' It was Jenrich, his new sergeant, brought in to replace Hart, who was on secondment. She was a pared-down woman with whipcord arms, who looked as if she pumped weights in her sleep. Her cheeks were so lean you could see the muscles move when she spoke. Her hair was cut as short as a man's round the sides and back, but was thick and layered on top, deep chestnut brown with gold high-lights. Her deep-set eyes were dark blue, you could have cut yourself on her cheekbones, and she had unexpectedly full lips. She was quirkily attractive, but she had rejected the sexual advances of the usual first-off-the-blockers at the station with a brusqueness that had, of course, led the more Neanderthal element to conclude that she must be a lesbian. The imputation slid off her like water off a greased duck.

'What was that about orange squash?' she asked.

'You could make a meal here, of sorts,' Slider explained, 'but then again, what sorts! Who eats Pot Noodles?'

She looked as if she didn't understand the question. 'The

veggie teriyaki's all right. And there's a kung po chicken that's not bad.'

Slider, who had the privilege of going home at night to a freshly-cooked meal, had obviously asked the wrong person. 'Have you looked upstairs?'

She nodded. 'That bed looks as if it's not been slept in. There's a couple of outdoor jackets and a pair of wellies in the wardrobe, some socks and plain white T-shirts and a pair of jeans in the drawers. In the bathroom there's just a bottle of Head and Shoulders shampoo and a bottle of Radox Muscle Soak. Oh, and a packet of twelve Anadin, three left.' She looked at him steadily, like a well-trained dog waiting for a command. Out of the corner of his attention he saw the ghostly figures of the SOCO team moving slowly through the garden. Searching for a murder weapon.

'What's the story with this place, boss?' Jenrich asked.

He shook his head, and walked across into the little sitting room. The paperbacks he had noticed earlier turned out to be very old Westerns: Louis L'Amour, Zane Grey, J.T. Edson – even Clarence E. Mulford. The more traditional end of the genre – not the graphic, brain-splattering modern sort. Here the cupboards yielded a fold-up chessboard and a box of chessmen, a very ancient and dog-eared Monopoly set, a Travel Scrabble, and a board game called It's Bananas – Loads of Fun for Ages 6 and Up! There was a pack of hopelessly grimy playing cards, and a couple of very elderly jigsaw puzzles – the colour tones of the illustrations suggested they dated from the seventies. Old Amsterdam was one; Wisley in Bloom the other. Guaranteed At Least One Piece Missing.

'It's the sort of stuff you'd find in the cupboards of a holiday let,' Slider said with dissatisfaction.

'Maybe that's it,' Jenrich said. 'Maybe the house was let out.' He looked at her steadily until she worked it through. 'But there's not enough furniture. Nobody'd pay good money to stay here. And the dead woman – that's a seventy-quid haircut she's got. Plus highlights. And her watch is a Nordgreen. They start about a hundred and fifty. She could be the landlady, but no way someone like that'd be stopping here. Anyway . . .' She hesitated. She was new to the team, didn't yet know Slider and how much he liked individual input.

'Yes?' Slider invited.

'Well, if anyone's living here, I'd bet it wasn't a woman. No make-up anywhere, no face or body cream, no sanitary products.'

'Good point,' said Slider.

Through the door on the far side of the sitting room was a small lobby containing a washing machine and dryer, the aforementioned lavatory and the back door, which was locked and also bolted top and bottom. Whoever did this came and went through the front door.

An intensifying of sounds from outside pulled Slider's attention away. He went back into the kitchen and saw, through the window, several ghosts heading in the same direction. 'Have they found something?' he said.

On the way through the hall he was stopped by one of Freddie Cameron's assistants, young Vaughan. The body, Slider saw, now decently zipped into its bag, was being carried out of the front door. 'Oh, I was looking for you, sir,' Vaughan said. 'Doc Cameron asked me to give you this. We looked through deceased's pockets. There was nothing in the back ones, but these keys were in one of the front ones. Nothing else.'

On a ring, with a dark-green leather tag, were three Yale-type keys and a mortice key.

'We tried them out,' Vaughan said. 'This Yale and the deadlock key are for the front door. The other two Yales are different – as you can see. They don't fit anything here.'

The leather tag, about the size and shape of a car key fob, looked new – it wasn't at all worn at the edges, as such things are by travelling in pockets or the bottom of handbags. It was embossed in gold on one side and had the look of the sort of tabs sold by National Trust gift shops, embellished with the name of the property. On this one, the writing said Historic Buildings National Drawings Archive, and a website address.

'Doc Cameron thought you might have heard of it,' said Vaughan, 'given your interest in architecture.'

'Nope, doesn't ring a bell,' said Slider. 'Would have been

better if it was the victim's name and address. Anyway, thanks, Vaughan. Let's see what's going on out there.'

Atherton was standing at a polite distance from the action. He glanced at Slider. 'They've found a nest of what looks like rubbish in the corner. High hopes of a blunt instrument.'

Slider told him about the keys.

Atherton frowned. 'That puts a slightly different complexion on it, doesn't it? We were assuming the murderer took away her handbag, but if she lived within walking distance, she might just have taken the keys with her and left her bag behind at home.'

'Thank you for complicating matters,' said Slider.

Atherton grinned. 'And what's this National Drawings Archive? Sounds like a fun destination. An exciting day out for you and the kids! Browse dusty shelves! See old drawings in their natural habitat! Is that the sort of place, I ask myself, that would have a gift shop?'

'You just never know. The Los Angeles Coroners Department has a thriving gift shop. Why not this? And if they don't have many visitors, someone may recognize her from a mugshot.'

'If she bought the key fob herself. Could've been a gift from an admirer.'

'There you go,' Slider complained, 'always with the negative vibes. Hullo! What's that?'

'False alarm,' Atherton said after a moment. 'Just a stick. You couldn't inflict a fatal wound with that.'

The nest of rubbish was lying in the corner made by the front and right-hand-side walls. The trunk of a tall old conifer of some kind growing about four feet back, and a couple of overgrown shrubs, made it a sheltered spot, and also prevented any grass growing in the corner. There were some bits of cloth and a few empty tins and bottles, some sheets of corrugated cardboard and a quantity of old newspapers.

'Looks like somebody's been chucking their rubbish over the wall,' said Bob Bailey.

'Cue the nine-foot man,' said Slider.

'Or the six-foot man with a step-ladder,' Atherton added.

Bailey froze them both with a look. 'People'll go to any lengths to dump rubbish. A high wall wouldn't stop them.'

'In any case, there's nothing there that could serve as a weapon?' Slider asked.

Bailey fingered the stick wistfully – about three feet of twenty-five-millimetre wide batten. 'You couldn't kill anyone with that,' he admitted reluctantly.

D'Arblay was still on the gate. The pavement was taped off on this side of the road, and a very small crowd had gathered on the pavement opposite, in the hope that something interesting might happen. Most people paused briefly on their way past, then carried on, but a little knot of those with nothing better to do had formed front and centre where the view was best.

Slider glanced across, and said to D'Arblay, 'Isn't that Very Little Else over there? Just moving away. I thought I recognized the hat.'

'Oh, yes, sir, that's her. I expect she spotted me as she was passing and wondered what was up.'

D'Arblay had always had a special relationship with the bag lady, who had long stomped about the streets of Shepherd's Bush with her meagre possessions in two plastic carriers. Where she slept no one knew, and as for eating, shopkeepers and café owners sometimes gave her leftovers, and D'Arblay would slip her a few coins now and then to buy herself a meal. She lived, literally, hand to mouth. There had never been very much of her – barely four foot eleven in thick socks, and thin as a rail, though her constant travelling had given her a wiry strength. She had a passion for biscuits and Slider had been known to pass her a packet of custard creams in return for telling him about something she had seen – though you couldn't have used her as a witness. In the first place, you'd never have got her to go into a courtroom, and in the second, no court would have accepted her as reliable. Still, there had been something vaguely comforting about the sight of her on her peregrinations, always in the same black wool coat and squashy black felt hat, and he had been sorry to think that one day they would find her dead by a wall, a poor huddle of bones, the sparrow that God didn't see fall.

'I haven't seen her in a while,' Slider said. 'I thought she must be dead.'

'We got her into a hostel, sir – you know, when we had that drive a couple of years back to get all the rough sleepers off the street.'

'And she's stayed there?' Slider asked in surprise. Street people could be very hard to persuade to leave their well-ventilated lives. The call of the wild generally dragged them back.

'Oh, yes, sir. She loves it at St Mark's. She sleeps there and eats breakfast and dinner, but she's still out walking all day.'

'Well, I'm glad she's settled,' Slider said.

The Bush was less colourful with the old-school street people gone, but you couldn't stand in the way of progress. And you couldn't have them untidily freezing to death under railway arches in winter. Elsie, he reflected, seemed to have achieved the perfect balance between civilization and freedom. Meals and a bed, and then . . . the open road! The dusty highway! Travel, change, interest, excitement. The whole world before you, and a horizon that's always changing. Poop poop!

In the CID room there was tea on the brew, and a bag of 'cheesecakes' someone had fetched from Greggs: those strange London confections made of puff pastry topped with white icing and desiccated coconut, and containing a blob of rasp-berry jam – but never, ever cheese.

Slider's share was brought to him by Gascoyne. 'I've been over to Westfields, sir,' he said. With mug in one hand and plate in the other, he looked puzzled for somewhere to put them down. Slider's desk was densely layered with piles of paperwork. Some of it was rumoured to be so old that, given there were probably food remains among the files, the bottom strata could well be undergoing some kind of biological process. Atherton swore he'd heard voices down there.

Slider made room by moving the telephone to the table behind him. 'Any luck?'

'There's no CCTV specifically covering the payphones,' said Gascoyne. 'There's various cameras covering the entrances and the main halls, but there'd be hundreds of people going back and forth, and we don't know who we're looking for.'

Slider got the point. 'Definite problem picking someone out when you don't know what they look like.'

'I've secured copies of the tapes anyway, just in case,' Gascoyne said. 'And . . . I was thinking—'

'Good. I always encourage that,' Slider said gravely.

'Well, sir, how did the informant even know about the body? Unless she was involved in some way.'

Slider pondered. 'She went to the door for some reason? And when there was no answer, looked through the glass?'

'But then she'd think deceased had fallen downstairs, and she would have called an ambulance, wouldn't she? That's what an innocent person would do.'

'I suppose so. So you think she was an accomplice and got cold feet?'

'Or a witness, and was afraid to get involved.'

'Good point.'

Atherton, who had been lounging in the doorway for the last few exchanges, said, 'Where could she have witnessed it *from*? Through the kitchen window? It's hardly likely she could have been inside, or the murderer would have done her too.'

'Unless she was hiding. If you witnessed something like that by accident, you wouldn't want the murderer to find you out.' He frowned. 'But then, if she was inside the house she must have had some connection with deceased surely? A friend, relative – client? So why didn't she give the victim's name to the emergency services?'

'Panic,' Atherton said. 'Panic answers every question.'

'True,' Slider said. 'Well, I'd better go and talk to Mr Porson about the press release.'

But first, the cheesecake. That was not to be hurried. It was one of those things, like an Australian meat pie or an American hotdog, that was so disgusting it was delicious.

When he got back to his office, he spent an hour or so clearing his desk. He didn't really clear it, of course, just skimmed a bit off the top without going deep. There could be a promising civilization developing down there, and he wasn't about to throw if off track by breaching the Prime Directive.

Then he phoned Joanna. She said, 'Hello,' against the background of the baby screaming like a steam whistle.

'It's Teddy,' she said, *mezzo forte* and *molto agitato*. 'She's been doing it for hours. I don't know what's wrong with her. George never did that.'

'I expect he did, you've just forgotten. It's probably colic – it usually is. Or maybe she's starting teething.'

'Teething? Don't toy with me, Bill Slider, I'm in a dangerous mood. I've had three pupils today and you know how I hate teaching.'

'Beginners?'

'Absolute.'

'That's probably it, then. She's imitating them.'

'If you think that helps!' The screaming, *per impossibile*, went up a pitch. He heard Joanna say, 'I don't—' and then break off. Behind her was a murmur of voices, she said something he couldn't catch, and then she was back on the line. 'Your dad's just come up. Thank God. Now at least I can—'

The screaming broke off short on a surprised-sounding hiccup, and a blissful silence ensued. Joanna said, at normal pitch now, 'He just picked her up. How does he do that?'

'It's a thing he has. He's always been good with animals.'

'I love your dad *so* much,' she said fervently.

'Wife's Surprise Confession. Policeman Slays Father and Self,' said Slider.

'Were you ringing for a reason?' Joanna said, sounding absolutely normal now. 'Or just to say you love me?'

'That, of course. And to let you know I'm about to leave. What's for supper?'

'Lobster thermidor from yesterday's leftover chicken.'

'Sorry I asked. Do you realize you called her Teddy?'

'Called who Teddy?'

'The baby. You know – Teddy.'

'Oh, *that* Teddy!'

'I think I'll have to buy her a teddy bear called Zoe,' said Slider.

THREE

Fortune Favours the Bald

'According to the Land Registry, Dunkirk House is owned by a Philip and Kate Armstrong,' said Swilley. The heatwave continued, but at least in the morning the day was fresh, and the sun was not on the windows yet. Swilley looked fresh, too, in a short-sleeved white shirt and light beige trousers. She was the firm's hand-to-hand combat expert, though her small-nosed, wide-mouthed, blonde beauty made her look like an American beach babe. Just now a deep biscuity tan increased the likeness.

'Have you had your summer holiday yet?' Slider asked.

'Not now Ashley's in school. Can't go until August,' she said. She gathered the import of his question. 'This is from the garden,' she explained, gesturing to her arms. 'We're trying to grow our own vegetables.'

He shook himself back from the vision that arose of Swilley digging – for some reason, in a bikini. 'You were saying? Armstrong?'

Swilley switched just as nimbly. 'They're joint tenants, not tenants in common, so I suppose they're husband and wife.'

'Well, that gives us a starting point, anyway,' said Slider. 'See what you can find out about them on the internet. And have Fathom check criminal records.'

'On it, boss. Also I did a quick check of the current electoral register. There's no one listed at that address.'

'Ah,' said Slider. That was a nuisance. Of course, lots of people were too stupid or too lazy or even too indifferent to their democratic rights to register. Others simply didn't get round to it. But it made their job all the harder. 'You'd better check back the last few years, see if you can find a name.'

Atherton appeared behind her. 'It's a hell of a property to leave standing empty.'

'Doesn't prove it's empty,' Swilley said stubbornly.

He ignored her. 'If they didn't want to live there, they could have sold it for – what? – over a million, anyway.'

'It's a developer's dream, with that big garden,' Slider said. 'Room to stick up a block of flats.'

'If the victim *is* this Kate Armstrong, maybe she *was* trying to sell it,' Atherton said. 'She could have been showing round a potential buyer. There was that Suzy Lamplugh case—'

'She was an estate agent,' Swilley objected.

'More and more people are doing it themselves these days, and saving the two-per-cent-plus-VAT,' said Atherton.

'But that doesn't explain the food in the kitchen,' Slider said.

'She'd had a caretaker in, but he'd left, so she decided to sell rather than find another one.'

'You're just spinning a fantasy about it,' Swilley said.

'Well, you won't let me spin one about you,' said Atherton with the sort of leer that was a man's equivalent of batting the eyelashes. Swilley, famously impervious to Atherton's charms, merely snorted.

'You might see how it's listed for Council Tax,' Slider suggested.

'Right, boss,' said Swilley. 'Find out who's *paying* the tax as well. If it's empty, we'll see how long for. The council charges double on empty properties, so you wouldn't want to keep it that way without a reason. And they can force you to sell if it's empty for a long time.'

She went away. Slider glanced at Atherton, noting his rather bleared look. 'You look hung-over.'

'Quite the reverse, as the man said on the Bay of Biscay when the steward asked him if he'd dined.'

'Eh?'

'My date last night insisted on a curry. You can't drink wine with curry. I was astonishingly abstemious.'

'And that's something you can't say with a load on. What are we doing to identify the victim?'

'We've got the fingerprints from Forensics, so we're checking those. I don't hold out much hope – she doesn't look like someone with a criminal record. Forensics'll send off for a DNA profile. Jenrich is co-ordinating the house-to-house. We'll do all the searches on these Armstrongs. And we've got the mugshots, though I don't know where would be the best places to circulate them.'

'We're not there yet. And it's too early for Mispers. You might see what you can find out about the house – come at it from that direction.'

'Right. I'll scour the internet – and ring round local estate agents, see if it's been put up for sale anywhere.'

'Don't get too attached to your theory, will you?'

'Hey – it's me!' Atherton said in hurt tones, and went out.

Freddie Cameron rang in the afternoon. 'I'll put the full report in the bag for you, but I thought you'd like the results of the PM verbally first.'

'Thanks,' said Slider. 'Anything out of the ordinary?'

'No, it's all as we were speculating,' said Cameron. 'Firstly, time of death – rigor had fully passed off by midnight last night, which puts death at around ten a.m. Sunday morning. That's taking a median time – you know rigor can be hugely variable, so it can only be an indication.'

'Of course,' said Slider.

'But my personal view is that it wouldn't be much *later* than that, and probably not more than two or three hours earlier either, as the contents of the stomach suggest. The last meal taken involved toast and eggs, suggesting breakfast, and was probably consumed about two hours before death.'

'There were no eggs in the house, and no eggshells or egg box in the kitchen bin,' said Slider. 'So unless the murderer emptied the bin and took the rubbish away with him, it looks as though she breakfasted elsewhere and then came to the house. Which again suggests she didn't live there.'

'That's your province, not mine. The cause of death was a single blow to the head with a heavy implement with a square profile. As I suggested, a long, heavy spanner would do the trick. It was a very powerful blow, shattering the skull and driving bone fragments into the brain. Death would have been pretty much instantaneous.'

'Any other injuries?'

'Nothing to suggest a fall down stairs, at any rate. But there were bruises on both upper arms, consistent with finger and thumb marks. From the span, I'd say they were large, probably male hands, and the bruising was deep.'

'He grabbed her by the arms at some point in anger,' Slider said. 'Perhaps in the course of an argument.'

'I'd say that's possible. There were no defence injuries, and nothing under the nails. She didn't fight back.'

'He was bigger than her and she was afraid of him.'

'And from the angle of the head wound, she didn't see it coming. He hit her from behind and to the side. Nothing else really to tell you. No tattoos or distinguishing marks. She was well-nourished and in good health. I've made a record of the teeth but there was no recent dental work for you to latch on to. And I've sent off the DNA and blood samples as per.'

'Thanks, Freddie,' Slider said.

'You haven't identified her yet. I can tell from your glum voice.'

'We've got nothing to go on so far except your bunch of keys. This one's going to be a sticker, I can feel it in my bones.'

'Oh well, nil desperate dan, as the scholars say.'

'And pip pip to you,' Slider returned amiably.

So she went to the house from elsewhere. Arranged to meet the murderer there. Or was there for some other reason and he called, and she knew him well enough to let him in. They talked, quarrelled. In the kitchen. Perhaps she was going to make him a cup of coffee. He grabbed her by the arms – towering over her, probably, shouting. He let her go. She turned away, by the sink, perhaps to fill the kettle, and he solved all his current problems (murderers rarely thought further ahead than that) by breaking her skull with . . .

Ah, yes. The murder weapon. Unless it was something you would find in that remarkably bare house (a spanner under the sink for unblocking the bend? But he'd have to have known it was there), he must have taken it with him, which meant he planned to use it.

And anyway, at least, took it away with him afterwards. Along with, putatively, her handbag, so that she would not be identified.

After he had dragged her to the stairs to make it look as though she had fallen down the flight. Dropped her shoes artistically halfway down. Cut a hole in the carpet at the top.

Someone who knew too little about forensics to realize the deception wouldn't wash. Well, the general public were notoriously – and thank God for it – ignorant of that sort of thing. Chummy thought the appearance of a fall would be accepted at face value. He was dumb, or smug, or out of touch. Or any combination of all three.

The answer to this problem was going to lie in the life of the mystery woman. And that meant the sort of long investigation without material evidence that was most likely to irritate Mr Carpenter and have Porson obliged to cut him off.

He got up and went through into the outer office. 'I'm going out to look for a gift shop,' he said.

According to the website, the mission statement of the Historic Buildings National Drawings Archive was to collect, collate, preserve and archive historical blueprints, architectural plans, original drawings, inventories, and all similar documents relating to the building, extending, repairing and altering of ancient edifices. The patron was HRH the Prince of Wales, and it listed some prominent sponsors, of the genus Lord This, Sir Somebody That, and Lt General The Other. It invited donations of documents, and of money towards the upkeep of the archive. Opening hours were ten till five Monday to Saturday, and some documents could only be viewed by appointment. The director was a Gideon Lankester, with enough letters after his name for a game of Scrabble: B Arch, D Phil, RIBA, ARB, FCIAT, FRSA and so on. He probably had a Bronze Swimming Certificate and a Blue Peter badge as well.

The address was in Bayswater, and turned out to be a tall, narrow, three-storey building of about 1860, part of a white stuccoed terrace a short walk from Queensway Station. The small front garden had been sacrificed to provide two parking places, and miraculously only one was occupied – with a British Racing Green soft-top TR4 in immaculate condition. Slider oozed into the space beside it, glad he didn't have to find a street spot.

Inside the front door he found himself in a large reception area/office, with the usual office accoutrements, lifted out of the ordinary by the beautiful original ceiling mouldings and central rose and a fine marble fireplace. A middle-aged woman with exquisite make-up and dark hair cut in a 1930s bob looked up from her keyboard, gave him a professional smile, and said, 'Can I help you?' in a pearls-and-twinset accent.

Slider gave her his card and said, 'I'd like a word with Mr Lankester, if that's possible.'

She smiled a little more roguishly as she stood up, smoothing down her sensible skirt. 'I hope he hasn't been doing anything naughty,' she said. 'We really couldn't afford to lose him.'

She tapped on a door on the other side of the room, opened it, spoke to someone inside, then held it open for Slider. Beyond the door was the rear reception room of the original house, with the same mouldings, the original chandelier still hanging from the rose, and an even finer fireplace. There was a lush, dark-blue carpet, office furniture made of real wood instead of MDF, and the two pictures on the wall looked like genuine oils. An office smart enough to receive the royal patron, should it be necessary. Slider's quick and comprehensive goosey even spotted a silver drinks tray with cut-glass decanters and identified what he guessed was the concealed refrigerator below. After all, what's a cheeky G & T without ice? This was a classy outfit, no doubt about it. It wasn't in one of the nicer bits of Bayswater for nothing.

'Mr Lankester?' he enquired for politeness sake.

The director came forward from behind his antique mahogany desk with the eye contact and outstretched hand that said he had a clear conscience. He looked to be in his fifties, lean, not very tall, with a lightly tanned face that missed being handsome by a small but significant degree. He wore his hair rather long at the back, perhaps to compensate for the fact that it was disappearing from the front, giving him either an impressively intellectual forehead or junior baldness, depending on your point of view. Instead of a suit he was wearing skin-tight dark trousers and a close-fitting, thin, black roll-neck. Plainly he was aiming for the carefree, trendy appearance of his joint-smoking university days, but as he had skinny legs and a bit of a pot belly, he just looked like a big chicken.

'How can I help you . . . er' – he glanced at the card – 'Inspector?'

Slider decided on the less formal approach. Despite the domestic fowl misfortune, Lankester had a firm mouth and intelligent eyes. 'I came to see whether you had a gift shop, but I rather suspect you haven't.'

Lankester smiled, which greatly improved his looks. 'We haven't, as it happens, but that's a good idea. Except that we're rather short of space. We just have the two offices on this floor, and the two floors and the attic above house the archive. Not enough spare room to swing a mouse. In fact, we'd ideally like to move to larger premises, but I doubt our sponsors could bear the expense.'

'Isn't there a semi-basement?' Slider asked, from old knowledge of this type of house.

'Well spotted,' said Lankester. 'But it's on a separate lease and occupied by a tenant who isn't interested in selling. Had you some particular reason for wanting a gift shop?'

Slider produced the key tag. 'It looks like the sort of thing you buy as a souvenir at a National Trust property.'

'Oh, yes – quite. In fact I think the same company makes theirs.'

'How would somebody come by one?'

'Oh, it was a little idea of mine, for advertisement and to promote good will,' Lankester said. 'I thought we could send one as a thank-you to anyone who made a donation. We always ask, when people come to consult a document, if they'll – er – drop a penny in the box, so to speak. And we sent one to each of our regular donors and sponsors last Christmas.' He gave Slider a rueful smile. 'Small beer, I know, but we aren't a wealthy organization. We get a tiny government grant, and the lease of the house was given to us in trust at the beginning, but otherwise we depend entirely on the generosity of donors, and we don't exactly have the emotional appeal of other charities. Can't get people worked up about old documents as if they were lost dogs or starving children.'

'I see,' said Slider. 'How many of these tags have you distributed?'

'Well, I ordered two hundred to begin with and we've probably got about forty left. Apart from our regular donors, we get about three visitors a week, on average, though that varies a lot. Sometimes it can be two or three a day.' He raised an eyebrow, to signify that he wanted to know why Slider wanted to know, but was too polite to ask.

'What sort of people visit here?' Slider asked.

'People researching the history of a building. Often it's students, or it might be someone who's just bought an old house, or an architect interested in a particular period or place. And we're consulted a lot about planning applications, both by the owner and the planners. When someone wants to restore a feature, for instance, and needs to know how a building looked in a previous time; or claims that an alteration would bring the building closer to its origins. In some cases,' he added proudly, 'the building has been entirely demolished, and we have the only proof that it ever existed. Or we can show evidence of a long-lost feature. For instance, there's a certain large house, originally built by an eccentric lord in the eighteenth century, which was acquired by the government for the Ministry of Defence. They came to us asking about a local rumour that the lord had built a labyrinth of rooms and tunnels underground, and we were able to produce the only plans in existence that showed the extent of them, and where the hidden entrances were.' He beamed. He plainly loved his job. Slider, who loved architecture, thought it must be just about the perfect one. 'Of course, I'm bound by the Official Secrets Act,' Lankester went on, 'not to reveal to you the name or location of the house. In fact, those plans are now locked in our most secure archive, in a fireproof box. In their way, they are beyond price.'

Slider left this beguiling thought and pondered. Obviously it would be impossible to trace every one of a hundred and sixty key tags. 'I suppose you could give me a list of the regular sponsors who were given one of these?' he said, as a way of paring it down.

'Ye-es,' said Lankester hesitantly, still not knowing what it was all about. 'I could. Each of the staff had one, as well, if that matters. I have one myself.'

Slider brightened. A staff member would be more likely actually to use such a tag than an outsider. 'Do you have a large staff?' he asked.

'Goodness, no!' Lankester exclaimed. 'I wish we had. There's me, I'm the director, and Pandora Ormsby-Cecil, who's the archivist – she's down in Yorkshire today, looking at some documents we might be acquiring. And then there's the two part-time secretaries: Hattie, who showed you in, and Prue. They share the job between them, Hattie does Monday, Tuesday and Wednesday, and Prue does Thursday, Friday and Saturday. And that's all.'

Slider drew out the mugshot. 'Would you have a look at this? I wonder if this is someone you recognize.'

Lankester looked. He was sharp enough to know what it was. He swallowed. 'Is this . . .?'

'Do you know who it is?' Slider insisted.

'It's Prue,' he said in a flat voice. 'Prue Chadacre, our other secretary.' He scanned Slider's face urgently. 'Is that where you found the key tag? What's happened to her?'

So, not Kate Armstrong, Slider thought. Oh well, who said life was going to be easy? 'I'm sorry to tell you she was found dead in a house in Shepherd's Bush.' That provoked no reaction from Lankester, who was still looking lightly stunned – a chicken on the way to slaughter. 'It appears as though she fell down the stairs,' he went on. 'Would she perhaps have been looking at the property on your behalf? It is an old house.'

Lankester shook his head. 'No – not at all. I would never ask her to do that. It's the documents we're interested in, in any case, not the actual building. Oh dear, how dreadful! Poor Prue. But . . .' He frowned as his brains caught up with him. 'Surely she must have had some identification with her. Why didn't you know who she was?'

'I'm not at liberty to discuss that with you,' Slider said. 'What can you tell me about her?'

Still frowning, Lankester shook his head. 'Very little, I'm afraid. She's worked for us for about five years. She was with another charity before that, a local wildlife trust somewhere in West London – the details will be on her file. That was a voluntary job, but it was the experience that mattered. And, frankly, it's more important to us to have someone who fits in, than someone with superior skills. We couldn't pay for superior skills, in any case,' he added with a shrug. 'The job is practically voluntary here. The government grant just covers fifty-six hours at minimum wage, which Hattie and Prue share between them. It's not enough to live on, that's for sure.'

'So how do they manage?'

'Well, Hattie has a husband, she just does the job for interest, something to get her out of the house. Prue – I don't think she's married. I think she must have a private income.'

'Do you know who her next of kin is?'

'I'm afraid not. I've had very little conversation with her over the years. And none of it was personal. I've never heard her talk about anyone. We had a little drinks party last Christmas, with some of the sponsors, when we all brought our significant others, but Prue came alone.'

'Did she seem a happy person?'

'Oh, yes. Well, not the life and soul of the party, by any means, but I'd say she seemed quietly contented. Arrived punctually, did her work, went home. Never said much. I got the impression she was a very private person. I think working here suited her – not much contact with the hurly-burly of the outside world. It wouldn't suit everyone – which is why, as I said, it's important to us to have staff that fit in.'

'Would your other staff be able to tell me more about her?'

He frowned. 'I don't think Hattie could help. They never worked on the same day. Pandora might have spoken to her on a personal level at some time. She'll be back in tomorrow, if you wanted to ask her.'

'You'll be able to give me Prue's home address.'

'Of course. Anything that's on her file is yours,' said Lankester, his face a seething mass of questions.

Slider distracted him. 'Is that your car outside?'

It worked. He grinned with pride. 'The TR? Yes, guilty as charged! She's my one great indulgence. Pandora laughs at me – says I'm a stereotype, clinging to my long-past youth – but I don't care. I wouldn't part with her for worlds.'

Back in the first office, Slider had a chat with Hattie Tolliver. He got her going by asking, 'What does the job entail?'

'Oh, it's ordinary secretarial work,' she said, scanning his face hungrily for clues. 'Answer the telephone, deal with the mail, receive the visitors, send out mailshots and press releases. Now and then there might be a little bit of research to enliven the day. And occasionally a celebrity visitor.' She gave a tight smile. 'But generally it's routine, and we're very quiet here on most days.'

'What can you tell me about Prue Chadacre?'

The searching gaze grew sharper. 'Has something happened to her?' she asked bluntly.

'Why should you think that?'

She gave him almost a pitying look. 'Because you're here.'

Point, thought Slider. 'I'm afraid she seems to have had an accident. She was found dead in a house in Shepherd's Bush, apparently having fallen down the stairs. Do you know if she had any connections there?'

'I really didn't know her at all,' Hattie said. 'We worked opposite ends of the week, you see, never together. The only time I saw her to talk to was at office parties. We have a small one here at Christmas, and a bigger garden party at Pandora's house in Berkshire in the summer. Pandora's husband is David Ormsby-Cecil.'

The name sounded vaguely familiar to Slider, so he nodded as if the information meant something to him. 'Did she ever come with anyone to those parties?'

'No, alone. I don't think she was married. She had a gold-and-diamond ring that she wore, but when I admired it once she said it was her mother's. The little conversation I had with her, I don't think she had anyone in her life. She was . . . a bit odd.'

'In what way?'

'Hard to define. Very closed-off. She only spoke if you spoke to her, never initiated anything. And at the parties, if one of us didn't go and chat to her, she just stood in a corner saying nothing.'

'Perhaps she was shy.'

'It didn't come across that way. More like detachment.'

'Did she seem unhappy?'

Hattie frowned. 'I didn't get that impression. Just that she was completely shut in on herself. Didn't need human contact. I don't think she was depressed – her body language wasn't right for that. She moved and spoke quite briskly – just didn't do either very much.'

'Did she ever mention someone called Armstrong? Philip Armstrong? Or Kate Armstrong?'

Hattie shook her head. 'She never mentioned anyone at all, really. The only conversation we had was on the lines of "isn't this a good party?" and the weather and current events. But,' she added, as if wanting to be scrupulously fair, 'one doesn't tend to exchange confidences at parties of that sort, does one?'

Slider couldn't really speak for One, but at work parties in the Job you tended to talk about the Job, exchanging news about troublesome lowlifes and bitching about the bosses. It was probably quite different at the sort of garden party in Berkshire at which you might meet Prince Charles.

He took his leave. At least now he had a name – Prudence Chadacre – and an address – in Notting Hill – but still no clue as to why deceased had been at Dunkirk House or what she had to do with Philip and Kate Armstrong.

Having an affair with Philip, perhaps? But that empty house was not much of a setting for illicit nookie. Gideon Lankester, the old swinger, would have done an assignation with more style.

Slider got into his car, and cast a middle-aged man's look of wistful admiration at the TR. But he had two small children. Even Joanna had swapped her boy-racer musician's car for something matronly. And Slider was just a humble copper. He hadn't Lankester's pizzazz.

He was reminded of the old rhyme:

> Roads and bridges, docks and piers, that's the stuff
>   for engineers;
> Wine and women, drugs and sex, that's the stuff for
>   architects.

Stereotype indeed!

FOUR

Sham Prue

Having drawn a blank on estate agents, Atherton rang up local historian Ada Forster, who had such a passion for Shepherd's Bush she had spent – some unkindly said wasted – her life learning everything about it. He didn't think she'd have much to say about one Victorian house in an area that was nearly all Victorian houses, but her voice perked up at once.

'Oh, Dunkirk House! That's quite interesting, actually. It was originally called Inverness House, you know.'

'Was it?' he said, and relaxed. He'd struck oil.

'Didn't you notice the stained-glass panel over the door? View of Inverness Castle?'

'Oh, is that what that was?'

'The house was built by a Scottish builder who came from Inverness – I suppose he was missing his home town. You know what a speculative builder was?'

'Remind me,' Atherton suggested.

'Well, before the mid- to late-Victorian time, houses were built, as it were, bespoke. Someone with money bought a bit of land and paid a builder to put up a house for him. But with the invention of the railways London started expanding rapidly and a new way to build houses was needed. A speculative builder borrowed or raised large sums of money, bought a plot of land, built a whole lot of houses on it, and then sold or let them – we might call it "off the peg". The successful ones made absolute fortunes. And it was a new investment vehicle for the wealthy. Some of our top landowners bolstered their estates that way, at a time when agriculture wasn't bringing in a return.'

'I presume the builder in question was one of the successful ones.'

'Oh yes, Morton Chadacre from Inverness. He's responsible for several whole streets in Shepherd's Bush. Remarkable, when he was only in his thirties.'

'So Dunkirk House was one of his speculations?'

'No, that was special. He'd just got married, to the daughter of one of his wealthy investors, and he reserved a large plot of the land he'd bought and built a "bespoke" house for her: Inverness House. That was in 1898. What's interesting is that he put in a lot of modern innovations – used it as a sort of testing ground for his ideas, if you like. New building techniques. Patent window-openings. A special kind of patent fireplace, labour-saving devices in the kitchen, a new kind of pump to take water up to the upper floors. It even had a lift that worked on some ingenious hydraulic system. I'm afraid they all got swept away in the post-war period when the craze for modernism took hold, so I've only read about them. There's a whole chapter on Chadacre houses, and Inverness House in particular, in a book called *Building Victorian London* – I have a copy if you'd like to consult it. The house that's left was horribly messed-about in the seventies and eighties and onwards, but I think there might still be some trace of the lift – it was built into a sort of false chimney, so it may just have been disconnected and still be there. I'd love to be able to excavate it and have a good look,' she added wistfully.

'When did it become Dunkirk House?' Atherton asked.

'Well, the Morton who built it had a son Morton, and he had a son David who was killed at Dunkirk, so the second Morton renamed the house in his honour. David's younger brother Willie inherited the building business in the sixties, but he only had one daughter, Sandra May, so I don't know what happened to it when he died, whether she inherited it or it was sold. The book doesn't go up that far.'

'And who inherited the house? Who owns it now?'

'I'm afraid I can't help you there. One assumes it was Willie's daughter, but the book doesn't say. And what happened after her time . . . The Land Registry would tell you, presumably?'

Atherton thanked her and rang off; and was writing up his notes when Slider arrived back and favoured the troops with his fresh identification of the victim.

'Chadacre!' Atherton exclaimed. 'Well, that's not a common name. It can't be a coincidence.' And he passed on Ada Forster's story.

'So who is Prue Chadacre?' Swilley said. 'If this Willie inherited in the sixties, she can't be his daughter, can she? She'd have to be a lot older.'

'Granddaughter, then,' said Lœssop.

'But she wouldn't be called Chadacre, would she?' said LaSalle. 'If Willie only had one daughter, and she got married, *her* daughter'd've had a different surname.'

Atherton clapped his hand dramatically to his head. 'Don't tell me, it's the Case of the Long Lost Heir! Prue Chadacre is some previously unknown descendent who's challenging ownership of the entire Chadacre Estate, and the current incumbents murdered her to get her out of the way.'

'Leaving melodrama aside,' Slider said, 'it could be something inheritance related. Love and money are the two great drivers of murder.'

'Which means we're still looking for Philip and Kate Armstrong,' said Lœssop gloomily. 'It's a common name. My Google search turned up thirty-nine thousand results for Philip Armstrong and forty thousand for Kate. It's going to take time filtering that lot.'

'We got a few hits on criminal records, but so far nothing to connect anyone with Dunkirk House,' said Swilley. 'Nothing yet from house-to-house or the council.'

'Well, we might be able to bypass those enquiries,' said Slider. 'Now we have an address, the obvious thing is to go and see if those keys fit.'

He took Atherton and Swilley. The address led them to a newish, three-storey block just behind the main road in Notting Hill. The street had once housed small factories and warehouses which had all over the years been converted to dwellings as industry moved out of London. Channing House was not a conversion, however, but a new build, and probably the worse for it: the converted factory next door at least had nice proportions and solid brick walls to keep out the weather. Channing House, unimaginatively cheap, flat and plain, looked as if it had been made of cardboard, and from a design done by a seven-year-old. All it lacked was a stick figure standing outside with MUMMY written under it in wobbly capitals.

One of the Yale-type keys opened the street door. This was not the sort of building to have a caretaker. 'So far so good,' said Slider. The victim's flat was on the middle floor, and the other key fitted it. Slider opened the door cautiously, fearing a burglar alarm, but nothing happened.

Inside was the sort of minimalist space, low ceilings and cheap finishes which was all you got these days for around three quarters of a million. Even the largest room – the sitting room – was only eleven by twelve. The front door opened into a short corridor which had a kitchen and bathroom on one side and a bedroom on the other, and led straight ahead to the sitting room, which looked down onto the street. The walls and ceiling were off-white, the flooring was wood-effect laminate all through with a plain square of beige rug in the sitting room in front of the beige sofa. The furniture was Ikea-cheap, and plain, and everything was super tidy. There were no pictures on the walls and no belongings in sight. It could have been a developer's show home, except that the purpose of a show home was to stimulate envy in the observer. Or at the very least, preserve the will to live.

'So dull!' Atherton wailed. 'I can feel brain cells dying. Who could live like this?'

'What d'you mean?' said Swilley. 'I think it's nice. Very modern, easy to look after.'

'It couldn't be more different from Dunkirk House, anyway,' said Slider. 'I'll take the bedroom. Swilley, bathroom and kitchen. Atherton, living room.'

The bedroom was as bland as the rest. Built-in wardrobe in 'light oak' veneer MDF. Double bed with white counterpane. Off-white blind pulled half down over the window. Bedside cabinets built in, lamps with off-white shades.

In the wardrobe were clothes neatly hung up, dresses, skirts, tops and trousers, plain, of good quality and un-emphatic colour. Some were in dry-cleaner's plastic wraps. One dress still had the shop's plastic shoulder-guard cape over it and looked as if it had never been worn. It was of some silky material, with a square neck, half sleeves, and a belt round the middle, unpatterned, sage green. The plastic cape was printed TED BAKER in gold. There were two wool overcoats, one navy, one camel. On the top shelf were two leather handbags, both empty, one brown and one navy, in their protective fabric bags. Below, side-by-side on a rack, were pairs of well-kept shoes, low-heeled, so sensible they could have done their own tax returns.

One bedside drawer was empty, and in the other was a pair of glasses in a case, a packet of Kleenex, a pack of paracetamol, half used, and a pack of diazepam with a pharmacy label. Behind them was a Katie Fforde novel. He pulled it out and flicked the pages. The corner of page fifty-eight was turned down, as if to mark progress. But if it was current reading, why was it pushed to the back? It was only his imagination, but he thought he heard the weary sigh as the page was marked and book set aside. If ever a dwelling said that life had no savour for the occupant, it was this one.

He went to join Atherton in the living room, passing Swilley who was leaving the bathroom for the kitchen and said, 'Nothing interesting. A few proprietary medicines, soap and shampoo and per. And everything's spotless. White towels!' she added in a head-shaking tone. 'You can tell she didn't have a husband and children.'

'White sheets as well,' said Slider.

In the living room Atherton was standing by a sort of low-level sideboard on which the television stood. It had a cupboard and three drawers, and he was just shutting the top one. 'Coasters, table mats and napkins,' he explained.

'No sign of her current handbag,' Slider said. 'It's not in the bedroom.'

'Or the bathroom or kitchen,' Swilley agreed.

'I haven't found it,' said Atherton. 'So it looks as if she did take it with her to Dunkirk House, and presumably the murderer nabbed it.'

'Good to have that cleared up,' said Slider.

Atherton opened the second drawer. 'Well, looky here,' he said. 'The story now has illustrations.'

It was a Three Candlesticks box, Slider saw, that had once

held writing paper and envelopes. Did they still sell those in this email age? The box was full of family photographs.

Among the older, black-and-white entries was one of a couple standing formally side by side, the man in a suit with waistcoat holding the hand of a small child in shorts and a Fair Isle jumper, the woman holding a baby of perhaps nine to twelve months. The baby was in a dress and sucking its finger. A golden retriever sat at their feet.

'Look at the background,' said Atherton. 'If that's not Dunkirk House I'll eat my chapeau.'

'Looks like it,' said Slider. The two bay windows, the door between with its stained-glass panels and fanlight were distinctive. The grass was cut short and there was a hint of flower beds over to the left – the house when it was occupied and loved. 'From the clothes and haircuts, I'd guess this was taken in the twenties or early thirties.'

'So that could be Morton Mark Two with the two sons,' Atherton hazarded. 'David that died at Dunkirk and Willie that was father to the lone daughter, Sandra May.'

Still in black and white were several wedding photographs from the early sixties. The woman, in a full-skirted, knee-length, white lace dress, had flick-up hair and a little hat instead of a veil, and the man was in an easy-fitting, double-breasted suit with turn-ups. Women guests had lampshade skirts and Cilla Black hairdos. The same flick-up-hair woman appeared in other photographs holding a baby in trailing Christening clothes.

'I'm betting the baby's Sandra May,' said Atherton, 'the putative inheritrix of the Chadacre empire.'

'You sound like the voice-over in a Charlton Heston film,' Slider complained. 'Is that even a word, inheritrix?'

Atherton didn't answer. He had turned over some more photos with Dunkirk House in the background. Some were of a woman with two children, some of the children alone, some included an older woman, of the age to be the children's grandmother. 'But no man in sight,' he commented.

'The man held the camera,' said Slider. 'Don't read too much into it.'

Swilley came to join them. 'Nothing interesting in the

kitchen. There's food in the cupboards – tins and packets mostly – I'm guessing she didn't do much cooking. In the fridge there's eggs, milk, butter and so on. And a ready meal for one – Tesco's Lancashire Hotpot. Presumably what she was having for supper on Sunday. The washing-up's been done and put away – there's no dishwasher – and everything's spotless.'

'Kitchen bin?' Slider asked.

'Two eggshells, two used tissues, a teabag and an empty milk carton. The one in the fridge is full, so she must have just finished it.' She frowned. 'That's odd, now I think of it. Nobody's rubbish gets collected on a Saturday. Where's the stuff from the rest of the week?'

'Perhaps she took it down on Saturday night. There'll be some sort of communal bin downstairs somewhere. There's a bin liner?' Slider asked.

'Yes, and the bin itself, you could eat your dinner out of it.'

'Everything does seem obsessively clean and tidy,' Slider said. 'I wonder if she emptied her bin every day?'

'That's a bit OCD,' Atherton said.

'Maybe she was,' said Swilley. 'I like a tidy house, but I've never known anyone live like this' – she waved a hand round the featureless room – 'with no belongings. What've you got there?'

'Family photos.'

Swilley looked through them, and picked out one in colour, of a girl of about ten, holding the hand of a skinny boy a little younger. The girl was smiling happily at the camera, full of the natural gladness of the child who hasn't yet understood life's basic awfulness; but the boy, shoulders hunched uncomfortably, was staring away out of the picture as if he wanted to escape. 'Could this be our victim?' she said. 'She must have had some connection with the house, or why would she have all these pictures with it in the background?'

'She could be just a cousin, who happened to inherit them,' said Slider. 'There's always one person in an extended family who ends up being the point of contact for everyone.'

'You mean, say, the family home was sold and everything

cleared and Cousin Prue was the only one who cared enough about the history to keep the photographs?' Atherton suggested.

'But then who are these Armstrongs?' Swilley said. 'And why does the victim have the keys to their house?'

'Good question,' said Slider.

Atherton opened the bottom drawer. 'Treasure trove!' he said, pulling out a cheque book. 'Now we can get her bank statements.'

'That'll help. What else?'

There was a large manila envelope, that proved to be full of documents. 'Leasehold agreement on this flat,' Atherton said. 'Insurance ditto. Long-form driving licence – I wonder if she had a car?'

'If so, there'll be a log book in there somewhere,' said Slider. 'What's that?'

It was a size ten envelope within the envelope. Atherton investigated. 'Birth certificates!' he said eagerly. 'Thank heavens for an orderly mind. Oh. Now this is interesting!'

He handed the first one to Slider. A baby girl, born in 1983 in Queen Charlotte's. Mother's name Sandra May Armstrong, formerly Chadacre of Dunkirk House, Uxbridge Road. Father's name Magnus Armstrong, building contractor, also of Dunkirk House, Uxbridge Road. Baby's name, Kate Prudence.

Slider showed it to Swilley. 'Voilà Kate Armstrong.'

Swilley examined the evidence. 'Can it be our victim? She changed her name?'

'She changed her name,' said Slider.

It explained everything.

Among the other documents neatly folded in the envelope was a marriage certificate from 1982, of Sandra May Chadacre to Magnus Armstrong, both aged twenty-one. The bride's address was Dunkirk House, the groom's Percy Road, Shepherd's Bush. Witnesses William Forrest Chadacre and Benjamin Trossel.

'Magnus Armstrong?' Atherton said. 'Could that be *the* Magnus Armstrong, millionaire property developer and philanthropist?'

'Magnus isn't a common name,' Slider said. 'I've heard of him, vaguely. What does he philanthropize?'

'Most prominently, disabled children, and childhood cancers. Very worthy,' said Atherton. 'I read somewhere he's financing a whole new wing at Hammersmith Hospital.' He frowned. 'Can he really be the father of our victim, though, who lives in this modest way and eats Tesco meals for one? It's a bit odd.'

'Maybe it's not him.'

'Maybe she's not her and I'm not me,' Atherton said, and Swilley snorted.

'The age is about right,' she said sensibly. 'If he was twenty-one in 1982, he'd be – what? – fifty-nine now. Which *the* Magnus Armstrong is. About. And our victim was mid to late thirties, so that's right.'

'She changed her name,' Slider said. 'So perhaps there was a falling-out, and she doesn't have anything to do with him now.'

'If my dad was a multi-millionaire,' Swilley said, '*I'd* damn well have to do with him.'

'Here's another birth certificate,' Atherton said, pulling it out. 'From 1987: Philip Arthur Armstrong.'

'He's her brother,' Swilley exclaimed. 'Not her husband. So why has she got it, and not him? I don't have copies of my brothers' birth certificates.'

Atherton said, 'Cousin Prue syndrome again? Maybe she was the keeper of family history.'

'Someone who disliked her family so much she changed her name?'

'You don't know that's why she changed it.'

'If she owned Dunkirk House,' Atherton complained, 'why didn't she live there, instead of in this' – he waved a hand – 'place?'

'I'd sooner live here,' said Swilley, who hated old things. 'It's clean, modern, easy to look after. That old house'll be full of dust and spiders and silverfish. And it'd cost a fortune to maintain. What I don't understand is why she didn't sell it.'

'It was jointly owned. Maybe brother Philip wouldn't sell,' Atherton said. He looked at Slider. 'You realize this makes him number one suspect? And the house could be the motive. He kills her so that he can sell it and trouser all the cash.'

'You just said he didn't want to sell,' Swilley objected.

'I've moved on from there.'

Slider had taken over the envelope. 'Here's a death certificate,' he said. 'From 2001. Sandra May Armstrong, formerly Chadacre, age forty. Cause of death: 1a, cardiac arrest, 1b hypoxia, 1c hyperkalaemia.'

'What does all that mean?' Swilley said.

'Drowning,' said Slider.

'Drowning?' Atherton said, pained. 'How come?'

Death certificates, of course, didn't give that sort of information. 'The PM was carried out at Charing Cross Hospital. They'll have the records there,' Slider said. And then he remembered. 'Sergeant Paxman said something about a woman dying at Dunkirk House about twenty years ago. He said it was accidental death, but some of them had been suspicious about it. This has got to be it, hasn't it?'

'Quicker to ask him than to trawl Charing Cross,' said Atherton. 'But this makes it all more tasty, doesn't it?'

'Yes, I'm afraid it does,' said Slider. 'And the most urgent thing is to find Philip Armstrong.'

'If he's still alive,' said Atherton.

'If that's what he's still called,' added Swilley.

There was one more thing of interest in the drawer. It was a child's colouring book, depicting fairy tales – *Cinderella*, *The Three Bears*, *Jack and the Beanstalk*, *Little Red Riding Hood* and so on. The pictures had been coloured in with varying degrees of skill, and the Big Bad Wolf had been given a pair of heavy spectacles, while Jack's Giant had been stuck with arrows and axes and knives, and had had his face scribbled out. But there was a loose sheet of paper inside the book, an ordinary white A4 sheet on which a child had drawn a house with smoke coming out of the chimney and lollipop trees to either side, and two stick figures in front. One had a triangle below the waist and wavy lines emerging from its head, suggesting it was female, while the other, lacking these signifiers, was presumably male.

In a house so notably lacking in personal possessions and keepsakes, the fact that it had been retained had to be significant. But who had drawn it, and of whom? Was it from the victim's childhood, and her own hand? Were the stick figures her mother and father? Why had she cared enough about it to hold on to it?

Of course, it could just have survived by accident. It was easy enough to pick up a bunch of papers with something unintended on the bottom. But in a case with so little to go on, you had to hope that everything meant something.

FIVE
The Invisible Woman

The office of the Widewater Wildlife Trust was a former lock cottage on the Grand Union Canal between Harefield and Denham. Gascoyne thanked providence for GPS, or he doubted he would have found it. He was also glad to find there was an access lane running down to the back of it, so he didn't have a long hike along the towpath. Not that the walk would have been a severe trial, on a nice summer day, with a tall shady hedge of blackthorn and sloe on one side and the flat-smelling water of the cut on the other, complete with three hopeful ducks trailing you (there were always three hopeful ducks, a female and two males, wondering if you were concealing bread about your person. It was a Law of Nature).

The place, when he reached it, was picturesque and the setting idyllic: a chubby little flint-knapped cottage in a wrap-around garden stuffed with pansies and marigolds, salvia and mallow, a row of runner beans in scarlet flower, and bees and butterflies abounding. The canal lock in front contributed the agreeable sound of trickling water, while on the other side of the lane at the back, past hawthorn hedges full of birds, were pastures dotted with grazing cows. All this within smelling distance of London: Harefield, about half a mile away, was in the London Borough of Hillingdon, hard though it was to remember.

As he got out of the car, a dog barked and came out of the cottage to inspect him, then ran back to the woman who had appeared at the door with an enquiring expression. The dog – a hairy, curly sort of cross-breed – came back and circled Gascoyne welcomingly. Gascoyne was a fair, well-built man, not exactly handsome, but with the sort of look about him that made women instinctively know he was married with two daughters. When he smiled at the woman, she smiled back with her whole face, and was instantly ready to trust him. It was a thing he had, and Slider made use of it. Women melted with Atherton, too, but that was a different sort of melt: they lusted after Atherton, whereas Gascoyne made them want to be seven again and skip along holding his hand.

'Would you be Sally Lawson?'

'That's me. Detective Constable Gascoyne? Come on in and tell me what this is all about. I've got the kettle on.'

The tiny inside rooms of the cottage had been knocked through to make one reasonable-sized office with a kitchen area at one end. There were two desks with computers, a table with a printer and scanner and another covered in leaflets, and the usual filing cabinets and cupboards.

'This is a nice place to have an office,' he said, with a faint question mark at the end.

'Yes, we are lucky,' she said. 'Henry Bleasdale, who first set up the charity, gave it to the trust, along with a legacy. We have talked about letting it out and getting a conventional office somewhere, but we all love working here so much. And it looks good on promotional literature.'

She headed for the kitchen area and the kettle. Sally Lawson was a tall, lean, tanned woman in her early forties. She was comfortably dressed in jeans and a check blouse in shades of plum and blue, with reading glasses pushed up into her short, sandy, fair hair. She wore no make-up, but she had the sort of firm, clear face of the woman who was put onto her first pony at the age of four, and considers a good wash and an application of Pond's Cold Cream a sufficient beauty regime. It went with the sort of self-confidence that never needed to state itself, and Gascoyne felt very comfortable with her. His father, also a copper, who now taught police recruits at Hendon, had it.

A very elderly terrier-type cross got up out of a basket and ambled across to sniff Gascoyne's shoes.

'That's Posy. The other one's Buffy. You don't mind dogs, I hope?' she asked.

'Not at all.'

'Sugar?'

'One please.' He took the mug from her – white china, with Widewater Wildlife Trust written around it, and a decoration of birds and butterflies. 'This is nice,' he said.

She smiled. 'They are, aren't they? We sell them to raise funds. Mail order mostly, but we do shift quite a few in the summer to the walkers. Best bone china, fourteen pounds each in a nice presentation box,' she concluded with an upward tone and a hopeful look. 'Awfully good cause.'

He evaded that one, and accepted the proffered visitor's chair. She perched herself on the edge of a desk, and seeing there was no sale, said briskly, 'So how can I help you?'

'I'd like to talk to you about Prudence Chadacre.'

'Oh,' she said. 'Well, she hasn't worked here for quite a while – must be five years. Has she done something wrong?'

'I'm sorry to tell you she's dead.'

Lawson looked genuinely shocked. 'Oh, how awful! What happened?'

'It appears she fell down a flight of stairs.'

'How *awful*,' she said again, but with more emphasis. 'Was it – did she – was it the pills?'

'Pills?'

'While she still worked here, she'd started taking diazepam, and they made her feel wobbly sometimes. That's why she left, actually. She had to drive to get here, you see – we're not near any public transport – and she didn't feel safe driving any more. She wanted to get rid of her car and get a job nearer home that she could get to by tube. And she did, in fact, get what sounded like a very nice job. Some sort of architectural charity. It would have suited her down to the ground, because she was interested in old buildings – when she first came, she wanted to know all about this cottage and its history, and she loved hearing about my family home – which is a bit of a stately,' she added with throwaway modesty. 'They asked for a reference for her and I sent them a glowing one. It couldn't be more perfect because the office was in Bayswater, and she lived in Notting Hill, so she could get there on the Central Line.'

'Yes, we know about that,' Gascoyne said. 'But we can't

seem to find out much about her. What can you tell me? You worked with her for some years?'

She frowned. 'Yes, quite a few. But she wasn't a very *forthcoming* person. Didn't talk a lot. She liked to keep busy – you never had to ask her to do a job, she'd just latch on and do it. But she didn't like having to deal with the public. We have open days from time to time, to get up public interest, and she'd always hide away inside. She'd make endless cups of tea and cut sandwiches and so on, but she didn't like handing them out. Terribly shy. Of course, there's no point in trying to force someone like that, so we just let her be. She was tremendously useful in other ways.'

'Her job was . . .?'

'Typing letters, sending out mailshots, all the usual back office work. There are two others apart from me and we did all the public-facing things, and the fundraising, dealing with landowners and government departments and so on. Campaigning.' She raised clear eyes to his. 'We're *terribly* harassed by HS2 at the moment. It's going to cut clear across a lot of *irreplaceable* reserves, if we can't get it stopped.'

He didn't want to wander down that thorny lane. 'Tell me more about Prue. Was she married?'

'Oh no,' she said promptly, and then thought about her answer. 'You couldn't imagine her ever being able to relate to someone in that way. She was very reserved, quite closed off. It took her a long time to get used enough to us to talk at all.'

'About what?'

'Oh, just what one talks about day to day. The weather. Current events. Television programmes watched. Books read. She read a lot,' she added. 'Always had a book on the go. I think she liked to lose herself in stories.'

'What sort of books?'

'Oh, romances. You know, Milly Johnson and Lucy Diamond and Jill Mansell and so on.' Gascoyne nodded wisely as if he did, in fact, know. 'She loved all that sort of thing. But, here's an odd thing – she never kept them. Most of us, when we've finished a book, we keep it on a shelf, or take it to a charity shop. But she threw them away. When I once suggested she gave them to Oxfam, she looked quite alarmed and said, no, she couldn't do that. She would tear off the covers and put them in with the paper waste.'

'Why do you think she did that?'

'I've no idea. It was as if . . .' She frowned. 'This is purely amateur psychology, you know, but it was as if she didn't want to leave any mark on the world. When she left here for her new job, she didn't have to clear her desk – there wasn't anything in it. No personal possessions at all. And she kept everything very clean and tidy – almost unnaturally so. Working out here, we tend not to mind about a bit of mess – muddy footmarks and so on. But she'd clean everything up straight away. Couldn't leave it. Washed up the cups straight after morning coffee, that sort of thing. Her clothes always looked as if they were fresh from the dry-cleaners. Even her car was clean.' She smiled ruefully as if a clean car was something she could only dream of.

'A bit obsessive?' Gascoyne suggested.

'OCD? Possibly. She could be quite nervous – jumpy, anxious. She seemed better some days than others. She'd be fine for a while, and then she'd seem to get depressed and nervous. That's why she started taking the diazepam. She told me she'd been having trouble sleeping and her doctor had prescribed them.'

'Did she mention the name of the doctor?'

'I'm afraid not.'

'Did she have any friends outside work? Who was her next of kin?'

'She never spoke about anyone. I got the feeling that her life consisted of being here, and being at home in her flat, reading, or watching television. She talked a lot about television. She never mentioned any relatives, though, except her brother. Phil.' She gave him an enquiring look, and he nodded. 'She really loved him, talked about him with great affection. He was so clever, so handsome, so artistic, and so on. The only time she talked about her private life was when she told anecdotes from their childhood. I suppose he would be her next of kin.'

'Do you have an address for him?'

'Don't you have one? I'm afraid I don't know where he lived. I got the impression that he moved around quite a bit. Sometimes she would mention having postcards from him. I never saw them, though – I suppose she threw them away, as well.' She frowned in thought. 'She said he loved fishing, and he loved painting. Did she once mention Cornwall?' She pondered. 'I'm not sure. Maybe I imagined that. She wasn't, as I've said, a great communicator.'

'Anything else you can tell me about her? Anything at all?'

She pondered again. 'She wouldn't have her photograph taken – that was an odd thing about her. Anybody came in with a camera she'd shy away like a startled horse. And absolutely refused to be part of group photos. I asked her why once, but she just shook her head and wouldn't answer.'

'That is odd,' said Gascoyne.

'She was an odd person. But very nice,' she added quickly. 'Very hard working. And she loved the doggies. I always think that's a good marker of character, don't you?'

'You could be right.' Gascoyne finished his tea and stood up. 'Well, thank you, ma'am. You've been most helpful. And thanks for the tea.'

She slipped off the desk and stood, too, fixing him with her direct gaze. 'If this was a simple accident, I don't believe you'd be here asking questions. Is there something else? You don't think . . . that she did it deliberately? I'd hate to think she was so unhappy she'd kill herself.' When he didn't immediately answer, she went on: 'It would be a very uncertain way to do it, throwing yourself down stairs. You could end up badly hurt and suffering but by no means dead. It would be *awful* to lie there needing help and not knowing if it would come.'

'We don't think it was suicide,' Gascoyne said, and watched the thoughts pass through her face. Her eyes widened a little more. 'Do you know if she had any enemies, anyone who might want to hurt her?'

She shook her head. 'Enemies? It sounds absurd applied to poor Prue. I don't think she had anyone, friend or foe, apart from her brother. Although, as I said, I haven't seen her for

. . . oh, it must be five years. We sent each other a Christmas
card, but that was all. She might have made new contacts in
her new job; though who could want to do away with her I
can't imagine. She was so . . . harmless.'

Gascoyne thanked her and took his leave. She accompanied
him to the door, and squinted out past him into the hot day,
through which fine threads of gossamer were floating, irides-
cent in the sunlight. A collared dove hooned monotonously
from the cottage roof; the woolly dog rushed past her and
stuck his head into a clump of grass, and sneezed. 'I've sometimes wondered,' she said in the least sure voice he had yet
heard from her, 'whether she actually *had* a brother Phil.
Whether perhaps she made him up.' He didn't answer that. 'It
would be awful to be so alone in the world you had to make
up a brother. If only she'd had a dog! The last time Posy had
a litter I offered her one of the pups. But she declined. Said
she wouldn't be able to look after it. And she couldn't leave
it shut up in her flat all day.'

'Probably not,' Gascoyne agreed.

McLaren didn't like doctors. He reasoned that they didn't
make any money out of you if you were well, so it was in
their interest to find something wrong with you. If you once
got into their hands, you were done for. Atherton opined he
was just scared to find out what his appalling diet of junk
food was doing to him, to which McLaren replied that he'd
had a mate who'd hooked up with a skinny bird who was all
Gwyneth Paltrow and clean eating, he went veggie and died
within the year. McLaren also had an aversion to skinny birds.
His new love, Natalie, was comfortably upholstered, drank
pints when they went out, and could beat anyone at darts. She
was also as fond as the next man of a takeaway, and since
McLaren was the next man, it was a match made in heaven.
So far McLaren had enjoyed remarkably good health despite
(or he would probably contend because of) his constant
snacking, and he hoped to remain that way by never getting
within twelve feet of a medic.

So it was ironic that it was him who, having back-traced
the prescription for Prue Chadacre's happy pills, via the

pharmacy on the label, to the prescribing GP, was told to go off and interview him.

The surgery was in Pembridge Road, in a new building, and was one of those multiple-GP set-ups where you took pot luck and saw whoever you saw. The days of the cosy old buffer who'd looked after your mum and dad and had known you since the cradle were long gone. Despite its newness, the surgery had that distinctive doctor's-waiting-room odour, and McLaren shivered like a horse that smells pigs as he urged the hostile receptionist to get him in straight away. Eventually she was persuaded to ring through, and after the sort of conversation where she spoke in a low voice and shielded her mouth with her hand while staring at McLaren over the top of it, she conceded he could go in next, but he'd have to wait for the patient who was in there to come out. So he still had to wait ten minutes, and a long ten minutes they seemed to him, staring at a poster warning him about Hepatitis B and listening to a coffin cough emitted, remarkably, by a child of about ten.

When he finally got in to see Dr Lal, he found a sleek, well-dressed, good-looking young man with a perfect Oxford accent, who smiled and said, 'I hope I'm not in trouble. I haven't got any unpaid parking tickets on my conscience.'

McLaren sat down gingerly, as though the action might lay him open to being seized from behind and having his blood pressure forcibly checked, and said, 'It's about a patient of yours called Prudence Chadacre. You prescribed her diazepam about three months ago.'

'Chadacre,' he said, turning to his keyboard. 'Unusual name. Sounds vaguely familiar. Do you have the date of birth? Thank you. Let's see.' He tapped and scrolled, and said, 'Ah, yes. April the eighteenth. It was a repeat prescription. I hadn't seen her before. Dr Sharma saw her the previous time, and Dr Chakrabati the time before that. Hmm, hmm. No contra-indications. The patient was generally in good health, blood pressure on the low side but within acceptable range. She seemed a little nervous and complained of feeling depressed and not being able to sleep. As she'd had diazepam before, and seemed a sensible, intelligent woman, I saw no reason not to give a repeat. Though I did say before any further repeat I should want her to have a blood test.'

'What for?' McLaren asked.

'Oh, we like to have a look at the blood of our regular customers, just in case there's anything going on.'

In other words, McLaren thought, you get paid if they have a blood test so you lose no opportunity of copping the proverbial armful. He shivered again, saw Lal automatically perk up and eye him hungrily, and hurried on. 'Is there anything else you can tell me about her? You say she seemed nervous?'

'That's what I've written here,' said Lal. He steepled his forefingers and rested his mouth on them while he thought. 'Yes, she's coming back to me now. Tall lady, late thirties, smartly dressed, would have been quite nice looking if she'd smiled more. She sat on the edge of the seat, very upright, like a good child at school. Looked straight at me the whole time, as if she wanted my approval. Well, we get that a lot, especially with older ladies who live alone. The romance of the white coat, you see.' He laughed deprecatingly. 'It makes us more attractive than we really are. And they long for one-on-one attention. Half the time, I think the depression is just living alone and having no one to bounce off. Loneliness is the great undiagnosed sickness of our society.'

'Yeah, but you said she was nervous and depressed,' McLaren insisted.

'She *seemed* nervous, she *said* she was depressed. She'd been on diazepam on and off for years, according to the records, but she didn't abuse them, didn't take them all the time, so it was felt she could be trusted with them. But I did tell her she must come back in six weeks for a follow-up.' He looked at the screen again. 'Oh. Now that's interesting. She made an appointment for the end of May, but she didn't keep it. According to the note here, she rang up and cancelled it, saying she was feeling fine and wasn't taking the pills any more. And there's been no contact with her since.' Now he looked sharply at McLaren. 'Why are you asking about her? Has something happened?'

'She's dead,' McLaren said, just for the pleasure of seeing him look disconcerted. It was all very well Atherton being cool and wearing expensive suits – he was a copper, so you knew he'd paid his dues – but there was something not right about a doctor being rich and sharp that way. He let Dr Lal open his mouth to ask the anxious question before continuing, 'Nothing to do with the pills. We're looking into a homicide. Did she say anything to you about why she was depressed?'

He frowned, trying to remember. 'Did she? Let me think. I wish we had longer with each patient – there just isn't time to chat. She said . . . she said . . .' If he frowned any harder his eyebrows would become a moustache. 'She said she worried a lot – yes, that's it – and I asked what about, and she said, "I know it's silly, but sometimes I just can't stop thinking, and everything seems to crowd in on me."'

'What d'you think she meant by that?'

'I've no idea.' Lal made an exasperated little movement with his hands. 'If I knew it was going to be important, I'd have asked more questions. But we only get ten minutes with each patient, and that includes taking the blood pressure, which we're supposed to do every time, and making up the notes afterwards. And often, you know, they don't want to tell you what's wrong right away – they want it coaxing out of them, and we just don't have the time. It's very frustrating. People slip through the net all the time. But . . .' He seemed to remember something that reassured him. 'She didn't commit suicide, did she?'

'No, doc, you're off the hook there,' McLaren said sourly – and unfairly, since it was nothing to do with the pills. Anyway, statistics said one in four women got depressed at some time. It'd been in the paper only last week – they'd talked about it in the office. Apparently they claimed things got on top of them. Swilley reckoned it was the sweaty bloke that got on top of them that caused all the trouble, but that was just Swilley. Women were always moaning about something – it kept them going, like talking about footy kept men going. You couldn't pay attention to every little thing they said. Luckily, he had one of the good ones – Nat wasn't a moaner, though she did throw things at him from time to time. But you could always duck. Better than having your ear bent.

SIX

When Shall We Chew Meat Again?

S lider was meeting Joanna after work at the Dove in Hammersmith. She wanted to celebrate her freedom: Zoe was now fully weaned off the breast, so she could go out again and have a drink. Now was the right time, too, when she could take advantage of Kate's presence to babysit. Slider's daughter Kate only stayed with them Monday to Thursday in term time – it was easier to get to her new school from there than from her mother's house – so this was her last week before the summer holidays started.

Atherton joined them just for one drink, as he had a date. 'So you trust Kate with your precious babies, do you?' he asked as they waited for Slider to come back from the bar. He had known Kate through her Goth period, and more recently the head-tossing, eye-rolling, *oh per-leaze!* aeon of disdain for all grown-ups.

'Oh yes,' said Joanna. 'She's really changed since she's been going to the North London. It's making a proper, sensible young woman of her. It's quite a pleasure to have her around the house now – and she does love the kids. Anyway,' she added, looking round as Slider approached, 'if she's worried at all, Dad and Lydia are just downstairs.'

'So they could have babysat?'

'Yes, but I don't want to keep calling on them all the time. They have a life of their own.'

Slider put down three pints of Pride on the table, and Joanna sighed with pleasure. 'Oh, I've dreamed of this moment for over a year. Bung ho!' She lifted the glass and lowered the creamy head by an inch. 'Nectar!'

'And I've ordered the appropriate food.'

'You don't mean . . .?'

'Ham egg and chips.'

Atherton laughed. 'You could have had anything in the world and you chose that?'

'You want proper pub food with a proper pint,' she said firmly. 'Anyway, what could be nicer? That egg, as bright as a Surrealist daisy. That proper carved ham, lifting its savoury fragrance to the waiting nostrils. Those glistening, golden chips, crisp on the outside and fluffy on the inside . . .'

Atherton nodded appreciatively. 'Nice encomium,' he said. 'But you want to lose the "nostrils". There's no way to make that word sound attractive. It has an offaly sound to it. Like "organs" or "tube" or "gristle".'

'Stop spoiling my moment,' Joanna said. 'I suppose you and your female are having something fancy-shmancy?'

Atherton chuckled indulgently. 'Fancy-shmancy! Is that the best you can do? And after the Surrealist egg, too.'

'Well, I presume it's not to be curry, after the last one. Even a fancy-shmancy curry.'

He sighed. 'She's vegetarian. And she wants to go for Thai.'

'What's wrong with that?' Slider said.

Atherton turned to him. 'You like Thai?'

Slider stared at him critically for a moment. 'Tie very smart.' He pointed to his own chest. 'You like shirt?'

Joanna intervened. 'Who is the date du jour, anyway?'

'I have hopes of this one,' Atherton said. 'She's smart. Works for a PR firm in Canary Wharf. Makes a packet. And she has a Mazda MX5.'

'Fun car,' said Joanna.

'That's what I thought.'

'It's a midlife crisis car,' Slider said. 'Are you sure she's not your midlife crisis woman?'

'Give me a chance,' Atherton said. 'This is only the first full date. I don't know her yet. I can only say, indications are mostly favourable. If I can get over the vegetarianism.'

Joanna thought he was beginning to look badgered and changed the subject. 'So how's the new case going?'

Between them they filled her in. 'I think we've done pretty well so far, considering we didn't even know who she was at the start,' Slider concluded. 'Obviously, Hammersmith want results yesterday. If the shout comes in at nine o'clock they expect an arrest by half past.'

'And as we have neither suspects nor motives yet . . .' Atherton said.

'Well, with no men in her life, doesn't the motive have to be money?' Joanna asked, having learned the maxim from Slider. 'You said she'd got a rich father? Maybe she was going to inherit from him.'

'Obviously we'll have to look into him. That's next thing on the list. But if you're going to kill someone for their inheritance, it's best to let them inherit first, don't you think?'

'Point.'

'The brother's the obvious suspect – or at least, person of interest,' Atherton said. 'As joint owner of the house, he comes into full possession of it automatically on her death. And it's worth a million-plus to a developer. That's enough money to stand up as motive.'

'But you don't know where he is?' Joanna asked. 'What about a phone number?'

'Her phone was presumably in her handbag, which is missing – probably taken away by the murderer,' said Slider. 'But we've got the number from her employers, so we can get the phone records and work from there. That plus her bank statements should give us something to get our teeth into.'

'Speaking of teeth,' Atherton said, as a waitress appeared with two plates of gastronomic heaven, 'I'd better be off.' He drained his pint and stood up.

'Have fun,' Joanna instructed. 'What's her name, by the way?'

'You're not going to Google her?' Atherton asked suspiciously.

'Of course not! Just interested.'

'Her name is Georgia Gresham-Hawke,' Atherton said, slightly defensively.

Joanna laughed. 'You're such a stereotype!' She watched him go, then turned to Slider. 'He's not happy, you know,' she said seriously.

'Nor are six out of seven dwarfs,' he replied. 'Tomato sauce with your chips? Or vinegar?'

'Both.'
'Hedonist!'

Slider went in early, and by the time the morning meeting started, breakfast was a distant memory, so he was glad that LaSalle had done the bacon sandwich run to Mike's coffee stall at the end of Shepherd's Bush Market. Mike was an epicure's dream in grease-stained whites, and always remembered that Slider liked streaky in his sandwich, not back.

The reports were all negative to begin with. Jenrich said house-to-house had revealed nothing, which was pretty much what they'd expected. 'We can't even put out a board, because it's not like an RTA: nothing to see,' she complained. 'And no CCTV covering that side of the road because there's no shops.'

'Transport for London cameras?'

McLaren spoke round the sides of a mouthful of a Breakfast Special, a Mike-conceived sandwich that featured bacon, sausage, *and* a fried egg – fortunately well cooked, or there could have been yolk-related sartorial disasters all around. 'There's a traffic camera on the lights at Askew Road that might cover the front of the house,' he reported. 'I'm looking into it, but it might be too far off to make anything out. And bus cameras, once I've got the numbers from TfL – but we don't know an exact time, so there'll be a lot of trawling to do.'

'There always is,' Slider said, not without sympathy. It was a tedious job, and only rarely rewarded by a *Eureka!* moment.

'The council's come back to me, boss,' Swilley said. 'Dunkirk House is not listed as empty. Occupants are registered as Philip and Kate Armstrong. I've asked them to let me know who actually paid the council tax, but you know how slow they are to come back.'

Slider nodded. 'What else?'

'Fingerprints have come in,' Atherton reported. 'The freshest are one lot male, one lot female. The female match the victim, so that's one thing less to worry about. The male come from the front door, the kitchen door, and some partials on other kitchen surfaces that are probably from the same person. Large hands, so we're probably looking for a tall man. There are also some less fresh male prints from a different male with different hands. They could be weeks old. Fathom's going to put them both through records.'

'Good.'

'And the PM report's here. I've put it on your desk.'

'Thanks. What about Philip Armstrong?'

'Still looking, guv,' said Lœssop. 'Nothing yet. We're trying social media as well, but it's a long job.'

'And I've put in for the phone records and the bank statements, but they've not arrived yet,' said Swilley.

'So we'd better have a look at Magnus Armstrong while we wait,' Slider said. 'In the absence of the brother, he would appear to be the next of kin, so at least we should inform him.'

McLaren swallowed the last of his sandwich – Slider half expected to see it travel down his throat like the tin can down the ostrich's neck – and said, 'I'll do it, guv.'

They gathered round his desk while he did an internet search and gradually assembled a lifeline.

According to Wiki, Armstrong had been born in March 1961 to George Armstrong, a motor mechanic, and Margaret Armstrong, of Dunraven Road, Shepherd's Bush. He had attended Christopher Wren School where he had excelled at technical drawing, woodwork, metalwork and mathematics. On leaving school at sixteen with five O Levels he had joined local building firm Larson Brothers, where he had shown such a grasp of the business he had been offered a partnership at the age of twenty-one.

In 1982 he married Sandra May, daughter of William Chadacre, head of the family building company of that name and was made a director.

'Hang on – he refused the partnership in Larson's to marry into Chadacre's?' Atherton said.

'Quicker way up the ladder,' Jenrich said tersely. 'Less like hard work.'

'It seems like it,' Slider said, reading the screen. 'He became managing director on the death of William Chadacre in 1984—'

'That's only two years,' said Swilley. 'Talk about marrying for love!'

'And changed the company's name to Armstrong Construction in 1992.'

'Tactful,' said Atherton.

'Well, but he knew what he was doing all right,' McLaren said in exoneration. 'Made his first million in 1999.'

'The same year he got the contract for the Millennium Arts Centre in the Clifford Dock renewal programme, which was completed in 2000,' Atherton read. 'Must have made his second million with that. And that gave him government contacts, put him in the front row. What you might call a meteoric rise from Dunraven Road.'

Swilley, impatient with waiting for McLaren to scroll where she wanted, had gone to her own desk and was doing her own search. She said, 'Personal life. He married Amelia Lovell, daughter of Lovell's Supermarkets in 2000, having divorced his first wife the same year. Children: by his first wife Kate and Philip, as we know. By his second wife, sons Amyas, 2002, and Frederick, 2003. Oh, look at this: second wife Amelia died in a tragic accident in 2019, aged forty-four.'

'He's remarried again,' Atherton said, over McLaren's shoulder. 'To Edith Alexandra, daughter of Lord Earnshaw, the former Lord Privy Seal, and granddaughter of the Earl of Sutton who was a cabinet minister in the seventies. Impeccable political credentials.'

Swilley was hastily clicking and scrolling. 'Got her. She's twenty-eight. Got a first in PPE from Magdalen. Works as a special advisor to the Department of Business, Energy and Industrial Strategy.'

Jenrich, who had defected to Swilley's desk, said, 'That could be useful. She's not hard on the eye, either.'

'I'm not sure he needs any more added usefulness,' Atherton said. 'He's hugely rich and successful and a noted philanthropist. If anyone's "arrived", it has to be him.'

'Interesting,' Slider mused. 'And it looks as if his eldest, our victim, got left behind in Shepherd's Bush. I think I'd like to have a squint at the great man. Someone find out where he hangs out, and get me an appointment for an interview.'

'I'll do it, boss,' said Swilley.

*   *   *

The family home turned out to be one of those huge stuccoed Kensington mansions in Phillimore Gardens, and there was a country house in Adlestrop in the Cotswolds; but unfortunately – for Slider would have liked to have had a goosey at either or both – it was at his office that Armstrong was discovered and made available. This was in a new glassy edifice on the corner of Byward Street and Trinity Square and had no architectural appeal, other than an enviable view of the Tower of London.

The inside of the building was expensively fitted out and had the atmosphere of hush and seriousness suitable to the making of uncounted boodles and the conscientious spending of same. Slider and Atherton were only kept waiting a nicely-judged eight minutes before being conducted by a fragrant young woman (who was surely called something like Lucinda or Camilla) up in an express lift to the top floor. The big man's vast office was a whole corner, with glass walls round two sides – solar glass that let in the light but kept out the heat – and the panoply of London was spread like a feast for the eyes of the person who could afford it. Slider felt like the Little Match Girl.

Magnus Armstrong was a tall man, with a decent head of silver-grey hair, worn *en crinière de lion*, and a faceful of firm, distinguished features that were near enough to handsome as to make no difference. Add to that a warm and charming smile and blue eyes that crinkled engagingly, and you could see why he was successful with people. Slider's quick once-over took in clothes and shoes so expensive and beautiful he couldn't begin to guess what they cost, and a well-kept hand extended for shaking, with no rings (he disliked jewellery on men). The shooting of the cuff revealed a slim-profiled watch whose very lack of flamboyance suggested it cost about what Slider earned in a year.

'Magnus Armstrong. How do you do. You're Chief Inspector Slider? What can I do for you?' He had a rich sort of voice – the sort you felt on your skin as well as heard – and a neutral accent, not over-posh but clear, like a BBC news reader.

'I'd like to talk to you about your daughter,' Slider said, and paused, because he didn't know which name Armstrong would know her by.

Fortunately, he solved the problem. 'Kate, you mean?' he said with a surprised look. 'Has she got into trouble?'

'Why would you think that?' Slider asked.

Armstrong smiled faintly as if he knew that lever. 'Because *you're* here. No other reason. I haven't seen her for . . . oh, twenty years at least, but I suppose if she did get into trouble she might think I could get her out of it. Though what trouble that would be I can't imagine. She was always a very placid, docile girl. I simply can't imagine her committing a crime.'

'She hasn't, as far as we know,' Slider said.

'Well, it must be something important to warrant a visit from a chief inspector,' he said genially. 'Where's she living these days?'

'I'm sorry to have to tell you, sir, that she's dead.'

It seemed to take a moment to register; the smile remained, but the rest of his face slithered away from it. 'Dead?' said Armstrong, blankly. The smile disappeared too, a frown took over. 'What do you mean, she's dead? How?'

'It appears she fell down a flight of stairs,' Slider said.

'I thought you were going to say it was a car crash. What stairs, where? And why are you here, if it was just a fall?'

'Further investigation suggests it wasn't an accident.'

'What – you mean she threw herself down? She was pushed? What are you saying?' The impatient questions rapped out. This was a man used to command.

'We think she was murdered, sir.'

'Murdered?' Armstrong sat down on the nearest designer chair and rubbed his hands over his face. 'Murdered!' he said again, with a different intonation. 'Who on earth would want to murder *her*?' He rubbed his face again, and then looked up sharply. 'But why have you come to me? Why are you telling me? You're not trying to tell me that someone killed her to get at me? I don't have any enemies that I know of. I'm not that sort of businessman. In any case, why would anyone even think of her? There's no connection between us any more. I divorced her mother twenty years ago and haven't seen or heard of her since. I doubt if I'd even recognize her now.'

'We hoped you might be able to tell us something about her recent life. She seems to have been a very private person.'

He waved Slider and Atherton, at last, to seats. 'I know nothing about her life or circumstances. I don't even have her address.'

'Really, sir?'

'It was not an amicable divorce, you see. There was a great deal of acrimony on my first wife's part. She made things as difficult as possible for me. I won't even mention the settlement, but it was punitive. And she turned Kate against me, and promised I would never see her again. And so it's turned out.' He shrugged. 'I don't claim to be unique. I'm not the only divorced father in the country cut off from his offspring. It was very painful for me, but I came to terms with it. I made myself a new life, I remarried, I had a second family, and I hope you won't think badly of me if I say I no longer think about the first one. If Kate had ever come to me asking for help, of course I would have given it, but that never happened. She shut me out of her life, and I did the same with her. So you see,' he concluded with a small, tight smile, 'how odd it seems to have you come to *me* about her.'

'Were you aware that she changed her name? She took her mother's surname.'

He didn't answer for a moment, but then said slowly, 'No, I wasn't. Somehow, that doesn't surprise me.' He sighed, and then stood up.

'Thank you for bringing me this news, unwelcome as it is. I may be technically her father, but as you see, I know nothing of her recent life, so I'm afraid there's nothing I can help you with. I don't know who her friends were, or what places she frequented, or anything of that sort. She has never tried to contact me in all these years.'

'Well, thank you for your time, sir,' Slider said, rising to leave.

Armstrong escorted them to his door, and said, 'You'll keep me informed about the progress of your enquiries? When all's said and done, she was my child. I'd like to see the perpetrator brought to justice. If there's anything I can do to facilitate things for you – I have a number of contacts in high places, including the Home Office.'

'Thank you, sir,' Slider said, sturdily neutral.

*   *   *

Stepping out from the frosty-cool air-conditioned building onto stifling hot Trinity Square was like having a large dog pant in your face.

'Was that last bit a threat, by any chance?' Atherton said. 'The bit about knowing people in the Home Office?'

'Not so much a threat as a reminder of who he is. But he was remarkably unarrogant about talking to us. I expected a lot more chill and why-are-you-bothering-me.'

'Can he really not have had *any* contact in all this time?'

'There are men all over the country who've lost contact with their offspring. He was right about that. Though, of course, in most cases the offspring wouldn't know where to find the father. That's not the case here. It would have been easy for Prue Chadacre to locate him if she'd wanted to. But an acrimonious divorce—'

'And a lot of wives under the bridge since then,' Atherton said. 'He never mentioned Philip. I wonder why?'

'We didn't ask about him.'

'Perhaps he was a bit of a dud, not one to add lustre to his father's name,' Atherton said. 'He's got two new ones now. Better models, perhaps.'

'Not forgetting the new-reg, GT wife. That's enough to keep a man occupied.'

'Do you realize we're standing out here in the hot sun when right next to us is a decent-looking pub?'

Slider turned his head. 'Oh yes – the Liberty Bounds. I suppose it wouldn't hurt to have lunch before we go back.'

'What a good idea. Then I can write up my notes while they're still fresh in my mind.'

'How did the double-barrelled date go, by the way?' Slider asked as they turned in.

'Disaster. We went back to her place after nosh, and she got out a bottle of white wine that she said was her favourite. I had to drink a glass.' He rolled his eyes.

'Embalming fluid?' Slider asked with sympathy.

'Worse. More like jet fuel.'

'Ah,' said Slider. 'I think I know that one. Isn't it called Vin Diesel?'

SEVEN

Old Families Last Not Three Oaks

B ack at the factory, he was reminded that he hadn't picked Paxman's brains yet. Waving Atherton on up the stairs he turned aside through the connecting door into Processing. Paxman was standing behind the desk ingesting a mug of tea. Somehow, with Paxman, you always wanted a grander word for the ordinary things he did. 'Majestically ingesting' was about right.

He gave Slider a look that was not exactly benevolent. Large creatures famously have long memories, and he had never quite forgotten that at one point in the past there had been Irregularity in Slider's life. OK, he'd made an honest woman of Joanna in the end, but that didn't expunge the preceding sinfulness.

'You've finally come to ask me about Dunkirk House, have you?' he said sourly.

Slider knew there was no point in buzzing around an already testy bull. 'Sorry, Arthur. I wasn't forgetting, just there's a lot to do in the first stages. So, what was this case you were talking about? Have you got time now?'

A soft answer turneth away wrath, especially when the answerer outranks you by several important rungs. Paxman settled his weight slightly, took a slurp of tea, and said, 'I've been thinking about it. Musta been 2001, thereabouts – you can look it up.'

Slider nodded. Paxman wouldn't have said 2001 unless he'd already checked it himself.

'Woman by the name of Armstrong – Sandra May Armstrong, age forty, divorced, two teenage children. They'd be – what? – fourteen and eighteen, both living with mum. Boy was at school, girl was doing a secretarial course. Both out all day, you see?'

'Yes,' said Slider.

'Boy gets home first, about four, ha-past, finds his mother dead in the bath.'

'In the bath?'

'Head under the water. Boy's testimony is the water was still warm when he found her, so she'd not long been in there. Who takes a bath in the afternoon?'

'So we were suspicious, were we?'

Paxman frowned. As an expression of disfavour it was as alarming as tectonic plates moving, but the disfavour was not directed towards Slider this time. '*We* weren't! *I* mighta been, if my opinion'd been asked, but it wasn't. It wasn't investigated as it shoulda been, and I'll tell you why. Mr Dickson put Alcock and Hough onto it.'

Dickson was the detective superintendent in those days, and Richard Alcock and Sharon Hough were detectives who had left before Slider had come to Shepherd's Bush, but their fame had outlived them. They had been inseparable workmates, spoke alike, finished each other's sentences, even looked rather alike – same height and build and with similar length and colour hair – so their department nicknames had been Alcock and Nocock, or sometimes Dick and Dickless. What made them notorious was that their closeness had segued into an affair, despite the fact that both were married. Contrary to the usual human experience, their passion only increased over time, and the affair had eventually become red hot and scandalously indiscreet. They were doing it everywhere, to the neglect of their duties, and the final crash was inevitable. A pregnant Mrs Alcock (the baby wasn't actually her husband's, but that did not emerge, like the baby, until some time later) stormed the station and demanded justice and heads on plates. She threatened to go to the press and the commissioner if the fornicating miscreants weren't hauled up, heaved apart, hosed down, and summarily punished. Everyone then had to admit to themselves what they'd known all along and were hoping would never come out. Dick and Dickless were suspended and, after a disciplinary hearing, sacked for misconduct and bringing the service into disrepute.

What no one knew, of course, was whether any cases had been affected, and if so how, and how many.

'It was brought in accidental death,' Paxman went on. 'She was on tranquillizers, so it was reckoned she'd got drowsy, slipped under the water and drowned. And the PM discovered she'd got twice the normal dose in her system, so that made sense of it – she'd taken a pill, forgotten she'd taken it, and taken another.'

'So what did you suspect?' Slider asked. 'Suicide?'

'Coulda been, coulda been that,' Paxman allowed grudgingly. 'But if she'd wanted to kill herself, she'd a' taken more than two pills, wouldn't she? They always do.'

'Homicide, then?' Slider asked.

Paxman's normally stationary gaze slid away for a moment, proving he felt he was on shaky ground. 'Like I said, who takes a bath in the afternoon? And water in the face when you go under'd wake you up unless you were heavily sedated – or held down. But they didn't even look into that. Didn't want the bother. They wanted it off the books as accidental death and that's what they got.'

'So who did you suspect?'

'Not my business to go suspecting people.'

'Come on, Arthur! You've been thinking about this for all these years.'

'Only just thought about it for the first time Monday when you come back from the house,' Paxman said stubbornly. 'But if it'd a' been me, I'd a' looked at the son. Queer sort of fish he was – not right in the head, if you ask me. He was the only witness. He *says* he found her dead, but who's to say? And – something you won't find on the files, because those two useless lumps never wrote it down – he bunked off school that afternoon. It was a Friday and they did cross-country all afternoon, and he'd got out of it. Sick note or summink. Supposed to be working in the library until home time, but he slipped out, went fishing instead. So he *says* – which means no one actually knew where he was all afternoon. Alcock assumed he had an alibi, but he never.'

'How do you know all that?'

'The kid told me, while he was waiting to be interviewed by Alcock and Hough. They were setting up the interview room – so they said. More like wanted a few more minutes alone so they could paw each other. So I was alone with the boy. He seemed to want to get something off his chest. Looked guilty as hell – nervous, twitchy, muttering to himself – like I said, I reckon he was a few sandwiches short of a picnic. He blurted it out to me that he'd not been at school. Course, I told Alcock when he come back, and he thanks me all smarmy and uppity and says, "I don't need you to do my job for me." But when I asked him afterwards, he said he'd not made a note of it because it wasn't relevant, because it was accidental death.'

'Well, thanks, Arthur. That's very interesting.'

'All I'm saying is, their minds weren't on the job. It wasn't investigated properly.'

'Right.'

'I had a feeling about that boy,' said Paxman with a martyred look, the Cassandra of Shepherd's Bush, doomed never to be believed. 'When you've been in the Job as long as I have, you get a nose for these things.'

'Shorn of Sergeant Paxman's prejudices, could there be anything in it?' Slider mused when he had filled Atherton in.

'Hard to say,' said Atherton. 'Two coppers being on the job when they should be on the Job? That would enrage him so much he'd see everything through a red filter. And a fourteen-year-old boy murdering his own mother? Seems unlikely. Unless he was severely unbalanced. We'd need to see the files and whether there was anything about a past history of mental disturbance. Of course,' he added, brightening, 'that would certainly help our case. Killed his mother and then killed his sister. I wonder if he's been institutionalized at any point. I don't think anyone's checked the mental health system for him, have they?'

'Good point. That could be why we can't find him.' Slider stared at the wall, thinking. 'It would be a very bad thing indeed if it turned out to be true.'

'Yes – a murder not discovered, and another death that could have been prevented if two randy coppers hadn't been going at it like knives. The press would love that.'

'It must never get to the press,' Slider said. 'But we need

the original file on the case – the paper file. Have a word with Connie Bindman at Hammersmith, will you.'

'Right. But you realize if Alcock and Hough weren't doing their job properly, there's not likely to be very much on the file.'

'I know. But you have to go through the motions.'

'Also,' Atherton said from the door, 'there's no reason a person wouldn't take a bath mid-afternoon. Particularly if that's the one time she can be sure of having the house to herself.'

'What about mid-morning?' Slider suggested.

'Housework,' Atherton said.

Swilley raised her head as Slider came through from his office and said, 'I've got the bank statements, boss. The utilities and the council tax on Dunkirk House as well as on the flat are paid by her by direct debit.'

'So that's one thing cleared up.'

'And there's a small mortgage on the flat, but nothing on the house. There are also two credit cards and two mobile phones paid for by direct debit. And here's the interesting thing: her income. Every month, a bank transfer comes in from solicitors Kenton Orr for £4,150. And every month £1,200 is transferred by standing order into an account in the name of Philip Arthur Armstrong.'

'Any other income?'

'Her salary from the Historic Buildings National Drawings Archive, but that's not even two hundred a week after deductions. She must just've been doing that for a hobby, to pass the time. This money from the solicitors – that's close on fifty thou a year. Must be some kind of trust fund, don't you think?'

'We'll have to ask them,' said Slider.

'They're a local firm,' said Atherton, who knew all the solicitors' firms in a wide area. There had been a time in his past when he'd had a thing about doinking solicitorettes. 'Interesting that she pays money to the brother. I wonder what that's all about?'

'Not enough to be blackmail,' McLaren said.

'Blackmail? You've got a nasty mind.'

'If he's got a bank account, the bank will have an address for him,' Slider said.

'Already on it, boss,' said Swilley. 'Just waiting for a reply. And the second mobile phone – I wonder if that's the brother's. Maybe she was taking care of him.'

'The suggestion has been made that he was mentally disturbed in some way,' Slider said, and told them what Paxman had told him. 'We don't know if it's true, of course, but it's something to bear in mind. And by the way, no whisper of this Alcock and Hough complication is to escape these four walls, am I clear?'

There was a murmur of agreement, then Jenrich said, 'Boss, what are the odds, this geezer Armstrong, two of his wives dying in "tragic accidents"?'

'Tragic accidents do happen,' Slider said.

'Yeah, but wifey one dies, he remarries, wifey two dies, he remarries. It's a pattern, isn't it?'

'Barely that, but it might be worth looking into.'

'You like Magnus Armstrong for the murder, do you?' McLaren asked her.

'He's a man, he's rich and powerful. What's not to like?'

'All right, settle down,' said Slider. 'That's not a reason. But you can see what you can find out about the second Mrs Armstrong's demise.'

Jenrich wrinkled her nose, but with a smile. '"Demise". You don't half talk funny sometimes, guv.'

'I'm a very funny man,' said Slider. 'But remember, wifey number one divorced him. What would be the motive for killing her? He was already remarried when she died.'

Jenrich grunted, in the manner of one not convinced but too polite to say so.

'Now, what's the address of these solicitors?' Slider asked.

Porson had a cup of tea and a document on the top of the filing cabinet and was reading while he sipped. He was not a great one for sitting down. Slider often wondered if he slept standing up, like a horse.

He looked up as Slider appeared in the open doorway, and said, 'Any progress?'

Slider updated him, and told him of Paxman's theory. It was before Porson's time, too, of course, but he had heard of Alcock and Nocock. He had always heard of everything. If he'd been universally available as an app, there'd have been no need for Google.

'We don't want baseless suppostitions, thank you,' he said with a mighty scowl. In his tempestuous wrestle with life and the Job, Porson's words frequently got mangled between brain and fresh air. 'If that got out, the spit really would hit the spam. Sergeant Paxman should know better than to go dredging up old alligators like that, with nothing to go on.'

'I think he disapproved of—'

'Yes, yes, we all do, but that's all water under the fridge now. Least said, soonest mentioned.'

'All the same,' Slider urged gently, 'Philip Armstrong . . .'

The scowl disappeared like a lizard down a crack. Porson sipped his tea in human mode. 'Oh, quite,' he said. 'Got to look at him. As things stand, he's in the hot seat. What are you doing to find him?'

'Well, so far the press release only says a woman was found dead. So we'll put out a follow-up, naming the victim, see if that flushes him out. And we'll put out a countrywide police alert for him. Difficulty is, we don't have a recent photograph. She only had old family snaps from when they were children. But there's one of him when he was about fourteen and we'll do what we can with that.'

'You need to be precautious,' Porson suggested. 'If he *is* a few bricks short of a shilling, we don't want the press howling after us for insensitivity.'

'Oh, certainly,' Slider agreed. 'Meanwhile, we might get a lead from the solicitor, and we'll keep looking for other contacts of hers.'

Porson nodded. 'I'll distract Mr Carpenter if he looks this way.'

'Thank you, sir,' Slider said. For all Porson's oddities, he knew his job – which was primarily to keep the spit off the spam for long enough for Slider and his firm to do theirs.

*   *   *

Kenton Orr had offices in a very smart new block in Glenthorne Road, with twenty-four-hour security, hot and cold running lifts, full height solar glass windows – every damn thing that opens and shuts, as Barry McKenzie used to say. They had transferred there only a year before from a cobbled-together, knock-through sort of suite above the shops on Shepherd's Bush Green, where they had been since 1902, so it wouldn't have been surprising if some of the older members of staff were suffering from a bit of culture shock. Just the increased amount of daylight would take some getting used to. Ask any vampire.

It was not to be wondered, then, that Mr Felbrigg looked a bit blinky and bewildered, like an owl woken at noon. He was elderly, with sparse grey hair, and a sort of downward-drooping face, the flesh descended like melting tallow in folds either side of the mouth to join up with the loose wattles under the chin. He looked like a bloodhound that had just received very bad news.

He had reason for it when Slider had finished his exposition. 'This is dreadful,' he said. 'Absolutely dreadful. Sunday, you say? Why wasn't I informed before?'

'Because we had no means of identifying the body at first. And when we were able to search her flat, we found nothing there to help us – no papers, nothing to lead us to you until we acquired the bank statements.'

Felbrigg looked a hint more sorrowful. 'Ah, yes, Kate was always worried about burglars. She asked us to keep all her important documents – passport, the Trust deeds, her Will, and so on. We have a whole box for her in the safe.'

'And I presume you are her executor?'

'I have that honour,' he said, with a solemn bow of the head.

'And you know her as Kate Armstrong?'

'You must excuse me. My connection with the family goes back a long way. I know she changed her name – indeed, I drew up the deed poll – but to me she is – was – always Kate.'

'I would like to hear about your connection with the family, if you would be so kind.' This courtliness business was catching. Slider felt Atherton look at him and deliberately not snigger.

Felbrigg sat back in his chair with the air of one with a story to tell. 'The Chadacres had been clients of Kenton Orr since the 1920s,' he began. 'I took over their affairs from the younger Mr Orr on his retirement in 1980. At that time William Forrest Chadacre – Kate's grandfather – was the head of the family, and of the company. A building firm, you understand?'

'Yes. And was it doing well?'

'Extremely well. The earlier generations of Chadacres had amassed quite a fortune over the years. But by the time I took over the files, William Chadacre, though not old, was in poor health, and not expecting to make old bones. So he was very pleased when his daughter Sandra May got married at the age of twenty-one, and to a fine, vigorous man who was also in the building trade. Magnus Armstrong cut his teeth at Larson's, a very respectable company. Sandra May was William's only child and he adored her. He confided to me that he had been worried about what would happen to her if he died suddenly, leaving her to cope all alone. A husband to take care of her, and run the company for her, was exactly what he'd hoped for.'

'So did he make any financial changes at that time?'

'Not immediately. I think he wanted to wait and see whether Armstrong lived up to his promise.'

'Very wise.'

'Yes, William was a thoughtful man. I'm sure he would have kept the reins firmly in his own hands had his health allowed. However, he had a mild stroke, which increased his fears of leaving his family unprotected. And when Kate was born, he worried that at some point she might be left unprotected, as he had feared Sandra May might be. So he drew up a new Will at that point, leaving a considerable sum in trust for Kate. She was to have access to the income from the trust from the age of eighteen, and any outlay of capital was to be at the trustees' discretion until she was twenty-five, at which time the whole was to be handed over to her. In the event, she asked us to continue to look after her inheritance, and the investments have realized such a good income that she has only once asked for a capital sum to be made liquid, and that was to buy the flat where she now lives.'

'She didn't buy it outright? There is a small mortgage.'

Felbrigg refrained from asking how he knew that. 'We recommended a small mortgage, to enhance her credit rating. People with no credit history at all are at a disadvantage in this modern world.'

Slider nodded to the point, and continued. 'William didn't make any provision for his grandson, Philip?'

'William died in 1984, and Philip wasn't born until 1987, or I'm sure he would have. But Kate has always taken care of him. She keeps Dunkirk House going entirely for him, and pays a proportion of her income over to him.'

'A proportion. Not half?'

Felbrigg looked as if a slightly indelicate suggestion had been made. 'The inheritance was made to her without condition,' he said disapprovingly. 'She is entitled to dispose of it as she sees fit. But the upkeep of the house is considerable. When that is added to the allowance she makes to Philip, it comes to very little less than half.'

Slider made amends. 'That's very generous. Not everyone would behave so well towards a sibling.'

Felbrigg sighed. 'That, I'm afraid, is very true. Much of our business is generated by squabbles between siblings over inheritance. But Kate and Philip were always very close.'

'How did they come to own the house?'

'Sandra May left it to them jointly in her Will. She died, as you may perhaps know, in a tragic accident in 2001.'

'Yes, we did know,' Slider said. 'What happened to the business?'

'That had already passed into the hands of her husband.'

Atherton spoke. 'She gave him the whole company?'

Felbrigg looked slightly defensive. 'It was he, after all, who ran it, and who had steadily built it up over the previous almost twenty years. She knew nothing of the day-to-day running, the contracts, the investments, and so on. Magnus Armstrong took a good business and made it better. As her solicitor, I would not of course have advised her to give up control entirely, but it was what she wanted, and there is no doubt that he ran it well, and she and the children never wanted for anything.'

'But when she was divorced, surely ownership must have been an issue?' Atherton said. 'Especially as it was acrimonious.'

'Who said it was?' Felbrigg looked surprised.

'Magnus Armstrong said so,' Slider answered.

Felbrigg shook his head. 'I did not, of course, act for him. I cannot speak to his state of mind, and naturally no outsider can tell what goes on inside a marriage. But as far as I was aware it was mutually acceptable to both partners.'

'What were the grounds?' Atherton asked.

'Unreasonable behaviour. According to Sandra May, they agreed on that between them. The instances cited were Armstrong's devoting too much time to his career, their having no common interests, and his pursuing a separate social life.' He looked from Atherton to Slider. 'Bear in mind that the court doesn't usually insist on severe allegations of unreasonable behaviour in order to grant a divorce. Relatively mild allegations normally suffice, if they are not contested.'

'So *she* divorced *him*.'

'Indeed.'

'And what settlement did she get?'

'She had been paid an allowance, a very generous allowance, out of the business ever since she transferred ownership to her husband. That was doubled. It was more than she asked for, but considering how well the company was doing, I believe it was reasonable.'

Slider pondered. An amicable divorce in 2000, and she died a year later in a 'tragic accident', by which time Armstrong was already remarried to a wealthy second wife and had a son. There didn't seem to be any reason to connect him to Sandra May's death. And, he reminded himself, it wasn't that, in any case, that they were investigating.

'Why did Kate change her name?' he asked abruptly.

Felbrigg took a moment to change direction. 'It was after the divorce. She wanted to take her mother's surname. She said she felt she was a Chadacre, not an Armstrong. I think she resented a little that her father had changed the name of the company. And it was, after all, the Chadacre fortune that was paying her income. I suppose it was loyalty to the family, keeping the old name going which would otherwise disappear.

And she said she had never really liked the name Kate.
Prudence was her grandmother's name,' he added. 'William's
wife. She died when Kate was ten. She was always very fond
of her granny.'

Well, all that made sense, Slider thought. It was crunch
time. 'Tell me about Philip,' he said.

EIGHT
Nuts. And Bolts

'Ah, poor Philip,' said Felbrigg. 'It must have been a dreadful shock to him to be the one to discover his mother's body. He was just a schoolboy, you know. And he had always been a rather sensitive child.'

'In what way, sensitive?' Atherton asked.

'Oh.' Felbrigg seemed to grope for vocabulary. 'Well, nervy, you know. Easily upset. Feeling things too deeply. I never had much to do with him, you understand,' he added. 'I am only going by what Sandra May, and later Kate, told me. I understood there was some question of his being a little . . . oh dear, I'm not sure what the acceptable word is these days. In my youth we used to say backward, but I'm sure that would be thought offensive now.'

'I get the idea,' Slider said, waving him on.

'Not severely, you understand. Just a little slow. And it would surely upset even a normal boy, his mother's sudden death. What it must have done to Philip is hard to imagine. And so soon after the shock of the divorce.' He shook his head at the thought. 'Kate in particular has always been very protective of him. She worries that he can't cope with modern life.'

'Has he ever had a psychiatric evaluation?' Atherton asked, keeping it brisk. 'Or treatment? Has he ever spent time in a psychiatric hospital?'

'Not to my knowledge,' Felbrigg said. He seemed to take the question amiss. 'Many people are made nervous and depressed by the traumas in their lives, without being classified as mentally ill.'

'We're simply trying to get the whole picture,' Slider said soothingly. 'And, in fairness, by your own account, you don't know Philip very well.'

Felbrigg bowed his head in acknowledgement. 'I only know what Kate tells me. Told me,' he corrected himself, putting his hands to his face for a moment, pulling it a mite further down. 'I was forgetting for a moment what brought you here. This is going to be devastating news to Philip. Devastating! To lose his mother, and now to lose the sister who meant everything to him. Have you spoken to him yet? How is he, poor chap?'

'We haven't found him yet,' Slider said. 'We were waiting for the bank to send us his address. But perhaps you can help us there – do you have an address for him?'

Felbrigg looked blank. 'Well, Dunkirk House is his address, of course. Kate keeps – kept – it up for him, as he was so attached to it. But I believe he is not there a great deal. He likes to travel.'

'Travel?' said Slider, heart sinking. If they had to trawl for him all over the world it would make a long job longer.

'By train, mostly,' said Felbrigg. 'Sometimes bus. He doesn't drive. He likes to pack a few things in a rucksack and go wandering about the country. Kate says he likes to fish, and to sketch – they are his passions. He stays a few days in a hotel or a bed and breakfast, then moves on. She gave me once a very pretty watercolour he had done of St Ives harbour, in Cornwall. I had it framed and I have it still, on the wall at home. I believe he favours Cornwall rather, which is not surprising, given how picturesque it can be. But there's no knowing where he might go next. He kept in touch with Kate by means of postcards, and latterly by mobile phone, just to say he was all right. Then every now and again he would come home to Dunkirk House – "to do his washing", she used to say.'

'How does he manage for money?' Slider asked.

'Oh, he has a credit card, and he can draw cash out from the bank when he needs it. His wants are few, and he manages, I believe, very well on what Kate gives him as an allowance. I suspect he seldom spends it all.'

'Are there any close family friends, or other family members, that we can talk to, who might have contact with Philip?' Slider asked.

'There are no other family members on the mother's side,' Felbrigg said. 'I never heard of any on the father's, but I had nothing really to do with him. Kate never spoke of any. As to family friends . . .' He pondered. 'No one comes to mind. I wish I could help you more,' he concluded. 'But Philip will turn up in the fullness of time.'

Slider rose to leave, then recollected. 'Oh,' he said, 'you mentioned that you had Kate's Will in your keeping. What happens to the Trust money now?'

'The Trust has long been dissolved, as I told you,' said Felbrigg. 'The money is soundly invested, and it would be up to the legatee to keep the investments going as they are, or to move the money elsewhere.'

'That wasn't what I meant. I meant, who inherits?'

Felbrigg raised his eyebrows. 'Philip, of course. There isn't anyone else. She left everything to him.'

'"He'll turn up in the fullness of time",' Atherton quoted, as they stepped out into Glenthorne Road – crisped air, and the smell of freshly baked car exhaust. 'Unless, of course, he was not merely sensitive but nuts, did something regrettable and bolted. It'll be hard to bring him in when we don't know what he looks like.'

'If he's bolted, sooner or later he'll have to use his credit card,' Slider said.

'True,' Atherton said, cheering up. 'And if he draws out cash we'll get an image from the ATM camera.'

'Though why he would suddenly kill the sister who's taken care of him all these years . . .'

'There's taking care of, and then there's smothering. She might have been unbearable – she sounds a bit strange, with the obsessive tidiness. Maybe she chucked away something of his – a painting he'd done specially for her, for instance. Hurt his feelings. The straw that let the cat out of the bag, as Mr Porson might say. On another level, the money certainly gives a motive the CPS would understand. Her income of fifty large suggests a fund of, what, a couple of million? Plus Dunkirk House, ripe for development, worth at least another. Enough to be going on with.'

'But if he killed her he wouldn't get it anyway,' Slider said.

'Only if he was nailed for the crime,' Atherton qualified.

'Hmm,' said Slider. 'Yes, and murderers seldom think that far ahead.'

'Or maybe he did it during a psychotic episode,' Atherton said, plipping the car. 'Maybe he heard the voices – maybe Opochtli told him to do it.'

'Who or what is . . .?'

'Aztec god of fishing.'

Slider got in the car. 'The things you know,' he said.

'Thank you,' said Atherton modestly.

'It wasn't a compliment. I was thinking of how much brain power you waste on arcane and irrelevant information.'

'It's all part of my ineffable charm.'

Atherton preceded Slider through the door, and Nicholls, the duty sergeant, looked up and acknowledged him. 'Jim. How's the dating going? Word is, you're seeing a different woman every night. Must be exhausting.'

'So many women, so little time,' Atherton sighed. 'I have to do my bit for womankind – spread myself a bit thinner than I have been doing. It's only fair to give them all a chance.'

'Arthur Paxman says you're a sex addict,' said Nicholls.

'Rubbish. Like the man who was addicted to brake fluid, I can stop any time,' Atherton said with dignity.

Nicholls shook his head, and said, 'Oh, and Bill – there's someone waiting to see you.'

'I think I was born with someone waiting to see me,' Slider complained.

'You'll like this one,' Nicholls smiled. 'A lady. Very fragrant.'

She stood up as Slider came in, stepped towards him and held out a hand. 'Pandora Ormsby-Cecil,' she announced, with such pure, unalloyed self-confidence that Slider actually took the hand and shook it without a thought, though usually he didn't like to touch members of the public. You never knew where they'd been.

'Detective Chief Inspector Slider,' he replied.

'I'm the archivist at the Historic Buildings National Drawings Archive.'

'Yes, I know,' Slider said.

'Gideon Lankester said you'd like to see me when I got back from Yorkshire.'

'Yes – won't you sit down?'

She was whisper-slim, probably in her fifties, but so beautifully presented – he didn't say 'preserved' even to himself because it had the wrong connotations – that she might have been ten or fifteen years younger. Her exquisitely-carved face had that watercolour-on-ivory delicacy of colouring that made her skin look slightly luminous; her hair was a thick and glossy dark brown bob, her eyes were hazel and bright and her look direct. She wore beige trousers and a cream silk blouse with expensive-looking nude heels; gold earrings and necklace; a wedding ring and diamond eternity ring on one beautifully-kept hand, and a watch with a leather strap on the other slim wrist which he knew instinctively, without being a watch aficionado, had cost in the thousands. She also smelled delicious. There was a certain sort of expensiveness that you pretty much had to be born into, and which looked very different from anything later-acquired wealth could achieve. No WAG could copy it. She was effortlessly perfect.

'I'm sorry I wasn't able to come sooner,' she said. 'There was a country-house sale that I wanted to take in while I was down there, and Gideon didn't say what you wanted me for. I hope it wasn't urgent.'

'He thought you might know more about Prudence Chadacre than he did, as you probably spent more time with her.'

'Yes, poor Prue – what a dreadful thing,' she said. 'Can she possibly have been murdered? Was it a house robbery gone wrong?'

'It was nothing like that,' Slider said. 'We believe it must have been someone who knew her. What can you tell me about her?'

'She was good at her job. She was interested in what we did, so that helped. Sometimes she would come upstairs after the ground-floor office closed and talk to me about the documents and the buildings they related to. It's nice to see a person make the most of their situation. She was particularly interested in Victorian church buildings, and now that so many are being converted to dwellings, we have quite a lot of documents on them, and quite a lot of people interested in them. It all helps fill the coffers.' She gave a professional small smile.

'Did you like her?'

She hesitated. 'She was a very reserved person. It was hard to get to know her. "Like" is probably not the word. I felt a little sorry for her. She seemed so . . . shut off from everyone. At our garden parties, for instance – did Gideon mention those?'

'That you have one for staff and patrons every year, yes.'

She nodded. 'You would always find her standing off to one side, on her own, not talking to anyone. Once or twice I tried to introduce her to people, but she just shrank back, and escaped at the first opportunity. I did my best to try to make her comfortable, but at these things, when one is hostess, one is kept tremendously busy, so I never had much time to be able to devote to her.'

'Did she ever talk to you about her family?'

'About her brother sometimes. He travelled, I believe, and sometimes she would tell me that she'd had a postcard from him. She seemed very fond of him. I believe her mother died when they were quite young, leaving just the two of them, and she had always felt responsible for him – he was younger than her. She spoke of him with affection and pride.'

'Do you know what he did?'

'She never mentioned what line of work he was in, only that he travelled a lot.'

'Did you ever see one of the postcards?'

'No, she . . .' She stopped.

'Yes?'

'It's rather hard to describe without sounding fanciful. She kept her desk very tidy. Most people keep some personal possessions in their desk drawers, but she had nothing, nothing at all. Everything *on* the desk was always lined up tidily while she worked, and at the end of the day she put everything away, and even emptied her waste-paper basket. It was as if she wanted to leave no trace of herself.' She looked down, and then up with a hint of shame. 'I saw inside her handbag once. It was on her chair as she was putting on her coat to go home, and the catch must not have caught properly, because it fell open. I was standing by the chair and could hardly help looking in. There was almost nothing in it. Most women carry their entire lives around in their bags, but Prue's was half empty, and the few things in there were arranged tidily, not just shoved in anyhow, as is usually the case. She saw me looking and hurried over and shut it. I was embarrassed, of course. One doesn't like to be caught snooping, even if it was unintentional. But she seemed . . . not so much affronted as alarmed.' She met his eyes. 'You'll think me over-imaginative.'

'No, this is very helpful,' he reassured her. Her voice was like Manuka honey stirred into high-quality Greek yoghourt, so he could have listened to her all day. She could have read him the shipping forecast and he'd have said, 'This is very helpful.'

He pulled himself together. 'What about friends?'

'She spoke once or twice about the people she'd worked with before, at her previous job.'

'At the wildlife trust.'

'Yes. She spoke of the staff there with . . . not exactly warmth, but as if she had liked them.'

'They told me that she did not like to interact with the public,' Slider said. 'I imagine there's a public-facing side to the job she did? How did she manage?'

'Well, there's not a great deal of that – I wish there were more. We would like a lot more foot traffic to bring in the funds. As I remember, she was apprehensive at first, but she got used to it. Most of the people who come in are regulars, and she only had to check their reader's card. They would know what to do and where to go. With non-readers, people coming in just for one occasion, she would have to make out a guest ticket, and explain the system. But they would generally have phoned beforehand and arranged to come, so they would not take her by surprise. It's rare we get a completely unheralded walk-in. No, she managed it all without drama. In fact, I think lately she had even started to enjoy it.'

'How's that?'

'I *should* say,' she corrected herself, 'there was one person recently who seemed to have punctured her reserve. A new regular. He comes in a couple of times a week, and it's Victorian architecture he's interested in, so that must have made a connection between them. I've heard her talking to him in quite a relaxed fashion. He's very attractive, and I've even wondered . . .'

'Yes?'

'Well, one day recently I was coming back from an outside job just about closing time, and I saw him standing outside, and she came out and they walked off together. So I wondered whether some kind of romantic friendship was growing up between them. I was really quite glad for her. She was too young to have given up all hope, and she was attractive, especially on the rare occasions she smiled.'

'Who is this man?' Slider said. 'Do you have contact details for him?'

'Oh, yes,' she said. 'Our documents are valuable, you know, and most of them are irreplaceable. We have to be very careful about allowing people access. Even for a guest ticket, the person has to show ID and give their address and a contact number. The person in question is a Tony Scrimgeour, and I can certainly email you the rest of the information.'

'Can you describe him?'

'I suppose he's in his forties, well-built, dark hair. As I said, rather handsome, though he didn't look like a scholar – much better built.' She smiled. 'We generally get the weedy, pale and bespectacled types, with the well-known scholar's hunch,' she joked. 'Perhaps that's why he appealed to Prue – quite a breath of fresh air. That, and the shared interest.' She paused, and the smile disappeared, to be replaced with alarm. 'You don't think . . .?'

'I don't think anything yet,' Slider said soothingly. 'If this man had more, shall we say, intimate conversations with her than you, he may know more about her life outside the office – who she knew and where she went and so on. You say this connection was quite recent?'

She answered more gravely than before, as if it suddenly mattered what she said. 'Yes, just a few weeks. He first came

in – let me see – it would be about a week after the garden
party, which was on the twenty-fifth of May, so that would
make it the first week of June.'

'Eight or nine weeks ago,' Slider said.

'The date will be on the record, if it matters?'

'And you noticed a difference in her from about the same
time?'

'It was nothing dramatic – just that she seemed a little more
relaxed, more cheerful, perhaps. At the garden party she had
been quite her old self, standing alone, keeping well away
from the crowd.' She stopped abruptly.

'You've thought of something.'

She frowned, pursuing memory. 'Someone at the party
asked me about her. I'm trying to think who it was.'

'Asked you what?'

'Oh, just who she was. I only remember because she was
so very *un*-noticeable as a general rule. I said, "Oh, that's
Prue Chadacre, one of my staff." Now, who *was* it?' He
waited while she thought, but at last she shook her head.
'There were so many people there. I expect it'll come to
me. Is it important?'

'Anything *could* be important. If you remember, let me
know.'

'Of course.'

'This Tony Scrimgeour, he wasn't at the party?'

'No, he couldn't have been, because it was for staff and
patrons, and he didn't take out a reader's ticket until after it.'

'Had you ever seen him before?'

'No, I don't think so. He wasn't familiar.'

'Have you ever heard her mention any other friends? Or
anything she did in her leisure time? Clubs she belonged to?
Places she went regularly – even if it was only the cinema.'

'No, I'm afraid not. She might sometimes mention a television programme she'd seen. But really nothing outside her
life in the office. Which is odd, now I think about it, because
Hattie, the other secretary, works the same number of hours,
and I know all about her life – her husband, her children, her
grandchildren, her garden, her charity work. I must have seen
hundreds of photographs of her family and the holidays she's

been on. Prue never even showed me a photograph of her brother.' She shook her head sadly. 'Talking of photographs,' she went on, 'we always take a lot at the garden parties. We put one or two up on the website, the best ones, but there are dozens more. Would you be interested in seeing them? I'll have a look through them when I get back, see if it jogs my memory about who it was who asked about Prue.'

'Yes, please send them,' said Slider. There might at least be a decent one of Prue, which would save having to show people the corpse mugshot.

She looked pleased, as though it helped to help. 'And I'll send Tony Scrimgeour's membership record at the same time. And if there's anything else I can do, please do let me know. I feel so awful about Prue. I keep wondering whether, if I had tried harder to get to know her, things would have come out differently. Have you made contact with her brother? If there's anything he wants to ask about her time with us, I'd be only too pleased to talk to him.'

'That's kind, I'll pass that along,' Slider said. She evidently knew nothing about Philip, so there was no point in spreading any further the dismal fact that they didn't know where he was.

NINE
Remember the Alamony

Detective sergeant was in many ways the perfect rank to be, combining wide freedom of activity with a lack of the paperwork and 'meetings' that haunted and hampered the inspector-and-upward ranks. Unless they were madly career-orientated and cared more about management structure than the streets, sergeants often found little incentive to aim higher.

Jenrich had the smarts to go further, but not the personality. She hadn't the patience. Her response to the sort of direction-less waffle that went on in meetings would have been to roll her eyes, shout, 'Oh for God's sake!' and bang heads together, which would have got her summarily ejected. On the trail of something, or with victims, she had the patience of a cat at a mousehole and Mother Teresa respectively, but she exercised her judgement on her own terms about when to use it.

It didn't take long to track down Sharon Hough. Kelly Deeping, the custody nurse practitioner, had been at Shepherd's Bush in her day and the two of them had been friends until Alcock started taking up all Hough's time. A casual chat revealed that they were still in touch. Kelly said that Hough had not remarried since the divorce and was living alone in Acton, after which it was easy enough for Jenrich to find her contact details.

'Poor Sharon,' mourned Deeping – her faint Irish accent had survived forty years of living in London. 'It was all that Dick Alcock's fault.'

'I thought they both got sacked,' Jenrich said.

'Yeah, but he was the one started it. It was *him* chasing *her*, not th'other way round. And it's easier for a man to get another job after something like that. It's the woman takes all the blame and the shame.'

Which gave Jenrich an approach. It turned out, though, that she didn't really need one. Hough, living alone in a tiny one-bedroom conversion flat in Mansell Road, and working as a security guard in a supermarket, was only too glad of someone to talk to. She was a bony woman with a pale, fleshy, freckled face and pepper-and-salt hair pulled back in an unbecoming ponytail. She didn't look likely to inspire a man to wild, job-risking passion. But as Jenrich always reasoned, it took two to do the horizontal tango, and from the newspaper photo she had pulled up on Alcock – a brick-faced, watery-eyed, sub-Burt-Reynolds type, still sporting his outdated 1980s 'tache – he didn't look the type to launch a thousand ships either. The Woolwich Ferry, perhaps – and not the smartly-painted present day one but the 1950's version with the broad bottom and the smoke stacks. It was a sad fact that uniformed policemen had to develop big hips to take the weight of the enormous kit belt. And the daily doughnuts and bacon butties didn't help.

But in spite of all that had happened to her – lost career, lost husband, lost home, stuck in a humdrum job and a poky, solitary flat – Hough was remarkably unresentful. 'Couldn't argue the toss at the hearing,' she said with a shrug. 'Had to put our hands up. No use denying it when everyone had seen us carrying on.'

They were sitting in a little café on the High Street, staring out through the big windows at the homebound traffic. The place was called Source. It was evidently going for an ethnic, earth-mother vibe, but was coming off more cheap and splintery, with unpainted wood façade, bare wood floors and very basic wooden chairs and tables. The smudgily-painted oxblood walls sported hand-written notices for all-day breakfasts, bacon paninis and chilli jacket potatoes, which showed they were trying at the same time not to alienate the natives. Jenrich had caught Hough coming off shift at the supermarket, and since she said she was starving, Jenrich had proposed getting her a snack on her way home while they talked.

'It was a relief to go, in a way,' Hough said, stirring her hot chocolate. Outside the sun was bright enough to throw blue shadows across the pavement from the standing buses, but Hough had still asked for a toasted cheese and ham sandwich and hot chocolate as if it were mid winter. Comfort food, Jenrich thought. She'd gone for an ice cream – she'd opted for the Peach Surprise. The surprise was that the peach was out of a tin, and the cream was squirted out of a can. *Gotcha!*

'There was so much talk, the looks, the nasty names,' Hough went on. 'Not him, of course, just me. He was a hell of a guy, I was the local bike. You know how it goes.' Jenrich nodded. 'All except for Sergeant Paxman. He hated us both.' She shrugged. 'At least he was even-handed.'

'Why'd you do it?' Jenrich asked, but with a sympathetic tone.

'Oh, you know,' said Hough, staring at her sandwich. 'Dick and me had been together a long time. We'd always acted flirty with each other – it didn't mean anything. That was just our way of getting through the day. Our working method. But my marriage was going south – Gary couldn't cope with my irregular hours, it was all rows at home, and the sex had dried up long ago. And Dick's wife was pregnant, so he wasn't getting any either. And suddenly the flirting got serious, and . . .' She stopped for so long Jenrich thought she wasn't going to add anything more, and was preparing her next question, when Hough continued, 'It was amazing. The sex. I mean, just mind-blowing. You wouldn't think it to look at old Dick, but . . . We couldn't get enough of each other. Like an addiction – the more we did it the more we wanted it. And after a bit, we just didn't even try to be careful. It didn't seem to matter any more – not compared with . . . you know. It was a sort of madness. Hot, mad, insane, out-of-this-world sex. Pure and simple.'

Actually, neither pure, nor simple, Jenrich thought. But at least Hough saw it for what it was, not 'love', but All For Orgasm and the World Well Lost. She smiled. 'Yeah,' she said. 'Not everybody gets to experience that. I hope it was worth it.'

Hough shrugged again. 'Can't do anything about it now. Water under the bridge.' She took a bite out of the sandwich and chewed. 'Dick's wife divorced him, you know. Gary and me split. But Dick and me never got together. After all the fuss and trouble, I dunno, the shine was off it, if you get my meaning. We kept in touch for a while, but it was no use. Thank God Gary and me never had kids. We split amicably. Dick and Rita was another story – battle royal, blood everywhere. He got taken to the cleaners by that bitch – had to take on two jobs to keep up with her. And it turned out later she'd been banging this window cleaner all the time while he was at work. Makes you laugh.' She gave a mirthless bark, then finished the half-sandwich she'd been working on. 'Anyway, what did you want to know? Not about me and Dick getting our rocks off, I'm sure.'

'No, girl, not entirely,' Jenrich said. 'There was a suspicious death on your watch back then. Dunkirk House – remember that?'

Hough shivered. It was an interesting reaction, though it may have been because the oscillating fan up by the ceiling, which did duty as air conditioning, had just swivelled her way and kissed the back of her neck. 'Yeah, I remember it. Woman drowned in her bath – what was her name?'

'Sandra May Armstrong.'

'God, yes, that was her. It was her teenage son found her. Came home from school and there she was. She'd taken a trank, apparently, got drowsy and slipped under the water. PM found she'd probably taken two – maybe forgot she'd swallowed the first one and took another. Went down as accidental death. What's your interest in it?'

'The son. Philip Armstrong. What can you tell me about him?'

'Him! He was weird. I mean, I know finding your mum dead in the bath'd throw anyone, but I reckon he was strange before that. And the whole house was weird. There was an atmosphere. I couldn't put my finger on it, but it gave me the creeps. Dick felt the same way. Made you want to get the hell out of there. Any kid living there'd have to be nuts – or he'd end up that way.'

'In what way was he weird?'

'It's hard to describe. He didn't cry or fuss, for one thing. He was dead calm about the body and everything. But his eyes were everywhere. He kept looking around as if he thought someone was going to creep up on him, or something'd come out of the woodwork. And his answers, when you asked a question, sometimes they didn't make sense. Almost like he was talking inside his head and you were only getting bits of the conversation.' She frowned in thought. 'I heard later they sold all the furniture but he went on living there in the empty house. Well, I suppose they might have needed the money,' she added fairly. 'And it was all old stuff, probably antiques. I'm not into that so I don't know, but it could've been valuable. But if he hated it that much, why go on living there? I couldn't have stood it.'

'Why?'

'Like I said, there was a weird atmosphere. All the rooms were dark, for a start, and sort of brown – looked as though they hadn't been painted in centuries, dark old carpets and this old brown furniture: it was like the haunted house in the movies. And it was so quiet. You couldn't hear a thing from outside. It was creepy. You started to think you could hear things – footsteps, y'know? Or people breathing just behind you. Made the back of your neck prickle. You'd think you could hear the dust falling. You couldn't wait to get out of there.'

'But you never had any doubts it was accidental death?' Jenrich asked.

'No,' Hough said simply. Then: 'There was no note, no reason to think it was suicide. And in any case, she had plenty of the tranks – if she'd wanted to kill herself, she wouldn't have taken just two, would she?' Jenrich continued to look at her, without speaking, inviting further confidence. A policeman is usually proof against that trick, but Hough had been out of the Job a long time. She shifted in her seat, and finally frowned and said, 'What? You're not talking murder?' Jenrich merely raised her eyebrows questioningly. 'It was never even considered,' said Hough. 'And in any case, who?' More silence. 'The kid? Philip?'

'He ought to've been at school all afternoon, but apparently he said he wasn't – said he'd gone fishing. So he hadn't got an alibi.'

She flushed – remarkably, after all this time. 'That was what Paxman said, but nobody else heard the boy say it. I reckon he was just trying to make trouble for us. He was always watching us, with that face on him, like bad fish, waiting to trip us up. I reckon it was him tipped off Dick's wife – you know? In any case, even if the kid wasn't at school, why'd anyone think he killed his own mother? That's just sick!'

'Yeah, sick,' Jenrich agreed. 'Did you check if he *was* at school that afternoon?'

'No, what for? It was accidental death,' Hough said. She looked away. 'Any kid'd bunk off cross-country if he could. Nobody likes double games, especially on a Friday afternoon.'

Actually, Jenrich had loved games. She'd been good at them. She'd loved stretching her body to its limits. But she didn't say so. 'You're right,' she said.

'And why would he blow his own alibi to Paxman if he'd done something wrong?'

'Right.'

Hough ate some more sandwich, her eyes on the far horizon. Eventually she said, 'When we first got there, he took us up to the bathroom, and there was something about the way he stood there, staring at her. I mean, no kid likes seeing their mum naked anyway, and she was dead as well, but he just stared, no expression on his face. And then he said, "I wanted to hide, but I thought I had to tell someone." I always remember that. And then he said, "I couldn't have seen him from there."' She looked at Jenrich interrogatively, and Jenrich made an indeterminate grunt of encouragement. 'It was one of those things he said that didn't relate to anything. I asked him what he meant, but he just shook his head. The kid was out to lunch.'

'So, looking back, do you reckon he was nuts enough – or nuts in the right way – to do something like that?'

'I didn't think so at the time,' said Hough. 'I mean, a scrawny kid like that doesn't kill his own mum. But I suppose anybody's capable, if the circs are right. Like, suppose she was suffering, for instance – terminal cancer or something – a kid might do it. Or if . . . well, suppose he was hearing voices? But there was no reason at the time to think it was anything but accidental death.' And she fixed Jenrich with a hard, determined look. 'No reason at all.'

She lapsed into silence. Jenrich ate the last of her ice cream and gathered her things to leave. 'Well, thanks for helping me out,' she said.

'No probs,' said Hough. She gave a faint smile. 'It's nice to talk to another copper, after all this time. I miss the Job.'

'You're still remembered at the Bush nick.'

'Yeah, I bet we are.' She snorted. 'Alcock and Nocock they called us. Famous police humour.'

'If I wanted to get in touch with Dick,' Jenrich said, 'do you have a number for him? Are you still in touch?'

'He's dead,' Hough said starkly. 'About – oh – five years ago. Heart attack. He went on the sauce, put on a ton of weight, and one day – boom. Poor old Dick. It hit him much harder than me, you see, in the end.' She spread her hands a little, to indicate the totality of her current situation, the stupid job, the empty life. 'At least I survived,' she said.

Porson rubbed his hands. 'This is better. A dark horse. We like that. Better than the weedy brother – wherever he may be.'

'But what motive would this Scrimgeour type have for killing her?' Slider said.

'You don't need a motive with a dark horse,' Porson said. 'That's the beauty of it.'

Black Beauty? Slider thought. He was pretty tired – his mind wanted to wander.

'Dark horses come self-motivating,' Porson went on. 'He could be some kind of predator. Obsessed with her. A stalker.'

'Oh, a stalking horse?' Slider murmured.

Porson frowned, not quite hearing. 'That sort of thing goes bad more often than not. That's the sort of villain you can enjoy taking down. The brother – even if you eventually find him' – Porson shot him a scathing look – 'what've you got on him when it comes down to it? Even if you found his DNA all over the house, he's got a right to be there, so it's evidence of sweet Fanny Ann. Unless he confessed, you'd be up a gum tree without a paddle. And even if he did confess, there's enough people calling him nutty to throw a confession into doubt.'

'Yes, sir. I was never too happy about the brother,' Slider defended himself.

Porson's gaze sharpened. 'That's not to say he didn't do it. Ninety-nine times out of ten it's the nearest and dearest, you know that. This Scrimgeour could be just what he seems.'

'He doesn't seem anything yet,' Slider said. 'But we'll be getting his contact details, so we can look into him ASAP.'

'You're tired,' Porson informed him, not unkindly. 'Go home. This'll all still be here tomorrow. At least now you can see the trees at the end of the tunnel. Go on home. How's the missus? And the nipper?'

'Both well, thank you, sir.'

'Envy you,' Porson said abruptly, and then turned his back, waving Slider away over his shoulder.

Slider went, aware that you needed a great deal of protective equipment in place – at least as much as an ice hockey goalie – before you offered sympathy to the Old Man. His beloved wife had died, leaving him all alone, his only daughter being married and living in Swindon so he didn't see much of her. But he was the boss, and bosses don't cry. Those last two words were, from him, a huge concession to the modern fashion for Sharing Your Pain.

Back in his office, Slider rang Joanna. 'I'm just about finished. All serene?'

'Yes,' she said. 'Kate's packed and gone.'

'Already?'

'End of term.'

'I know, but I thought she might wait to say goodbye.'

'You can't really expect them to hang around when freedom beckons. And your dad and Lydia are out tonight, so it's just me, all on my lone.'

'I shall come home toot sweet and remedy that.'

'Speaking of tooting – I had a phone call today.'

'Huh! That's nothing. I get phone calls every day.'

'Shut up, or I won't tell you. It was Martin Hazlett – you know, he used to be second trumpet in my old orchestra. He fixes now for the London Mozart Consortium.'

'I remember you talking about him. He wasn't one of your beaus, was he?'

'All my bows are in my violin case,' she said firmly. 'Honestly, if I'd had affairs with all the musicians you get jealous about, I'd never have got any macramé done.'

'I know musicians,' Slider said darkly. 'So what did he want?'

'To offer me work, of course, dummy!'

'That's great,' he said, pleased for her. He knew how much she missed it.

'Don't get too excited. It isn't a top gig. The LMC field a sort of second eleven to go round the provincial towns in the summer and fly the flag, and he's asked me if I can do Sunday, in Reading. Last minute drop-out. The main orchestra's going on tour, Germany and Austria,' she added wistfully.

'This Sunday,' he said, not pursuing the wist. Nothing to be done about that.

'Yes, if you don't mind taking care of the kids. The really good thing is that if I make myself available at short notice like that, he's in my debt, which means he'll find something else to offer me to make us even. And if I get back on his list—'

'You might get back on other fixers' lists,' Slider concluded for her.

'You said a bundle. You don't mind, do you?'

'Of course I don't,' he said with valiant untruth. Of *course* he would have preferred her to be at home on Sunday for family pleasures together after a stressful week. But she had to put up with his many absences, often cancelling things at the last minute. What's good for the goose is sauce for the other. Thinking of geese, he added, 'What's for supper tonight?'

'Chicken with red onions, red peppers and preserved lemons.'

'You must love me after all, to do that.'

'Come home quick and I'll show you how much,' she said.

*   *   *

He cleared his desk – or rather, scooped the sensitive things off the top layer to lock them in a drawer – and came upon the large manila envelope containing the hard copy of the PM report. He thought he'd just give it a quick squinny to make sure there was nothing important that Freddie hadn't told him over the phone. A minute later, he was ringing Freddie's mobile.

It connected. From the background hum, he was in his car – going home, presumably. 'This is a late call,' he said. 'What can I do for you?'

'This bit in the PM report about the uterus—'

'Have you only just read it?'

'It got lost on my desk.'

'Amazonian tribes have got lost on your desk. What about it?'

'You're saying she had a baby?'

'Nothing of the sort. I said there had been a pregnancy. The uterus does not go back to its pristine state after a gestation. But there's no way to know what the outcome of the pregnancy was – whether birth, miscarriage or abortion.'

'All right, but you're saying she had been pregnant at one time?'

'At least a little bit,' said Freddie wryly.

'Could you say when?'

'Not a chance. Not recently, however. It would be some, probably many, years ago.'

'She wasn't married, you see,' Slider said, brain working furiously.

'So aren't very many women who get pregnant,' said Freddie. 'It's a large club.'

A large club was what Slider felt he needed to cudgel his brain. What did this mean? Or was it nothing? So easy to get things out of proportion when you were studying them so hard. 'Go home,' he told himself, forgetting he was still connected.

'I am doing,' said Freddie. 'How about following your own good advice?'

TEN
Err on a G String

Joanna listened attentively while he told her the latest between mouthfuls. She was a good listener, one of the many reasons he loved her.

She cooked the chicken, onions, peppers and lemons on top of the rice, so all those good juices trickled down and were captured by it, and the flavours were competing with his brain for notice. But his training and long experience had made of him a man who could definitely walk and chew gum at the same time.

'You said she was really closed off and couldn't relate to people,' Joanna said when he finished. 'If she'd lost a baby, one way or another, that could be a reason. A bad love affair. The man didn't want to know so she felt she had to have an abortion. Or she wanted it and had a miscarriage. Any of those could affect a woman deeply, turn her into a shell.'

'Yes,' said Slider, 'but without any friends or relatives there's no way of knowing what the story was. If we even knew *when* the pregnancy was, we could search hospital records, but Freddie couldn't date it.'

'The brother might know, when you find him.'

'*When* we find him. And *if*. Maybe she invented him.'

'I thought there was a birth certificate.'

'Yes, and he was there when the mother died. But supposing he died too, and she couldn't face the truth, and invented an afterlife for him in her imagination, as a happy-go-lucky roving boy, painting and fishing and running free?'

'That's unusually fanciful for you, my level-headed detective hubby.'

'You're right. I *must* be tired. And to go back one step, the pregnancy probably had nothing to do with the murder, and I should remember it's the murder we're supposed to be investigating, not the condition of her soul.'

'Right. This Tony Scrimgeour type sounds much more hopeful.'

'Odd choice of word.'

'You know what I mean.'

'I do. And fortunately we have contact details for him – or we will have by tomorrow morning.' He finished the last mouthful and put down knife and fork. 'That,' he said, 'was delicious. What's for—'

'*Pas devant le petit homme*,' said Joanna.

George was in the doorway, pyjama pants at half mast, nostrils a-quiver. 'Are you having dinner?'

'Finished it,' said Slider, putting paid to any idea there might be pudding to scavenge.

George took it philosophically. 'I had chicken too,' he said. 'And jelly.'

'What are you doing out of bed?'

'Can I have a drink of water?'

'That's a transparent excuse,' Slider said, offering his glass.

George sipped from the glass for form's sake. 'What's transparent?'

'See-through. Like a glass of water.'

George considered this, then searched for a topic more likely to engross. 'Daddy, did you know? In the olden days, they had pyramids. Who builded them?'

'Egyptians. And Aztecs,' Slider said.

'Why?'

'Why what?'

'Why did they build pyramids?'

'Because they're much harder to knock down.'

That stalled him. 'Did they have electricity?' he tried next.

'I don't think so.'

'Did they have bicycles?'

'No.'

'They didn't have lots of things in the olden days,' George said with the satisfaction of nailing a fact. 'Daddy, you were the olden days, weren't you?'

'Up to a point.'

'Like the pyramids,' Joanna murmured.

'Grandpa says you didn't have electricity when you were a boy.'

'Only when I was very little.' The farm cottage he'd grown up in had been a bit remote, down a muddy lane. 'We had oil lamps. But I don't really remember that far back.' Modernization had caught up with them by the time he went to school.

'Did you have a bicycle?' George asked innocently.

Slider could see where this was going. Bicycles had cropped up quite frequently in conversations lately, and he was, after all, a detective.

'Not always. But I didn't have a pyramid, either. And pull up your pants, you'll frighten the horses.'

'What horses?' George said, hauling ineffectually on his waistband.

'No horses at all. Back to bed now.'

'Will you come and tuck me in?' George asked with all the pathos of Jo the crossing sweeper.

On the way upstairs, George said, 'You didn't come and see me have my bath.'

'Sorry. I had to work late. Tomorrow, maybe.'

'I helped Kate give Teddy her bath. Daddy, did you know? Teddy has *two bottoms*.'

Slider knew the next question would be *why*. Not tonight! 'It's one of life's little mysteries,' he said. 'We'll talk about it tomorrow.' With any luck, he'd have forgotten about it by then.

Slider got his son tucked in without further alarms, kissed him goodnight and got almost to the door when George said, 'Daddy, I've *got* to ask you something.'

'Not now, George. Go to sleep.'

'But Daddy, it's really, really important. Honestly, it's *vital*.'

Slider was impressed by the vocabulary, and hesitated, fatally. 'What is it, then?'

'Daddy, can I have strangled egg for breakfast, 'stead of boiled?'

'Weighty questions like that have to be addressed to your

mother, but I'll put in a good word for you,' Slider promised. '*If* you go to sleep now.'

Back in the kitchen, Joanna was making coffee. 'No pud?' Slider said in wounded tones.

'I thought you'd finished. D'you want something else?'

'Never mind, I'll just have coffee. I've just stepped across a minefield. Apparently the baby has two bottoms.'

'Oh dear. Well, it had to happen some time.'

'The only good thing is that it deflected him from the bicycle question.'

Joanna brought him his cup and ruffled his hair. 'You do have a hard life, don't you? You come home for a bit of peace and relaxation and instead you have to grapple with problems of gender identity.'

He put his arms round her waist, pulled her close, resting his head on her belly. 'Have I mentioned how glad I am you are a woman?'

'It *is* awfully convenient,' she agreed.

'Tell me about your gig on Sunday,' he invited. She sat, drank her coffee, and told him, and he felt himself relaxing at last. And there was still bed to come. That was the nice thing about marriage. He felt so sorry for Atherton, with a different woman every night, when he, Slider, went home to the same one. Of course, Atherton probably felt sorry for him for the same reason.

There was some debate in the office about whether the pregnancy meant anything or nothing. Swilley proposed do a search for a birth certificate for a child, or a local hospital search for a birth, but Slider said she was better employed chasing up the phone records for the two mobile phones Prue Chadacre had been paying for.

McLaren, meanwhile, was off to Soho, to the address in Dean Street that had appeared on Scrimgeour's record sent over by the Archive. He had tried the telephone number but the phone had been turned off – slightly suspicious to begin with.

A lot of Dean Street had been cleaned up, not to say poshed up, in recent years, the brickwork cleaned, original old doors and windows replaced with smart, straight-edged modern replicas; upmarket firms moving in to what was, after all, prime real estate in the centre of London, the world's most desirable address. But there was still a slightly tacky Cinderella remnant awaiting the transformation scene. The address McLaren found himself outside was a flat above one of the few remaining strip joints, which had a shiny modern frontage in clashing shades of purple and puce. It was called E-Z Strip, which didn't work in English, of course, and simply left people wondering what had happened to the A to D section.

The door to the upstairs premises was also painted an intolerable shade of synthetic lavender to match, and had an entry phone with four buttons – a flat on each floor, he presumed. They were numbered, without names, but the address he had been given was flat four, so he stuck his thumb on the button and left it there a good, long time.

After an appreciable pause, an irritable female voice said, 'What?'

'I'm looking for Tony Scrimgeour, love. Is he in?'

'No he's friggin' not. Go away.'

'It's the police, love. Just want a chat. Better let me in.' A pause full of static. 'You know I can *get* in if I want. Let's keep it friendly, eh? Friendly chat, and I'll leave you alone.'

Another pause, thoughtful this time, and the buzzer went. The door gave on to a bare stairway – the entrance was too narrow for any sort of hall – but it smelled clean. The cream paint on the walls was fresh-looking, and the stairs were covered in green lino, which looked a bit grubby, but was also evidently of recent date. He climbed. There was a tiny landing on each floor giving access to a closed panelled door – Georgian style but modern repro – each with a Yale lock. When he got to the second floor he heard a sound up above, and as he reached the third floor he could see a figure hanging over the banister at the top. There was a skylight above the stairs on the top floor giving light, and an open door, and a woman in a dressing gown watched him mount the last flight, her arms defensively folded across her chest. She had a cross face, bed hair, and sleep creases in her cheeks.

'Let's see your ID,' she said sharply, stepping between him and the door.

'What's your name?' he asked as he showed his warrant card.

'Roxie Hart,' she said as she inspected it suspiciously.

'Real name?'

'Ruby Harris. So what d'you want?' she demanded, as uncooperatively as she could make a short sentence.

'Tony Scrimgeour. I want a word.'

'I told you, he's not here.'

'When's he coming back?'

She rubbed her hands over her face. Last night's make-up had given her panda eyes. '*I* don't know,' she snapped. 'How would I know?'

'What are you, then?' McLaren asked. 'Girlfriend? Wife?' She snorted. 'Mother?'

'Fuck off, you cheeky bastard.'

'You don't mind if I just have a look round, then, see if you're hiding him?'

'I told you, he's not here,' she said, but resignedly. She stepped back and made a weary gesture. 'Have a look if it'll get rid of you. You woke me up.'

'Nurse, are you? On the night shift?' he asked, stepping past her.

'Gawd, everyone's a comedian,' she muttered, following him in. The interior was plain and smelled faintly of new paint, and the tiny space – once a servant's bedroom under the roof – had been turned by a miracle of geometry into a studio flat, with a tiny kitchen, minuscule bathroom, and a single bed-sitting room that probably measured ten by ten. The bed, a double, took up most of the space, but everything, to his surprise, was clean and tidy, apart from the tangle of bedding, evidence of her hasty uprising. It was clear from a single glance in at each door that you couldn't have hidden anyone anywhere in that flat. If more than one person was in any room at once, they'd have had to breathe by numbers.

There were pretty voile curtains over the main room's window – the only window in the flat; a modern Regency-style chair, white with pink velvet, in the corner; a full-length mirror with a fancy gilt frame on the wall; and a box of tissues in a frilled cover beside the bed. That and the large box of condoms in the bathroom gave the hint.

'You on the game, love?' McLaren asked.

'No, I'm the chairman of ICI,' she said. 'What d'you think?'

'So what's Tony Scrimgeour to you?' She shrugged. 'He your pimp?'

'Get lost,' she said witheringly. 'I work for myself.'

'Good for you,' he said. 'So who is he, then?'

'What's he done?' she countered.

'You don't want to know that.'

'Wouldn't have asked if I didn't, would I, genius?'

'Don't piss me off, love,' McLaren said, putting an edge in his voice. 'I don't want to make trouble for you.'

'Be the bloody first time, then, you bastards,' she muttered.

'Look, he's using your address, giving it out to people, so don't tell me you don't know him. Tell me where to find him and I'm out of your hair. Or' – he drew out his notebook – 'we can find a reason to make your life difficult. S'up to you.'

'What is it with you coppers?' she said wearily. 'Getting on our backs when we're just tryin' to earn an honest living. Look, I don't bloody know Tony Scrimgeour, all right? He just come one day and asked if he could use the address. He said it was just for correspondence. If a letter come, I was to keep it, and he'd ring every couple of days and check. But nothing ever come.'

'How did he know you? Was he a customer?'

'I thought he was. He rung one night. I got cards out all over the place. He says he's seen one. He comes round, but he don't want nothing, just to use the address. He swore there'd be no trouble – and there hasn't been. Not until now. So what's he done?'

'Nothing, as far as I know. We just want to talk to him. Did he give you a contact address?'

'Never give me nothing. Said *he*'d contact *me*. Ring me or come round.'

'When did he last ring you?'

She thought. 'Last week some time,' she said. 'Come to

think of it – not since before last weekend. Has something happened to him?'

McLaren avoided that one. 'And when did he last come round?'

'It'd be – first a' July, to pay me.'

'Pay you?'

'Well, I wasn't going to let him use the address for nothing, was I?'

'How much did he pay you?'

'A monkey. For a month. Paid me the beginning of June. I reckoned that'd be the last I saw, but he come round first a' July and paid me for another month. And he said, maybe he might want to use the flat to bring someone to, and if he did, I'd have to make myself scarce.' She shrugged. 'He said there'd be another two hundred to use the flat for an evening. I told him fuck off, I make three times that a night, so he upped it to five. But as it happened, he's never asked to use the flat. So all I've had off've him is the two months' payments.'

'What's he like, this bloke?' McLaren asked.

'What, to look like?'

'Yeah, that as well.'

'He's a bit taller than you. Looks well fit – like he works out. Dark hair. Not bad looking.'

'Age?'

'Forties, maybe.'

'What kind of man? You must've trusted him.'

'Well, sort of. I mean, he looked a bit leery, but not, like, dangerous. Not a john, but not a player either. Sort of professional. 'S if he knew what he was doing.'

'Professional like a bodyguard or a bouncer?'

'No-o,' she said doubtfully. 'I wouldn't a' got mixed up with someone like that. More like . . . like he ran his own business. Expensive shoes,' she added, as though that were a signifier. Which it was, in a way, given most people went around in trainers.

McLaren gave her a card. 'If he gets in touch again, you let me know. Right away. I'm serious, girl. This is important.'

Her eyes widened. 'What's he done? Is he dangerous?'

'Not to you,' McLaren said. Well, he had to. He didn't

know, of course. But there was no point in putting the wind up her.

'An accommodation address?' Slider said. 'Well, that does make him a person of interest. Why would anyone use a false address to access the documents in the archive?' He meant it rhetorically, but Gascoyne answered.

'Maybe he wanted to steal one,' said Gascoyne. 'That Gideon Lankester said some of them were valuable.'

'I think they're probably more priceless than valuable,' said Atherton. 'I doubt they have any resale value.'

'But do you really think he took out a reader's card there just so he could get to know Prue Chadacre?' Swilley said. 'Seems even more unlikely. She's not exactly Marilyn Monroe, is she?'

'She may not live like it, but she is pretty well off,' Atherton pointed out. 'The trust fund, the old house.'

Swilley shrugged. 'Getting friendly with her's not going to get your hands on either of those. Anyway, if he just wanted to meet her, there's other ways. Bump into her somewhere and ask her out for a drink.'

'Bump into her where? She never went anywhere.'

'We don't know that.'

'And from what we know,' Atherton went on, 'she'd be the last person to accept a casual drink from a stranger. She hardly even talked to people she *knew*.'

'I think that could be the point,' Slider said slowly. 'Becoming a regular at the Archive – maybe that was to get her to trust him. Possibly the only way it *could* be done.'

'And it worked,' said Lœssop. 'She *was* talking to him, according to that posh female. Chatting. Seemed relaxed with him.'

'The fact he said he might want to bring someone back to the flat,' McLaren said, peeling the paper down a Boost bar. 'That sounds like a date kind of thing. I mean, if it was just business, there's caffs and pubs all over the kip.'

'True,' Slider nodded. 'But we don't know it was her he wanted to bring there – since he never did. We don't have any evidence at all to connect him to our victim. Joining the Archive and taking on the accommodation address—'

'At around the same time, the beginning of June,' Atherton inserted.

'But you know that could be coincidental. Certainly any lawyer would say it was. We need to get hold of him, that's for sure.' He looked at McLaren. 'What about security cameras?'

McLaren hastily swallowed a chocolatey lump. When it came to swallowing, he was in the python class. 'I thought of that, guv,' he said. 'The strip joint's cameras were no good – wrong angle. But there's a posh gambling club across the road and it's got cameras galore. I checked with 'em, and one of 'em covers the door to the flats. And they keep their tapes for thirty days. Pretty good definition, as well. 'Course, there's a lot of people going up and down the street and in and out of that door, but not so many going in during daytime, and Ruby Harris said he called in the afternoon, before she started work, so that'll narrow it down a bit. Dunno if we'll get a good enough image to run through the system, though.'

'Well, do what you can. And keep monitoring that phone.' He looked at LaSalle. 'I presume he has no criminal record, or you'd have told me.'

'Not under that name, guv,' said LaSalle. 'And I've not found anything on the internet so far. Scrimgeour's not a common name. No Tonys. I've found a couple of Anthonys, but they're legit, can't be him.'

'That's another point, isn't it, sir?' Lœssop said. 'Who doesn't have a social media presence these days?'

Slider smiled. 'I don't.'

'Yeah, but . . .' Tactfully, Lœssop didn't finish the sentence.

'Yes, I know.' Slider finished it in his mind. 'Well, there's no doubt that he's someone we want to talk to, but it doesn't make him the murderer, so let's not get too excited.'

'If he was the murderer, wouldn't he have covered his trail more carefully?' Swilley said.

'I expect he thought he had,' said Slider. 'And we haven't found him yet.'

ELEVEN
The Bland Leading the Bland

Rita Alcock was now Rita Kaminski, having been born Rita Fowler. Jenrich could see the point, in these days of impermanent marriages, of not changing your name to your husband's. When you thought of credit cards and bank accounts and club memberships and so on and so on it was a lot of work the average woman could do without. There was no way *she* was ever going to take some hairy bugger's handle. Though of course 'Jenrich' was her hairy bugger father's handle. Everybody ought to choose their own surname at the age of eighteen, she thought, walking up the concrete path that linked the pavement to the glass front door of the 1980s terraced house in Dormer's Wells. It was one of those flat-faced, pale-brick efforts with the white bargeboarding on the top half. It looked as though the plan had been to make sure the house had nothing whatever you could remember it by.

The door was opened by a hulking young man in T-shirt, tracksuit bottoms and white athletic socks, and for a moment Jenrich thought old Rita was doing exceptionally well for herself before she took in the razor burn, a few spots and the guileless milky eyes, and realized the size had misled her and this was a teenager.

'If you want me dad he's not here,' the boy foghorned. 'He's out at work.'

'No, it's your mum I want a word with,' she said, presenting her ID.

He examined it with a sort of pioneering interest, as if he'd never seen anything like it before. Well, maybe he hadn't. Then he looked up and said, 'Police?' with a trace of anxiety.

'It's not trouble,' she said. 'I just want a chat about the old days. Can I come in?'

He stepped back, bellowed, 'Mu-u-um!' – the teenager's three-note call – and then went off up the stairs three at a time, clearly washing his hands of the whole situation.

Jenrich waited in the narrow hall, made narrower by a series of hooks just inside the door laden with outerwear, coats on top of coats, caps and scarves precariously balancing, pairs of shoes and trainers lined up on the floor beneath. Otherwise, everything was as featureless as the outside, off-white paint, beige carpet, doors with the minimum of architrave. And when a woman appeared, she was all in beige too, trousers and short-sleeved jumper, on top of which was a face-coloured face, neither pretty nor ugly, and neutral-coloured hair in that short, slightly waved style that spells 'housewife' in any advanced western country. The hairdresser's probably had a name like A Cut Above or Hair We Are; whereas it should really have been called Narcolepsy R Us.

'Hullo, Rita,' Jenrich said. 'I'm Leanne Jenrich. Shepherd's Bush nick. You don't know me, but Kelly Deeping told me about you. She sends her best.'

'Kelly Deeping? What'd she be sending me anything for?' Mrs Kaminski said blankly. 'I hardly knew her.'

'I just mentioned her name so's you wouldn't be alarmed. This is just a friendly talk, OK? Like I told your son?' She added the question mark because Rita Kaminski was small and narrow in build and didn't look capable of podding anything the size of that youngster.

'Michael,' she supplied, with a faint sigh. 'School holidays don't start till next week, but he's off with a cold. As if they weren't long enough. I suppose you'd better come in.'

She led the way into the lounge, with the window onto the street; more beige carpet, off-white walls, a three-piece suite in a sort of light-brown tweed fabric, encircling a glass-topped coffee table and facing the electric fire set into a low, modern fireplace of beige tiles. Rita perched on one armchair and waved Jenrich vaguely to the sofa. 'What's up?' she said. 'I suppose you want to talk about Dick,' she added drearily. 'I got no other contact with Shepherd's Bush. You know he's dead, don't you?'

'Yes, I did hear. I'm sorry.'

'Don't be,' she said shortly. 'I divorced him long before he died. Married that useless Arty Pollock, didn't I? Then he buggered off. Now I'm married to Micky Kaminski. He's a builder. Polish, but he come over here when he was a little kid, so you'd never know. He's all right, as they go. You married?'

'No,' said Jenrich, and added inside her head, *Never likely to be after talking to you.*

Rita gave a grim nod, as if approving the self-denial. 'Haven't thought about Dick Alcock in years. He never married that trollop, you know – that Sharon Hough. Much good it did her, messing around with other people's husbands.' The tone of voice did not match the emphatic words. She sounded as if all colour and contour had been worn out of her by the passage of time, three husbands and at least four children – two with the policeman, one with the window cleaner, and one Jenrich now knew about with the builder.

'Can you cast your mind back?' Jenrich asked. Rita sighed again, instead of saying, *If I must.* 'I expect Dick talked to you about his cases sometimes.'

'Not much.'

'There was an unexplained death case, Dunkirk House, a woman drowned in her bath,' Jenrich persevered, though thinking she had come to the wrong oracle.

But Rita's face sharpened a little – from dough to plasticene, perhaps. 'Dunkirk House! That was the one there was all the trouble about. It was after that they copped on to his little shenanigans. I reckon that Sergeant Paxman dobbed him in, you know? He come up to me after the hearing, all smarmy, said anything he could do – given Dick'd lost his job and I was in the family way. I thought, you done plenty already, mate. Reckoned Shepherd's Bush was one big family and they all looked out for each other, did Paxman. That was a laugh.'

'How *did* you find out, as a matter of fact? If you don't mind my asking?'

She shrugged. 'Ancient history. I couldn't give a monkey's now. As a matter of fact, I'd suspected about it for months. Men think they're so clever, but a wife always knows. Smug gits! Anyway, I got an anonymous note, and that was the last straw. Bad enough suspecting, but knowing everyone knew about it and were laughing behind my back, well, I wasn't having that. So I went down the station and told old Dickson he'd got to do something. And that was that.'

'So Dick talked to you about Dunkirk House, did he?'

'Not then. It was afterwards.' She looked down at her hands for a moment, and it was almost as if there was a human emotion buried down there somewhere in the Silly Putty. 'I lost the baby, did you know? That's why that git Arty left, in the end. Well, it gave him the excuse, anyway. He didn't last two years. It was after he buggered off that Dick come round to see me. Brought me flowers – soft pillock. Said he wanted to apologize for everything. A bit bloody late, I told him. But I was a bit down and everything, and, well, a bit of sympathy was . . .'

'Balm to your wounded feelings,' Jenrich supplied, guessing that softer vocabulary did not come easily to Mrs Kaminski.

Rita looked at her for a moment as if she thought she was taking the piss, then nodded. 'I wasn't sorry to have a chat with him, anyway. Cuppa tea, bit of a bunny. He told me he was ashamed of the way he'd been, not just cheating on me, but letting down the Job.' She sniffed. 'I reckon the Job meant more to him than I did. It's the same with all you coppers, isn't it? Us wives always come second.'

'I'm not married,' Jenrich reminded her.

'Yeah, well.'

'And he mentioned Dunkirk House in particular, did he?'

'Yeah. Him and that Sharon Hough, they fudged a lot of the reports. Said they'd interviewed people when they hadn't – were off doing it somewhere when they were supposed to be on the Job. He said he reckoned at the time it didn't matter because it was just an accidental death, and anyway the boy was obviously a bit dippy.'

Jenrich felt a looming on the back of her neck, turned her head to look, and saw the youth leaning in the doorway, staring at them blankly while idly fingering one of his spots. She waited to see if Rita would send him away, but his presence didn't seem to bother her. 'What boy was that?'

'You know – the kid. The dead woman's son. The one that found her.' Jenrich rolled her eyes towards the doorway, and Rita looked too, shrugged mildly, and said, 'Michael, go and put the kettle on. Your dad'll be in any minute.' The boy heaved himself to vertical and disappeared.

'Go on,' said Jenrich.

'Well, the kid apparently said something about a man coming to the house, and said his sister'd tell them all about it. But they never interviewed her. And they never logged what he'd said. Thought he was a bit daft and imagined things. But Dick said he'd got to thinking about it lately, and he wondered if there had been anything in it, and if maybe it wasn't accidental death after all. Well, I said it was too late to do anything now, and least said soonest mended. Couldn't see the point in stirring things up again. He didn't want an enquiry and a court case on top of everything else. Well, then he said I was right and it probably *was* accidental. The kid talked a load of rubbish, apparently. Too much telly, probably. Rots their brains. It's the internet now, and these games. Can't keep 'em away from it. Mine's as bad. Sits there at the tea table, tapping away like a bloody woodpecker. Can't get two words out of him.'

There was a click of the front door opening, and Jenrich felt loomed on again. This time it was a tall, heavy-shouldered man in work clothes with cement splashes on his boots and trousers. He had short-cut, bristly, fair hair and a wide weather-beaten face, and the same mild milky-blue eyes. He didn't say anything, just looked passively.

Rita gestured her head towards Jenrich. 'Old friend. We're done now. Go in the kitchen, I'll be through in a minute.' The man nodded and went. Evidently the strong, silent type. The leery policeman and the up-for-it window cleaner had changed her taste in men.

'Did Dick say anything else about the case? Anything about this man that was meant to've called? Any other evidence they'd fudged?'

'Can't remember,' Rita said. 'Too long ago. What's it to you, anyway?'

'The sister's turned up dead,' Jenrich said. 'And the boy's gone missing. Thought we might get a lead on them from the old case.'

Rita shook her head, indifferent to the suffering of strangers. 'Maybe Dick *should* have asked a few more questions while he was at it. But it's too late now.'

She roused herself to see Jenrich out, but only because she had to get up to go to the kitchen anyway. At the front door, she said, 'You talked to that Sharon Hough as well?'

'Yes.'

'What's she like now?' Jenrich didn't answer, not knowing what aspect was being enquired about. 'She married?'

'No.'

Rita grunted. 'Shows you,' she said.

McLaren had gone through the downloaded security camera images, and having located what looked like the right person, checked it frame by frame and printed out the most useful. It was late afternoon by the time he was ready to show them to the assembled troops.

A tall, well-built man with dark hair, wearing grey trousers, brown loafer shoes, and a blue, short-sleeved, open-necked shirt stood at the lavender door and was seen to go in. The cue time was 4.38 p.m.

'This is just his back view,' McLaren explained, 'to show he wasn't just walking past. Take it back a few frames, and you get him coming round the corner from Carlisle Street. That's the way he'd come if he came up by tube to Tottenham Court Road – round Soho Square. If he drove, gawd knows where he'd park. It's a nightmare. Anyway,' he continued, when Slider waved the point away as a 'not now' issue, 'these are the best frames that show his face.'

He fanned out three, two showing the man in increasing proximity to the camera, the other showing him facing in the other direction. It was a good-looking face, if a little grim: the features were good, and a smile would probably lift it to handsomeness. A firm face, probably in its mid-forties, with nothing weak or indecisive about it, and from the posture it was a decisive walk, as well. The hair was near black, wavy and abundant, and brushed back from the forehead. The eyes were narrowed slightly against the sun.

'I missed him at first because he walked right past the door,' McLaren said. 'Walked as far as the Soho Theatre and stood there for a minute, then came back. That's how I got him from both sides.'

'Cautious?' Slider hazarded. 'He must have known where it was from the first visit.'

'Yeah, I reckon he was just making sure no one was watching him,' said McLaren. He pushed the third print with a finger. 'This is when he comes back and straight to the door.'

All three prints were three-quarter profile, and since they had him from both sides, it would be possible to assemble a good likeness of his face. Slider pulled the third print towards him and bent closer. 'What's this?' he asked, pointing to something half-revealed on the neck by the drop of the shirt's soft collar.

'Tattoo, guv,' said McLaren with some satisfaction.

'Can you zoom in on it?'

'Already did.' He produced, like a magician, a close-up, a little grainy with the magnification, but possible to decipher. Though you couldn't see the bottom edge of it, you could work out that the tattoo showed a round object on top of stylized crossed lightning bolts.

'What's that round thing?' Swilley asked.

'A football?' LaSalle hazarded.

'Looks like an onion,' said Gascoyne.

McLaren shook his head, enjoying his moment of power. 'It's a pomegranate.'

'You can't tell that,' Swilley argued. 'It's just a round blob. Could be anything.'

'It's a pomegranate,' Jenrich put in tersely. 'Afghanistan. He's ex-military.'

'How do you know that?' Slider asked with interest.

She shrugged. 'I got friends in the military.'

That was something to file away, Slider thought. 'And the lightning bolts?'

McLaren wasn't letting Jenrich steal his thunder. He spoke before she could. 'Bomb disposal squad, guv. I've seen that before. Sometimes they have 'em crossed over a hand grenade, but a lot of people who served in Kandahar have the pomegranate. It's the national fruit, or something.'

'Very powerful symbolism, the pomegranate,' Atherton mentioned. 'Fertility and fruitfulness – all those seeds.'

'Yeah, well,' McLaren dismissed him, 'point is, we got a way to find out who he is, now.'

'I thought they weren't allowed tattoos on the face or neck,' Swilley said – there was the same rule in the police.

'It wouldn't show with a proper collar and tie,' said McLaren. 'It's 'cos he's wearing an open shirt.'

'It'd show above a T-shirt,' LaSalle pointed out.

'He probably had it done since he got out,' Jenrich said impatiently.

'Bomb disposal – that's Engineers, isn't it?' Slider asked.

'Royal Logistics Corps, guv,' McLaren said quickly. 'I looked it up.'

'Yeah, but EOD is part of the Rapid Reaction Force,' Jenrich said, 'and it comes under 33 Royal Engineers. Carver Barracks,' she added helpfully. Slider raised his eyebrows. 'Essex. Debden.'

'EOD?' Slider queried.

'Explosive Ordnance Disposal.'

'I see. You know all about it.' She shrugged. He turned back to McLaren. 'All right, see what you can find out about him. Jenrich can help you.'

They looked at each other with the faint hostility of two cats.

'Meanwhile, what about this man who was supposed to have come to the house on the day Sandra May died?' Atherton said. 'Are we thinking that was Tony Scrimgeour as well?'

'The two incidents are so far apart,' Slider said. 'Why would Scrimgeour wait eighteen years if he wanted to kill the daughter as well?'

'Even if it was true, and Philip didn't make it up,' said Swilley. 'Or Alcock mishear it.'

'In any case,' said Atherton, 'if Scrimgeour had killed the mother, he'd probably have been known to the children, wouldn't he? So he could hardly have started up a new relationship with our victim.'

'We need to get hold of Philip,' Swilley said. 'He's the key to everything. How can he disappear like that?'

'You haven't got the phone records yet?'

'I've chased them twice today,' she complained. 'I have got the credit card records, though. The second card is jointly for Prue and Philip – I suppose to give her some control and so she can pay it off – but it hasn't been used since last Thursday, for B & B in a pub in Dorchester. I've asked the local police to interview them, and put them on alert. But he doesn't use it much. The previous use was a week before that, to withdraw one hundred pounds cash from a machine in Bridport.'

'So we know he's in the West Country,' Fathom said helpfully.

Swilley looked at him witheringly. 'We know he *was* in the West Country. And it's a big area. I've been on to the Bridport police as well, and asked the bank branch if they can get an image from the cashpoint camera. It may provide a better mugshot for distribution. If we go public – asking anyone who's seen him to get in touch?'

She added the question mark as she looked at Slider. 'We may have to,' he said, with a sigh, because that sort of public appeal always generated so many false sightings it was a major task, like panning for gold, to sort through them for the tiny grain of truth they might contain. 'Let's give it another day, however. If you can get the phone records, it may give us a better fix.'

'Not if he's got it turned off,' she said.

TWELVE
A Soldier to Cry On

The RLC captain had a young face and old eyes. They assessed Gascoyne thoroughly and apparently found him acceptable, because he was offered a seat. Slider had deliberately chosen Gascoyne to go down to Debden because matching your detective to the task was a management skill. Gascoyne, big and strong, but calm and transparently honest, was his man most likely to win trust in a frightened woman, a shaken victim, a nervous dog or a career soldier.

'The person in the photograph you sent through was not, in fact, Anthony John Scrimgeour,' Captain Challoner said.

'But you do have someone called Scrimgeour?' Gascoyne deduced.

'This is his record,' Challoner said, opening a file, and pushing over a sheet with a photograph at the top of it. 'That's Tony Scrimgeour.'

A fair-haired, high-cheekboned face stared back. The roundness of head and breadth of face suggested a stockily-built individual. It was certainly not the dark-haired man at the lavender door, even allowing for a dye-job.

Gascoyne pushed it back. 'We were afraid of that. But if Scrimgeour is a real person, then there must have been a reason for our man to use his name. Perhaps they were known to each other. Is it possible for me to speak to Tony Scrimgeour, show him our photograph, see if he can help us?'

'Quite impossible, I'm afraid,' said Challoner. 'He's dead.'

'Oh,' said Gascoyne. 'That's probably why—'

'He felt it safe to use his name, yes.' Challoner moved some papers around on his desk. 'It's fortunate that we are a tight unit and pretty much all known to each other,' he went on. 'So it was not too difficult for me to track down your man.'

'He's one of yours?'

Challoner nodded. 'Tony Scrimgeour was shot by a sniper in Kandahar in 2014 – one of the last casualties before we pulled out. He had an exemplary record, and was well-liked, a very popular officer. This was the photograph that was used at his memorial service in 2015.'

He pushed across a twelve by eight glossy. Three men in light desert camouflage, capless, were pictured against a glaring background of dust and high sunshine. Two were sitting on a low bit of broken wall, the one on the left with a friendly headlock round the one on the right, both grinning in high spirits at the camera. The third was squatting in front of them, forearms resting on his knees, smiling, but in a more reserved way.

The soldier on the right was Tony Scrimgeour. The squatting soldier was clearly the Shepherd's Bush person of interest, the man who had borrowed his name.

'That's him,' said Gascoyne, and looked up.

Challoner seemed to sigh very slightly. 'His name is Jason Andrew Shalcross. He gave his notice just after Scrimgeour was killed and left the service in July 2015.'

'Do you know what he did then?'

'We do try to keep in touch with our personnel. EOD is dangerous work and can be very stressful, and sometimes they cannot settle comfortably back into civilian life. We do all we can to support them. But Shalcross rather went off the radar. He didn't call on any of our services, according to his records. Well, if they don't want help in any way, there's nothing we can do about it. Can I ask – is he in trouble now?'

Challoner looked genuinely concerned, and Gascoyne said, 'Not as far as we know. He seems to have been associated with someone we are investigating, and we hoped he might be able to tell us a bit more about them. Do you have an address for him?'

'Of course,' said Challoner. 'But it's the address he gave when he first left, and there's no knowing if he'll still be there.'

'It's a place to start,' said Gascoyne. He tapped the photograph. 'Who is the third man, here?'

'That's Val Farringdon – Valentine Farringdon. He left the service not long after Shalcross. The three of them, Farringdon,

Scrimgeour and Shalcross were close friends.' He hesitated. 'Losing Tony Scrimgeour was hard for them. He was a gentle, sympathetic person, the sort you go to with your troubles. The sort you would turn to for support when your best friend was killed in action.'

'Yes. I see the problem,' said Gascoyne. 'Perhaps Mr Farringdon could talk to me about Jason Shalcross?'

'I'll give you his address as well, but whether they kept in touch with each other I couldn't say.'

Gascoyne stood to go, and offered his hand. 'Thank you for your help.'

Challoner took the hand and looked into Gascoyne's face. 'Afghanistan was one of the hardest places to serve,' he said, 'especially in EOD. A six-month tour there was like two years anywhere else. I hope you take that into account when . . . if . . .'

'He's not in trouble, as far as I know,' Gascoyne said kindly. 'And we do understand what stress in the job means.'

'Yes, I suppose you do,' said Challoner.

The Shalcross address turned out to be a former council flat in Denmark Hill, in one of those solid thirties' estates sold off by the GLC in the eighties. From the upper flats of the block on one side, you would have had a wonderful view over to the opposite hills and Crystal Palace. Jason Shalcross's flat was on the other side, on the first floor and overlooked the block opposite, albeit to the other side of a strip of grass and a diminutive tree.

The door was opened by a young woman with reverse-badger hair – dyed platinum–white with a black streak down the parting – and two silver rings in her left nostril. She had two small children clinging to her, while in the background a baby wailed with a stolidity that suggested it had settled in for the long haul and could keep this up all day if need be. It was hard to get anything across to her against the distractions until she abruptly shoved the toddlers back and shut herself out on the balcony with Gascoyne, holding the door behind her against determined small hands.

'Now, say it again,' she said. He asked for Jason Shalcross, and she shook her head. 'He don't live here, love. It's just me and the kids.'

'Is he someone known to you? Or maybe to your husband?'

'Husband? Don't make me laugh! I got enough to do looking after three kids, never mind some lazy bastard of a man as well. No offence.' She gave him a belated look-over that suggested she wouldn't kick him out of bed for eating biscuits. Such was the lack of planning that had landed her where she was. 'What was the name again?'

'Jason Shalcross.'

She shook her head. 'No, never heard of him.'

'What about Tony Scrimgeour?'

'Nah. Who's he when he's at home?'

'It's a name he sometimes uses.'

'Never heard of him, neither. You say he lived here?'

'It's an address he gave.'

'Musta been before my time, then.'

'Do you know who lived here before you?'

'Nah. Why would I?'

'There might have been mail come for the previous tenant? Or someone asking after him?'

'Never seen no mail, never seen no one, not while I been here. I moved in five years ago.'

Five years or three kids ago, Gascoyne thought. He didn't want to keep her too long from the howling baby, just in case – though she didn't seem in any hurry to get back inside – so he said, 'Can I just quickly show you a picture, see if you recognize him?'

She looked, and said, 'No, never seen him before. Nice-looking bloke, though. What's he done?'

'Nothing, as far as we know. He might be a witness to something we're investigating. Well, thanks for your time. I'll let you go now.' One or both of the little ones was banging feverishly on the door behind her.

'Well, if I hear anything, I'll let you know. You got a number?' He gave her a card. 'Ta,' she said, inspecting it. Then she looked up. 'He's not dangerous, is he?'

Good question, Gascoyne thought. But there was no reason

on earth he would come back here after all this time. Or trouble this child-infested woman. 'No,' he said.

In the car he made his notes and rang the factory with the negative news. He was now on entirely the wrong side of London, with the rush-hour traffic just starting up. He wouldn't get back to Shepherd's Bush before the end of his shift, so he told McLaren, who had answered the phone, that he would go straight home. He had a wife and two little girls, and the interview he had just conducted made him even more eager than usual to see them.

'So we'll have to try and trace him through this other bloke, this Farringdon,' said McLaren, balling the wrapper of a cheese-and-onion pasty and lobbing it expertly into the waste-paper basket.

'What about ex-servicemen welfare schemes?' Swilley said. 'There's lots of them. Ministry of Defence do all sorts, plus there's First Light Trust, Military Members Club, Turn 2 Us—'

'How do you know all that?' Atherton asked.

She shrugged. 'Looked it up – Citizen's Advice, British Legion, not to mention the DSS,' she concluded.

'They'll have to be checked,' Slider said. 'But if he didn't reach out first to his regiment, it's possible he didn't want help. Have a look at Farringdon first, before bothering the Ministry of Defence.'

'If the address for him turns out to be current,' Atherton said.

Slider's phone rang, and he went back through to his own office. It was Nicholls, the duty sergeant downstairs. 'You'd better get down here, Bill,' he said. His Western Isles accent was so mist-and-heather soft he could make the simplest statement sound like poetry.

'What's up, Nutty?' Slider asked.

'Philip Armstrong. Bloke's just come in giving that name. Seems a bit upset.'

Nicholls had put him in the soft room, with a uniformed policewoman, Jillie Lawrence, to keep an eye on him. He stood up as Slider entered, a tall, thin man with a couple of days' growth of beard, unkempt hair and grubby, travel-worn clothes. He was wearing khaki canvas trousers, an olive green shirt with the sleeves rolled up, and dirty trainers. An army backpack was on the floor at his feet, together with a long, canvas, fishing-rod bag.

'He came in off the street, said his name was Philip Armstrong and something had happened to his sister,' Nutty had told Slider when he got downstairs. 'I could see he wasn't the full nine bob so I didn't question him, just sent for you right away.'

Now Slider took in the face that looked young until you spotted the fine, deeply-etched lines round the eyes. He noted the dry skin, with the little sore patches at the mouth corners from too much nervous licking of them; the unevenly-growing hair, sticking up here and there as though it had been carelessly grazed by goats; the fingernails bitten down to the nub; the eyes that flitted, and found it hard to fix on another person's. He looked drawn and haggard, and pale despite an all-weather tan.

'I'm Detective Chief Inspector Slider,' he said gently. 'Can you tell me your name?'

'Philip Arthur Armstrong, Dunkirk House, Uxbridge Road, London W12,' he said in a light, almost childish voice. He recited his name and address as though he had been taught it at a young age in case of emergencies. 'There's a policeman standing outside my house. I watched him for a long time, but he didn't move. Then I came here.'

'I see,' said Slider. 'Why did you come here?'

'I was here before,' he said, his eyes wandering round the room. 'Not this room. A different room. It wasn't very nice. That was when my mother died. There was a Sergeant Paxton. I didn't like him.'

'Sergeant Paxman,' Slider corrected.

'He didn't like me.' The eyes rested a moment on Slider's face for this revelation. 'He thought I'd done something. I could tell. I can always tell when people don't like me.' He looked away at the wall, at Lawrence, at his hands, and began picking at a fingertip. 'People think I'm a bit . . .' He put the finger to his mouth and gnawed a moment, then pulled it away as if with an effort. 'People look at me sometimes. I don't like that. So I keep away, mostly. I think something's happened to my sister.'

'Why do you think that?'

'Because, because, because she doesn't answer her phone. She always answers her phone. She worries about me. But she didn't answer so I came home and there's a policeman guarding the door. Did I do something? I think maybe I did something. I think maybe I killed her. I don't remember things sometimes, you see.' He looked at Slider from under his eyebrows, a haunted look. 'Did I kill her? Sergeant Paxman thought I'd killed my mother. I saw him whispering. He told the others I'd killed her.'

'And did you?'

'I don't *remember*!' he cried. He put his hands over his face and rubbed and rubbed at his eyes. 'I'm so tired,' he moaned. 'So tired.'

I'm so tired was often the trigger phrase for mentally unstable people, the warning that things were about to go fruit shaped.

'I expect you're hungry,' Slider said. 'Did you have anything to eat today?'

'I don't know,' he said, muffled, from behind his hands. 'I don't remember.'

'How would you like a cup of tea? And a sandwich?'

'Yes, please.' It was a small, childish voice.

'What would you like in your sandwich?' Giving a small choice to make, a small bit of autonomy, could deflect from tumbling thoughts. Armstrong said something too muffled to make out. 'I'm sorry, did you say ham?'

'Cheese, please,' Armstrong said in a tiny but clear voice, his hands held away from his face an inch for the purpose. 'Cheese please,' he said again, dropping his hands, and smiling vaguely. 'Cheese please, Louise, that's what Kate says. Cheddar and Cheshire, Wensley, Caerphilly, Lancashire, Leicester and Derby.' It was a rhythmical chant. 'But Stilton's true blue, for Milton, not you. Do you like cheese?'

'I do, very much.'

'I like cheese. I'd like a cheese sandwich, please. And then I'd like to go to sleep, because I'm *ve-ry* tired. I killed my sister, and it makes you tired, killing people. I couldn't sleep before, but I could now.'

'You'll get a psych evaluation before you question him?' said Porson.

'Of course, sir. Labouchere's on her way.'

'Can't be too careful with someone like that. One wrong step and you're up a gum tree without a ladder. Make sure you tick all the boxes, dot all the t's. What's your gut feeling about him?'

'Too soon to say, sir. He's tall, and though he's skinny, he looks strong enough to do it. Beyond that . . .' Slider shrugged.

Porson nodded. 'There's the mother as well. If he cops for that, it'll be two cases cleared up. A lot of bon for us. *Not*,' he added, drawing down his brows as Slider opened his mouth to speak, 'that that's what matters. But just on the side and by the way, they want to cut our budget again. There's talk of amalgamating us, moving us to Hammersmith. So handle this right, and it could make a big difference to all our futures. Savvy?'

'Yes, sir.'

He was almost at the door when Porson said thoughtfully, 'It's a teller, that he jumps to the conclusion his sister's dead. If he was innocent, he'd ask what happened to her, where she is, ask to see her.'

Slider didn't answer. That was also what he'd have said if he was guilty.

As Slider stepped out into the corridor, he saw Paxman just arriving at the top of the stairs. A glance at his watch told him it was change of relief time – Paxman must have just come in. He was evidently seeking Slider. It was never good to have Paxman actively wanting to talk to you. His silent disdain made for a much easier life.

'I heard we found Philip Armstrong?'

'He just walked in off the street,' Slider said, edging away.

'You checked his ID?'

'Nicholls did. Credit card, and a printed card with the Dunkirk House address on it in his wallet. He's not Dunnit Duncan.' There was a slightly disturbed local man called Desmond Duncan who liked to present himself at the police station and confess to things. He enjoyed the attention, and since he was harmless and actually quite likeable, they sometimes gave him a cup of tea and a biscuit before sending him back to the hostel. 'Dunnit's shorter, and he's got less hair.'

Paxman's lip curled. One of the things he disliked about Slider was his tendency to make jokes. Paxman didn't do jokes. He often didn't understand what Slider was on about, which made him think he was unsound.

'A little bird told me he put his hand up for his sister's murder,' Paxman said.

'Budgie, was it? Or a mynah bird?'

Paxman made a tut of annoyance. 'You know this makes it likely he did his mother as well? Like I always said. If them two bozos had investigated the case properly, instead of spending all their time . . .' He stopped and rolled his eyes. He never used swear words, or sexually explicit language, but his silences could seem somehow the more obscene.

'Everything will be done according to the book this time,' Slider said. 'Including getting a psych consult and a medical check.'

Paxman turned away sourly. 'You're just giving him time to get his story straight,' he muttered.

Slider turned the other way without comment. Alcock and Hough were Paxman's beef – adulterers and fornicators for whom hell wasn't hot enough. As Slider knew, the question of who killed Sandra May Armstrong and Kate Prudence Armstrong came second to his outrage over coppers tearing one off when they should have been on the Job. But if Philip Armstrong were to be righteously fingered for two murders it would prove that Paxman had been right all along, about Armstrong in particular, and in general about sexual misconduct being the greatest of all evils.

Kelly Deeping had already given Armstrong a once-over and pronounced him dehydrated, exhausted and underweight but otherwise physically OK. 'He's in pretty good shape, considering,' she reported. 'Not an ounce of fat on him but good musculature. I'd say he does a lot of walking or running – he's got that sort of physique. Like Mo Farah, y'know?' There was no sign of drug use or alcohol abuse. 'From my point of view, he's fit to be questioned.'

Danielle Labouchere, the police psychiatrist, spent a long time in with Philip, so long that Slider had rung home to say not to wait supper for him, and had gone up to the canteen for a meat pie and chips. He was back at his desk by the time she came to report.

'Interesting case,' she said. 'Arrested development, and he has some classic symptoms of schizophrenia. Disorganized thinking. Dislike of talking to people. Possible delusions. On the other hand, he seems, by his own account, to be quite high-functioning. Of course, many schizophrenics lead normal lives, but generally that's with help – drugs or therapy, or both. He seems to have been managing without either. He talks a lot about his sister. "Kate says" or "Katy says". He seems to have developed techniques to cope, possibly with her help. With the disorganized thinking, for instance, he recites lists of things to aid his focus on the topic in hand.'

Slider thought of the cheeses. 'Yes,' he said. 'Has he said any more about his sister's death?'

'No. He doesn't always seem to know she's dead. He talks about her in the present tense, as if she's alive, but then suddenly remembers.'

'Even normal people do that,' Slider said.

'Quite so. He weeps when he remembers.'

'Do you think he did kill her?'

'I couldn't possibly say. It's possible he did – or it could be a delusion. He spoke about his mother dying when he was a teenager – do you know about that?'

'She did die, in what was put down as accidental death.'

'Ah, so that wasn't delusional. Schizophrenia not uncommonly develops in adolescence as the result of a trauma, like the death of a loved one, so that could be the source in this case. Or it can develop because of a particularly troubled childhood.'

'Abuse, you mean?'

'Not necessarily. There are other sorts of trouble. A sensitive child, misunderstood, lonely, too aware of his elders' troubles – or it could simply be a child with too much imagination.'

'Is he fit to be questioned?'

'It's my opinion that he is. He'll have to have a solicitor present, of course, and if he doesn't nominate one himself, my advice would be to appoint one who understands the intellectually and emotionally fragile. I can recommend someone to you.'

'Yes, please. That would be kind.' He thought a moment. There was always the difficulty in cases like this that any evidence you acquired from the interviewee would later be dismissed by the court. You had to cover your back. 'You were in there a long time. Do you think he trusted you?'

'I got along with him all right,' Labouchere said. 'I see where this is going.'

'Would you sit in on the interviews, to reassure him, and in a professional capacity to see that everything's done right?'

'I will, but I shall have to rearrange a few things. I can make myself available tomorrow morning. It would be best, in any case,' she added, 'to let him rest overnight. A good meal and a night's sleep would help his mental state. He seems, from his own account, to have been wandering about and not sleeping for several days.'

THIRTEEN
Pale Ire, Envy and Despair

When he got finally home, Joanna came down, just out of the bath, wrapped in a dressing gown and steaming gently. The garment in question was not even first cousin to a negligée – it was tough, impervious, all-concealing. It occurred to him that a sensible dressing gown like that was a mark of motherhood. She hadn't owned even a frivolous one when he first met her, being more inclined to wander naked about her own home.

'Are you hungry?' she asked.

'I had something at work,' he said. 'I could do with a cup of tea, though. It's all right, I'll make it. D'you want one?'

'Make mine rooibos, or it'll keep me awake. So the missing brother just walked in?'

'It'll save us hundreds of man-hours looking for him,' he said. 'Mr Carpenter ought to be pleased.'

'Not more budgetary threats?' she interpreted, sitting down at the kitchen table.

'According to Mr Porson, they're talking about amalgamating us.'

'Why do I always think that means coating with zinc?'

'I'd prefer coating with zinc to moving into Hammersmith. Carpenter's the sort of boss you like better at a distance. A different continent would be ideal.'

'So what's he like? The brother, not Carpenter. I remember when you moaned about Mr Wetherspoon,' she added parenthetically. Wetherspoon had been the borough commander before Carpenter.

'I'd almost have him back,' said Slider. 'At least he came up through the ranks the hard way. Carpenter parachuted

in from university. He doesn't know his ACAS from his
EMRO.' He made the tea in two mugs, put them on the table
and sat down opposite her.

'So?' she prompted. 'How is Philip Armstrong?'

'A bit pathetic – strung out and exhausted. If he killed his
sister, he's suffering for it. We've had a psych evaluation and
we'll start questioning him tomorrow.'

'Saturday,' she said flatly.

He looked apologetic. 'Can't be helped, I'm afraid.'

'I mean, you'll probably be working on Sunday as well.'

'Oh, God, yes, your concert! What time are you on?'

'Three thirty to five thirty rehearsal, seven thirty concert.
It's in Reading, so it won't be worth coming back in between.'
She cocked him a warning look.

'I might be able to keep it down to only the morning on
Sunday,' he said, 'but just in case, I'd better have a word with
Dad.'

'If you were rich, we could have a live-in nanny, and none
of these problems.'

'Policemen don't get rich.'

'And if you hadn't been a policeman, I'd never have met
you.'

'You should have married George Clooney when you had
the chance.'

'Yes, silly me, I hesitated too long between him and
Leonardo DiCapricorn.'

'What's the programme on Sunday?'

'Bit of a scrub-fest. William T. Hell *Overture*, Dvorak *Scherzo
Capriccioso*, and Beethoven "Seven". Strings do all the work
and the brass gets all the glory.'

'William Tell – isn't that the Lone Ranger music?'

'There's my man of culture! It's a bugger to play – we
really need more than one rehearsal, but we won't get it. All
those down-bow ricochets on the sixteenths. If you don't get
it on exactly the right part of the bow . . .'

'I'm happy to say I didn't understand any of that. So there's
no soloist?'

'They can't afford one. Wear out the galley slaves instead,

that's their policy.' She held up her hands and waggled them. 'I shall have to practise tomorrow.'

'Practise?' he said in mock horror.

'Sometimes a girl's gotta do what a girl's gotta do. Well, at least it's work.'

'And everything has the defects of its virtues.'

'True.' She drained her cup. 'Bed?'

'Is that a defect or a virtue?'

'Let's go and find out.'

He was in so early the next morning that O'Flaherty was still the relief sergeant. He was the polar opposite of Paxman, an overweight, smiling, fatherly figure with an Irish brogue which he exaggerated for effect, when it suited him to play the Simple Man o' the Bogs. His eyes were usually so crinkled up with smiles you had to be a canny observer to see they were as hard and noticing as any copper's.

'How's our boy?' Slider asked.

'He's thirty-four years old, Billy. If he's a boy, I'm Gwyneth Paltrow.'

'To whom you bear a striking resemblance, let it be noted.'

'All you fellers say the same thing.' He did an alarmingly convincing toss of the head. 'We're much better, thank you. We had a good night's sleep, had a shave this morning and a good breakfast – eggs, bacon, the lot. Wolfed it all down, with seconds on the toast and jam. I reckon he's been half starved this week past. It's made a difference to the cut of him. By the way, the keys in his pocket fit the locks on Dunkirk House. And I heard one o' yours has matched his prints to some of those from inside the house, so that confirms his ID. In case you were wondering.'

'I wasn't, but thanks.'

'Maybe you should a' been,' O'Flaherty said in a low, warning voice. 'A little birdie tells me Mr Carpenter's on his way over.'

What was this bird that got so vocal around uniform sergeants? And Carpenter coming over? Slider was outraged. 'On a Saturday? At this time of day?'

'Have sense! He can't come any later or he'd miss his slot at the golf course.'

'Oh, silly of me. I hadn't thought,' said Slider.

Commander Carpenter was smiling, which was unpleasant on two fronts: first because he wasn't very good at smiling – like a crocodile he had the teeth for it but not the lips – and second because it meant he thought he had the drop on you.

After asking a lot of questions about progress, and lack of it, he showed his hand. 'What I can't understand is why you are investigating this in the first place. It seems to me you have no reason to suppose it's *not* an accidental death.'

'The head wound—' Slider began patiently.

'Yes, yes, I read the report. Not consistent with a fall down the stairs. You don't seem to have considered that she could have got the head wound earlier. For instance, what's to say she didn't slip and strike her head on, say, the corner of the bath, then wander in a daze to the top of the stairs, catch her foot in the hole in the carpet, and fall?'

'The bruises on the arms—'

He waved that away. 'She could have got those at any time. You're tying up manpower and a large chunk of budget looking into something that never needed looking into. And now you've pulled in a psychotic schizophrenic for questioning.'

'He actually walked in under his own—'

'Makes no difference. Do you know how the press is going to react to the idea of interrogating a mentally ill person?'

Porson, who had been standing by his window, arms folded and chin sunk on his chest, now spoke. 'I know what they'll say if it turns out there's something in it and we never investigated at all. I'd sooner be caned for doing my job than not doing it.'

Carpenter looked at him, opened his mouth and shut it again. The room was full of unspoken accusations, flitting about like invisible bats. The last time Carpenter had pressed for an accidental death write-off, it had turned into a high-profile murder case, in which Porson's firm had brought home the bacon, proving Carpenter wrong. On the other hand, Carpenter would probably reason that nobody would ever have known it was a murder if Slider hadn't refused to roll over, so there wouldn't have *been* any bacon in the first place.

Carpenter swung round and jabbed a rigid finger in Slider's direction. 'You'd better be damned careful about this. Take every precaution with this suspect – witness – whatever you think he is. Everything by the book. Kid gloves all the way. The first sniff I get of a complaint from anyone, and you're on report.'

'Sir,' said Slider.

'If you get nothing from him, I'm shutting you down.'

'Sir.'

'And if I don't see some very serious reasons for continuing this investigation by Monday, I'm shutting you down anyway.'

'Sir.'

'And stop saying "sir"!' he shouted suddenly. 'You're like a bloody parrot!'

Another little birdie! Slider shut his mouth on a possible reply that would have got him into trouble. He caught Porson's eye, and the old man gave him a hard jerk of the head, which meant *get out while you still have all your body parts*. Slider got.

Philip Armstrong did indeed look like a new man. The drawn, haunted look had left his face, there was a bit of colour in it, and the shave had made him much less like a tramp, though there appeared to have been nothing anyone could do about his hair, which still seemed to be having a party all on its own. It reminded Slider of a precautionary rhyme from his childhood: *Live wires, boy with pliers. Blue flashes. Boy ashes.*

'How are you feeling this morning?' Slider asked.

'All right,' Armstrong said cautiously.

'Do you feel up to answering a few questions?'

'What about?'

'Well, we'd like to know where you've been for the last few days.' Armstrong shrugged and looked away. 'You've met the lady solicitor, Dale Markby. She's going to be there to help you. And the lady you met yesterday, Danielle Labouchere, she'd like to sit in, if that's all right with you?'

'She's a psychiatrist,' he said. 'I know that.'

'She'll just listen, but she'll be there if you want reassurance.'

He was looking around him, as if he was only half listening. Slider persisted. 'So are you ready to come with me now to the interview room?'

Armstrong looked at him directly for the first time. 'I want to go home. Why can't I go home? I should call Kate. She'll come and fetch me. Kate says I should always call her if anything happens. But I haven't got my phone. They took my phone away. Please can you call Katy, so I can go home?'

'You can't go home yet,' Slider said, 'because something happened at your house. Don't you remember? Kate can't come, Philip.' The puzzled eyes were fixed on him. 'You remember, don't you? Kate's dead.'

The eyes filled slowly with tears. He didn't say anything, or make any sound, but the tears spilled over, and he shook his head slowly back and forth.

He seemed more at ease with women than men, so Slider chose Swilley to interview with him. Markby sat opposite beside Armstrong, and Labouchere took a chair in the corner of the room behind him. He looked at the mirror several times as if he knew it was a two-way glass, though he seemed resigned to it. He was such a mixture of normal and odd, Slider wondered what was the best way to get to him.

'Philip – do you mind if I call you Philip?' he began after the cautions. Armstrong shrugged. 'Now, we know that you were in Dorchester on Thursday last week, because you used your credit card to pay for bed and breakfast at the Borough Arms. Do you remember that?' No response. 'A week before that, you were in Bridport. How did you get from Bridport to Dorchester?'

'Walked,' he said, as if it were obvious.

'It's about fifteen miles,' Slider said, 'so you didn't go straight there.' Armstrong shook his head slightly, but didn't speak. 'It was lovely weather that week – hot and sunny. I expect you took your time. Enjoyed the scenery. You wouldn't go by the main road.'

He looked up. 'Of course not.'

'No. It's a busy road, the A35. That wouldn't be pleasant walking.'

He looked impatient. 'I go *fishing*,' he said. 'I follow the rivers. That's the Bride, nearly all the way. Then the Winter-bourne. Then after Dorchester it's the Frome. I know all the rivers. I like fishing.'

'So you walked a roundabout way, between Bridport and Dorchester, fishing here and there, as the fancy took you?' Armstrong nodded. 'Where did you stay at night? Where did you sleep?'

'Out, mostly. It was warm. There was a barn one night, I think.' He frowned a moment, then gave it up. 'Used to be lots of barns, but now they turn them into houses. But there's still some farms that have Dutch barns. It's nice in the straw, if you don't mind the mice. But when it's warm I just sleep under a wall or a hedge. Like the sheep.'

He was talking normally now, and seem relaxed. Slider was encouraged.

'But on Thursday, when you got to Dorchester, you wanted a proper bed.'

'To have a shower, and recharge my phone. And . . .' He looked shy, and lowered his voice. 'I washed some things out. In the basin.' Even lower, he confided, '*My pants.*'

'Of course. I see. And was that when you phoned Kate? Thursday night?'

He shook his head. 'After breakfast. On Friday. To tell her I was coming home. She meets me there. Gets things in for me.'

'You told her you'd be home – when?'

His mouth turned down and he shook his head. They were getting close to something he didn't want to think about.

'How were you going to get to London?' Slider tried. 'Walk?'

'Train,' he said, hardly moving his lips.

'Is that why you stopped in Dorchester, because it has a railway station?'

He began to chant under his breath. 'Southern Railway. Great Western Railway. London, Midland and Scottish. London and North Eastern. Great Central. Liverpool and Manchester.

London, Brighton and South Coast. London, Chatham and Dover.'

'You were in Dorchester on Friday morning,' Slider said over the chant. 'When did you get to London? Philip! What day did you get to Shepherd's Bush?'

'Bush, bushes, shrubs and trees. Plane tree, apple tree, sycamore, holly, laburnum.'

'I think we should stop now,' Dale Markby said. 'My client is getting upset.'

Slider ignored her. 'Where were you on Sunday, Philip? Is that when you saw Kate?'

'Don't know. Don't remember,' he said. His voice had become childish. 'Saturday, Sunday, Monday, Tuesday. Kate's dead? She can't be! No, no.' He set his fingers to the flesh of his face and drew it downwards in a horrible mask. 'I did a bad thing. He was right, I'm a bad person, I'm no good. I'm sorry, I'm sorry, Daddy, I'm sorry, Katy. Don't be dead, *please.* No more Mondays, no more Tuesdays. Katy, bar the door!'

'How did you kill her, Philip?'

'Drowned her in the bath.' His eyes were wide, staring at nothing, staring at memory. 'She looked up through the water but she was dead, she didn't see me. She had no clothes on. I didn't like that. I wanted to run away but I couldn't. I had to tell someone. Someone who's someone is no one who's anyone.'

'No, that wasn't Kate. That was your mother. That was a long time ago. Try to concentrate, Philip. You went by train from Dorchester to London. You went home. Was Kate already there when you got to the house?'

'I don't *know*. I don't *remember.*'

'I think you do,' Slider said, gently but remorselessly. 'Sunday, remember last Sunday. Sunday morning, at the house, at your house. Was Kate already there, or did she come in later?'

'She made the bed. Girls do. But you mustn't touch. He told me. I watched, but I shouldn't have. I hid and I watched, and I'm a bad person. I want Kate! I want Katy! Don't be dead! Please don't be dead!'

Labouchere shook her head at Slider, and he stopped the

tape. She came over and touched Armstrong gently on the shoulder, and he turned and pressed his face against her and shook.

When they resumed, he was quiet but, rather than relaxed, he seemed tired, almost sullen. Slider tried to start him by asking about where he had been since Sunday, but nothing was forthcoming. He either shook his head, or said he didn't know, didn't remember, or just said nothing staring blankly like something in a cage staring through the bars. Slider made it a short session and broke again to let him rest and get lunch.

'He can't remember? Or won't remember?' he said to Labouchere in the corridor.

'In his case it's probably the same thing,' she said. 'He has an emergency cut-off switch in his head when his thoughts come near something he doesn't want to deal with. On the whole, though, I'm encouraged. He's coping with the situation much better than I expected. I think if you can find the right way in, you'll get him to open up eventually. He doesn't seem afraid of you, which is huge. Something about you reassures him. If they're pushed too close to the fear trigger they can turn violent, or shut down entirely, and he doesn't seem to be close to that. Take your time, lead him rather than push him.'

'It's all very well saying take your time,' Slider said to Atherton as they headed up to the canteen, 'but we're on the clock. Not sure the magistrates will accept the difficulties of questioning him as a reason to give us an extension.'

'You've just got to find the right way in, like she said,' Atherton urged encouragingly.

'I particularly enjoy your use of the word "just" in that sentence,' Slider complained, pushing through the canteen doors. He sniffed. 'Macaroni cheese!'

'God, your arteries!' Atherton said, heading straight for the salad bar.

'My arteries can take care of themselves. It's my brain cells that need feeding,' Slider retorted.

When they reunited at a table, with matching looks of horror for each other's plates, Atherton said, 'I hope this lot's not going to mean I have to cancel my date tonight.'

'Something special?' Slider asked.

'Something different. You see, after some reflection, I realized that my serious relationships have always been with women with brains, and they've always gone wrong. There's always a clash between their requirements and mine. So maybe what I need is a woman—'

'Without requirements?' Slider suggested, working his fork through the crusty bit at the corner.

'Fewer requirements, anyway. So that our lifestyles don't constantly pull in different directions.'

'God, I'm glad I don't have to think about things deeply all the time like you,' Slider said, easing the crusty corner into his mouth.

'That's just it,' Atherton said. 'I'm tired of thinking and dating at the same time. It's time to get fundamental, access the core me, let things take a more natural course. Hence tonight's candidate.'

'Candy date? You've got a date with a girl called Candy? I bet she spells it with an "i".'

'If you could suspend your cynicism for a moment . . .'

'*Me* cynical? I make Pollyanna look like Dorothy Parker.'

'Her name isn't Candy, spelt either way. It's Rebecca, but she likes to be called Bex. With an "x".'

Slider forbore to comment. 'Don't tell me, she's young and gorgeous.'

'She's a wild, silky beauty. Smells like the ground floor of Selfridges. Wears the sort of underwear you can floss with.'

'You've met her underwear already?'

'I'm deducing it from her photograph and profile.'

'What does she do? I'm guessing, her GCSEs.'

'She's a photographic model. Don't snort like that or you'll do the nose trick with pasta and I don't want to be here to witness it. She models for clothing catalogues – upmarket ones. You can make a very good living that way. It's a proper, long-term career.'

'You've got your brains caught in your zip again,' Slider said kindly.

'I'm serious.'

'I know exactly how serious you are.'

Atherton sighed. 'You've snaffled the only perfect woman in the world. The rest of us have to do the best we can.'

Slider was slightly taken aback, but rallied. 'Well, I shall keep my fingers crossed we have a breakthrough this afternoon,' he said. 'I wouldn't want you to have to cancel such a dazzling opportunity.'

'This evening could be the beginning of the rest of my life.'

'It pretty much has to be,' said Slider.

FOURTEEN
Farewell to Alms

When Gascoyne said he wanted to talk about Jason Shalcross, Valentine Farringdon agreed, cautiously, to meet him. 'My office is in Bishopsgate. Do you know the King's Arms on Wormwood Street?'

'I'll find it,' said Gascoyne.

'I'll meet you there for a late lunch – say two thirty?'

'That's fine.'

'Upstairs. It's quieter.'

The King's Arms was a nice, old-fashioned sort of pub that specialized in well-kept ale and traditional food. Upstairs featured leather banquettes, some very old-fashioned brown wallpaper and framed sepia photos of Victorian street scenes, and it was certainly quiet, containing only one man, sitting at a table with a pint in front of him. He rose to his feet as Gascoyne caught his eye enquiringly. He was very tall and lean, clean-shaven, looked late forties, with the sort of firm face that belonged to someone who was definitely a grown-up. He looked like someone who could take care of himself. He was wearing a suit, but it had an impatient air about it, as if it wasn't his usual garb. Gascoyne could effortlessly translate him into combats. His hair had abandoned the front and top of his head, and he had shaved the remainder close to the skull, but despite that Gascoyne had no difficulty in recognizing the third man in the photograph.

'You don't mind if we eat while we talk?' he said briskly. 'I don't get much time for lunches. You hungry?'

'Very.' Gascoyne trimmed his style to match.

'They do a good steak and ale pie here.'

'That'll do me.'

A waitress had heaved herself up the stairs, and the order was placed. Farringdon sat again, on the banquette facing the stairs, and Gascoyne eased himself in catty-corner, having a dislike to sitting with his back to an entrance.

'So what's up?' Farringdon asked.

'I was hoping you could tell me something about Jason Shalcross.'

'Like what?'

'Well, where to find him, for a start. The address I've got for him is an accommodation address, and he doesn't answer his phone.'

Farringdon surveyed Gascoyne measuringly. 'Jason is an old friend of mine,' he said at the end of the inspection. 'If he's in trouble I want to help him.'

Gascoyne decided honesty was the best way forward with this man. Fudge just wouldn't cut it. 'A woman is dead in suspicious circumstances, and no one seems to know anything about her. Your friend Jason seems to be one of the last people she spoke to, and we're hoping he can give us a line on her.'

Farringdon's eyes narrowed. After a moment of thought he said, 'Jason would never hurt a woman. Never.'

'Then there can be no harm in your helping us,' Gascoyne said evenly. He felt Farringdon needed priming, and went on: 'Captain Challoner at the barracks said you and Jason and Tony Scrimgeour were all good friends in Afghanistan.'

Farringdon thought for a bit. The waitress toiled back up with a tray, bearing a pint for Gascoyne, two plates of steak and ale pie with mashed potato and vegetables, and two little bundles of cutlery wrapped in paper napkins.

'D'you want anything else? Any sauce or anything?' she asked. She sounded martyred, and Gascoyne hadn't the heart to send her all the way down and up again for salt.

When she was gone, Farringdon said, 'In Kandahar, a friend is someone you rely on. It can literally mean life or death. We looked out for each other. Anyone who didn't watch his mates' backs wouldn't have lasted long.'

'I understand,' Gascoyne said. He understood Farringdon would have to be led up to the fence. He cut into his pie. It was a proper, individual one with crisp pastry, and the filling was generous and fragrant. It was a pity it was going to come second to an interview – it deserved to be concentrated on. 'What happened to Tony Scrimgeour? How was he killed?'

'We were checking out an abandoned truck by some ruined buildings on the Ghazni road – the locals said it was rigged. Tony was checking it out, while Jason went up the road a bit, with half the patrol, looking for IEDs, and I checked the buildings with the other half, because it was a classic ambush situation. The buildings were clear, but there was a bomb in the truck, a big one. I went back to help Tony deal with it. There must have been snipers hiding in the scrub behind, they must've crept into the buildings from the rear while we were busy. As soon as Tony stood up, they shot him through the head.'

'I'm sorry,' Gascoyne said.

He shrugged. 'Could just as well have been me.' He ate some pie, chewing efficiently. 'At least it was a clean death. He always said he'd sooner die right out than go back home with no legs and half an arm. There's a heavy toll in our line of work.'

'It must have been hard for you to lose a friend.' Farringdon did not deny it. 'Did Jason take it particularly hard?' A raised eyebrow. 'I'm wondering why he used Tony's name, you see. When he gave this woman his address he told her his name was Tony Scrimgeour.'

Farringdon looked thoughtful. 'I think he did take it hard,' he said slowly. 'Look, I'll tell you something about Jason – something he never talks about himself, but it might help you understand.' He ate some more, thinking, then began. 'We lived on the edge out there. You knew you could die at any moment, and the only way to cope with it was not to think about it, to pretend everything was normal. You have to assume the IED won't go off, that you'll all be there at supper time, that you'll all go home eventually with all the bits you came out with. If you thought about what might happen, you'd go to pieces.'

Gascoyne nodded. 'I understand.'

'Part of this – pretending everything was normal . . .' He broke off again. 'There was this girl. Asal Afridi. Daughter of one of the Afghan nationals. One of our jobs out there was to train the locals, so they could carry on when we were finally withdrawn. We all took a turn at teaching, but Jason was especially good at it – he could get people's trust. Tony used to say he could charm the birds out of the trees. Not that there were any birds by that time, but you know what I mean. Everybody liked him. Anyway, Jason got very friendly with old man Afridi, got invited to their house for dinner. That was a big honour with them, getting asked home. They didn't do it lightly. And he . . . fell in love, I suppose, with the eldest daughter, Asal.' His eyes grew distant. 'She was lovely. Asal means "honey", and it suited her. She had skin the colour of honey, and a sweet face. Those luscious dark eyes you felt you could drown in, you know? Jason was crazy about her. No funny business, he wanted to marry her – but her old man wasn't too keen on his daughter going out with a Brit soldier. But he liked Jason, and Jason reckoned he could win him round in the end. I don't know if he would have,' he added. His voice grew cold. 'Some of the locals were hardliners when it came to the women, and some of them were just scared of the Taliban. No way to know who it was, but one day Asal was found in a ditch near our barracks with her throat cut.'

'I'm sorry,' Gascoyne said quietly.

'It finished Afghanistan for Jason. It was that, finally, rather than Tony's death that made him pull out. Well, losing Tony *was* part of it – it hits harder when it's a mate – but then Asal . . . It was one thing on top of another, and all the heart went out of him when they found her. He didn't want to risk his life protecting them when they'd do something like that to one of their own girls.'

'Did he get any psychological help, do you know? I believe there are lots of organizations dedicated to helping servicemen get over traumas.'

'Jason would never have any truck with that sort of thing. Too independent. He'd never take charity – that's what he'd see it as. Charity. Or pity. Some guys end up on the scrapheap, but he didn't believe they couldn't help it. You write your own story, that's what he said. No one else can help you.'

'So, do you know what he did when he got back to England, then?'

'When he got out? Well, he worked for Red Shield for a bit. That's a private explosives disposal company. They operate all over the world. A lot of us went there – it worked like a sort of stepdown facility, if you like, to ease you out of the service and into civvy life. Some guys like it so much they stay – bitch about the job all the time but don't feel comfortable without it. I was there for about five years myself, then I set up my own company. I get a lot of ex-servicemen too. Mostly I do risk assessment and the managerial side now – I've got a wife and kids, so I don't want to get down and dirty with the pliers any more.' He smiled to show it was a joke. 'You can grow out of risking your life in the end.'

'And did Jason grow out of it?'

'I guess he did. He left Red Shield before I did, went into personal security – you know, private bodyguard?' Gascoyne nodded. 'There are some clients who appreciate the extra expertise of an EOD specialist – clients who think someone might be after them. Sometimes they're right, mostly they're wrong, but it doesn't hurt to have a bloke check out your house and car for explosives, does it?'

'Do you know who he's working for now?'

'He was with an agency, but I think he went freelance a couple of years ago. I couldn't tell you who his clients are now. They must be pretty high-powered, because if I know Jason he'd charge a bundle.'

'Do you keep in touch?'

'Oh, I get a ring now and then. We went for a drink – what – must be a year ago, now. That'd be the last time I saw him.'

'What did you talk about?'

Farringdon gave him a quizzical look. 'You expect me to remember a conversation, after all this time? Just general chat, I suppose – the old days and so on. He'd ask about my family. I think I asked if he was seeing anyone, and he said no – said that was all over for him. Still hung up on Asal. I remember I gave him a lecture about putting the past to rest and getting on with life. I think,' he added, frowning, 'it wasn't so much heartbreak at losing her, though that came into it, but guilt, because he reckoned if he hadn't dated her she would still be alive. He blamed himself for her death. So you see,' he said with a clear look straight into Gascoyne's eyes, 'why I say he'd never hurt a woman.'

'I hear you,' said Gascoyne. Of course, it was an adage in the Job that anyone was capable of anything if the circumstances were right. 'So where's he living now?'

'He's got a flat in Limehouse. I'll give you the address.' He consulted his phone, and Gascoyne wrote it down – Flat 14G, Barley Wharf, Narrow Street, and the phone number. Different from the burner phone number he'd given the Archive. When Gascoyne had done, Farringdon gave him an earnest look. 'Jason's a mate, you know. And he's a good bloke. If he's in trouble I want to help. Will you call me if there's anything I can do?'

Gascoyne nodded. 'But so far he's just a potential witness,' he said. 'Nothing to worry about.'

Yet, he saw Farringdon was worried. Was that just loyal friendship, or did he have doubts about his friend's supposed inability to hurt anyone? They had done a hard job, in some ways an impossible job, and just surviving it would have to take its toll. Gascoyne wouldn't be so very sure Jason Shalcross was a fully rehabilitated pussycat.

Again, after food, Philip Armstrong seemed restored. The tiredness and sullenness were not in evidence. He was quiet, but seemed normally alert, and his air, if anything, was of puzzlement, as if he was not quite sure why he was there.

Slider reverted to the time he had not minded talking about. 'Tell me about Friday morning, when you were in Dorchester, at the hotel. You had breakfast there? What did you have?'

'I had a lot, so I wouldn't need anything later. I had corn-flakes with milk and sugar and peach slices, but they were only out of a tin, then I had bacon and eggs, then I had toast and marmalade. I like hotel breakfast. You can keep going back for more and they don't say anything. You can have enough to last all day, and it's all in the price.'

'And then after breakfast you rang Kate. To tell her you were coming home.' He nodded. 'How was she, on the phone?'

'All right,' he said, looking puzzled at the question. Slider waited, and he responded by searching for something to say. 'She said we could go out for something to eat. To Nando's. I like chicken peri-peri.'

'On Sunday?'

'On Monday night. When I got home.'

'Didn't you go home on Friday?'

He looked away, and his lips moved as if he were reciting something soundlessly. Lead, don't push. Slider thought. 'What did you do on Friday, when you left the hotel? Where did you go?'

He seemed to think for a long time, then he said, as if it had just come to him, 'Poole. I went to Poole. A man took me out on his boat on Sunday. Then I got the train on Monday.'

'Where did you stay on Sunday night? Did you stay in a hotel?' He shook his head. 'Where did you sleep?'

He screwed his face up, as if with a violent effort at memory. 'Park,' he said. 'Then I got the train, early. Early early. Early one morning just as the sun was rising, I got the train, to take the strain, to stop the train pull down the chain.' The childish voice again. 'I want to go home. Please let me go home.'

Change direction. Slider pushed the child's drawing from Kate's flat across the table. 'Do you know who did that?'

Armstrong glanced at it warily without moving his head, as if he could see it without looking, then leaned forward and pulled it towards him. 'It's mine. I drew it for Kate. Where did you get it?'

'She had it in her flat. How old were you when you drew it?'

'Don't know. Little. She kept it?'

'She did. And is this your colouring book?'

He pored over it with apparent pleasure, turning the pages, stroking the figures with a forefinger. 'We did it together. We liked colouring-in. But you mustn't go over the edges.'

'Who drew the arrows in the giant, and scribbled out his face?'

At that Philip closed the book and pushed it away hard, his mouth tight. But he picked up the drawing again, and softened. 'I drew lots of things for her. I draw much better now. And paint. I didn't know she kept this. She didn't like keeping things. She tore them up, threw them away.'

'Why do you think she did that?'

'Don't know. She was scared, I s'pose.'

'Scared of what?'

He shrugged. 'Just scared.'

'Was she married, your sister Kate?'

'No,' he said indifferently, still looking at the drawing. Then: 'But she had a boyfriend.'

'Did she? When was that?'

'Just now,' he said, the drawing seemingly occupying all his attention. 'She told me on the phone.'

'What did she say about him?'

'She said he was very nice.' A long pause. Then: 'She met him at work. She said I could meet him one day when I was home. She said he was kind.'

'What else did she tell you about him?'

'Don't remember.'

'Did she say his name?'

'Tony.' The name seemed to prime him. 'He liked old buildings. He was interested in our house. She said she would show him one day. She said I'd like him, he was kind. I said, not show him *everything*. She said not if I didn't want, it was my house too. She said he was just a friend, not a boyfriend, but I know. Her voice said she liked him another way. It was sort of . . . *lifty*. She said she'd bought a new dress. And she told me not to be jealous.'

'What did that mean?'

'She meant I wasn't to be jealous of him, because she loved me best and she always would.'

'And were you jealous?'

He looked up, but not at Slider. His eyes were blank, opaque. 'I was worried for her. I told her to be careful. She never had to do with men. Never. She didn't like them. Only me. But she said I was away so much. Maybe she was lonely. I thought she ought to have a kitten. For when I was away. She didn't *say* she was lonely. But sometimes they don't tell you things. Like Mummy. Kate's always looked after me. She was going to take me to Nando's. Just me, not him.'

'Is that why you killed her?' Slider asked, very gently, just slipping it in. 'Because you were jealous of this new man?'

'I never saw him,' he said. 'She didn't like men. They do things. They always do things. He said not to look, never to look. He said he'd know if I did. A little bird would tell him. Birds in the garden, blue tit, great tit, marsh tit, willow tit, coal tit, long-tailed tit. Goldfinch, greenfinch, bullfinch, siskin. No birds in the garden now, they're all dead. They're little and they all die. It was too little and it died. She didn't like the house because people die in it. Did I do something? I can't remember.' He put his fists against the sides of his head and pressed in until his knuckles were white. 'Oh I'm so tired. So tired.'

Labouchere lifted a hand, but Slider had already reacted. 'Interview suspended,' he said, and stopped the tape.

Porson looked grim. 'If he was in Poole Sunday, it lets him off the hook.'

'And that's going to be a tricky alibi to check,' said Slider.

'What about this man who took him out on his boat?'

'He doesn't remember his name, or the name of the boat. He says it was white. I imagine there are a lot of white boats in Poole.'

'Most of 'em, I wouldn't wonder. Worse than that, it'll be a bugger to disprove. If no one comes forward, that doesn't mean it didn't happen. Sleeping in a park – did anyone see him? Poole railway station – is there a camera at the ticket office? How many people take the early trains – and how early was early? Waterloo station – see if he appears on a camera anywhere. That's a lot of work. That's going to tie up a lot of people, just when Mr Carpenter's getting antsy.'

'It'll have to be done,' Slider said gloomily. 'I wonder . . .?' He didn't go on. It would take a very clever person deliberately to make up an alibi so hard to check out; clever and confident. Was Philip Armstrong both? He'd come in of his own accord – but could that be a ploy to deflect suspicion? *If he was guilty, he'd never have done that*, was a thing that was said, and it was generally true, but a clever and confident person might try the old double-bluff. How mentally unbalanced was he? That was something it was impossible to know.

'But this Tony Scrimgeour's looking tastier, sir,' Atherton was saying. 'We still have to find him – Jason Shalcross, as we now know he is.'

'Yes, there were two lots of fingermarks in the house, remember,' Slider said.

'And even if Shalcross is not involved,' Atherton went on, 'he's seen the victim more recently than anyone else.'

'I wonder if that was misdirection,' Swilley said. 'Philip putting the suspicion onto the new boyfriend because he was jealous of him.' She looked at Labouchere. 'Could he be that cunning?'

'He's disturbed, not unintelligent,' she said. 'Certainly he has the mental capacity to be cunning. I couldn't say without much longer study than I've had so far whether that's the way his mind trends.' She looked at Slider. 'You notice he often refers to a "he" who told him things – not to look, not to touch.'

'Yes, I noticed. Is that the voice in his head, do you think?'

'It could be. Or it could be a recurring memory. I'm thinking about the most traumatic event in his life – the death of his mother. Discovering her body. It might be fruitful to try to get him to talk about that. If he did kill his sister, talking about his dead mother might trigger a proper confession.'

Slider frowned. 'I don't like the word "trigger". If I push him on something as sensitive as that—'

'I only meant that there might be some help for you in the association of ideas. And,' she added, 'from the point of view of *his* mental health, rather than just your case, he needs to confront his worst memories in order to heal properly. If he killed his sister and doesn't confront it, he might sink so far into psychosis he'll be beyond help.'

'One of our officers from the time of his mother's death thinks that he might have had something to do with it,' Slider said cautiously. From the corner of his eye, he saw Porson give him a sharp look.

Labouchere looked troubled. 'Poor young man! In that case,

it really would be a mercy to get him to talk about it. It should have been done at the time. He should have had professional help back then.'

'He had his sister instead,' Slider said.

'And perhaps she became inextricably tangled up in it in his mind. The acquiring of a new boyfriend – the disturbance of the status quo – could have been the thing that pushed him over the edge.'

She went off to make some phone calls. At the door of the CID room, Porson stopped before going on to his office and said, 'I don't like all this psychological pavlova. But I can see it's going to take time to get him to spew it all out. Put in for a twenty-four extension and I'll sign off on it. And I'll keep Mr Carpenter updated.'

'There's the question of where he could go if he is released,' Slider mentioned. 'Back to Dunkirk House, all alone?'

'We'll cross that road when we come to it. You can have another go at him after tea, see what transpires.'

FIFTEEN
Jason the Argue-Not

The heat had turned oppressive, and though the sky was still blue it had a thick look to it, with a greyish tinge around the horizon. Slider, who was a country boy by birth, could have told Gascoyne that a front was coming over, but Gascoyne only knew that he was sweating, and didn't look forward to putting his jacket on when he got out of the air-conditioned car.

It was usually better down by the river – a little more air movement. It seemed thousands of Londoners had already concluded that, because the many restaurants and bars that lined the old commercial wharves were packed with smart young people, sitting at tables outside, or inside by retractable windows, enjoying an early drink, the view and the flat river smell as the Thames rolled immemorially by.

Barley Wharf was not one of the old brick warehouses that had been converted: it was a brand new building, all polished concrete and solar glass, with every dwelling angled to give it a little bit of a balcony looking over the river. High gates complete with a uniformed guard in a box gave access to the ground level and parking: this was not a place for casual visitors. The guard wanted to ring up to flat 14G before letting Gascoyne and Jenrich in. Having ascertained from the log that Shalcross was at home, Gascoyne had to come the heavy to prevent his doing so.

'He's probably going to ring him the moment we're out of sight,' Jenrich complained as they drove through the gates. 'He'll be ready for us.'

'Can't do anything about that,' Gascoyne said with a shrug.

She didn't like the shrug. 'You don't care if he jumps us?'

'I'm sure you can protect me all right, sarge,' Gascoyne said, straight-faced.

She snorted. 'That's why you wanted me to come, is it?'

'I've heard on the grapevine you're the best at unarmed combat.'

'Hell with that. I'm putting my vest on.'

'In this heat?'

'It'll be cool inside,' she predicted. 'Price of these places, they'll have AC.'

She had an NIJ II which was super lightweight and would fit under a suit jacket. Gascoyne watched her as she buttoned her jacket over it, and thought that she was so lean and muscled and dangerous, she didn't look as if she would ever sweat anyway. Heat wouldn't dare diss her like that.

No money had been wasted on the public areas and stairs – they were bare and minimal, concrete and iron; the lift was the most basic model: a stainless steel box with buttons. G was the seventh and top floor. 'Most expensive,' Jenrich said. 'He must make a decent screw at this security lark. We're in the wrong job.'

On floor G, another bare concrete corridor, they approached a bland, flat, UPVC door ('Steel reinforced – betcha,' said Jenrich) with a plastic fourteen on it, and a spyhole below. Jenrich nodded to Gascoyne and he rang the doorbell and held up his brief before the spyhole, while she took up position to one side and tensed for action.

Shalcross opened the door. He was tall – he had been squatting in the only photo Gascoyne had seen of him, so it had not been possible to tell – and though not bulky, was obviously well-muscled and extremely fit. He was wearing chinos and an untucked chambray shirt, loose enough to have concealed a shoulder holster or a knife at the belt. His face was lean and handsome, but watchful, his eyes steady and emotionless; his thick, dark hair was expensively cut in layers, his skin tanned.

Above all, he had a stillness about him, the stillness of the policeman or the soldier, who can stand motionless in the shadow of a tree or building for as long as it takes to get the opposition to show itself. It was the stillness of the hunting cat watching the mousehole, the leopard the clearing where the deer feed. Was it possible – was it even feasible – that a man of such power and self-control would have fallen for ordinary Prue Chadacre?

Shalcross did not speak, even to ask what they wanted. He just waited. It was impressive.

Well, they couldn't stand there all day. Jenrich was forced to introduce themselves, and said, 'We want to talk to you about Prue Chadacre. Can we come in?'

Inside there was all the luxury that had been spared outside. The style was minimal, but it was worlds away from the bareness of Prue Chadacre's flat; this was the starkness that cost real money. The living room was wide and open and walled on one side with floor-to-ceiling glass doors onto an outdoor terrace looking over the river. The woodblock floor was proper hardwood, the walls were done in alternating wide panels of matt cream paint and what looked like dark-blue silk; the lamps were brushed steel and so modern it took a minute to work out they actually were lamps. There was an enormous flat-screen TV set into one of the walls, and a bank of electronic equipment almost covering another; a huge cream leather sofa faced the window-wall and was flanked by a black leather Charles Eames with its attendant footstool. Through a doorway to the rear was a glimpse of a kitchen so modern and tech-equipped you could probably have done brain surgery in it. The air was cold and odourless, and there was no sign anywhere of personal clutter. It was the sort of room Gascoyne felt you wouldn't dare untidy. It looked like a film set.

'Nice,' he said. 'Terrific view.'

Shalcross merely observed him, as the lion might observe a butterfly while it waited for the herd of bok to wander near enough: nothing here yet that required action. He had quickly and comprehensively examined his two visitors, and now stood, relaxed but alert, in the centre of the room, waiting for them to begin. They were not invited to sit.

Gascoyne took out his notebook, and looked at Jenrich.

'When did you last see Prudence Chadacre?' she asked sternly.

He thought about it, which might have been a normal pause for recollection, or a calculation of whether or not to lie. Impossible to tell with someone whose face gave so little away.

'That would be Thursday of last week,' he said. His voice was a surprise, now they heard it for the first time – not harsh in any way, but pleasant, rounded, almost warm in tone – what Jenrich classed to herself as a furry voice. Its effect was to induce relaxation – which she resisted, of course.

'And where was that?'

'At her place of work. In the afternoon. I went in to look at some documents, and stopped to chat to her on my way out.'

'What documents were they?' she asked quickly.

'Plans of the original Barley Wharf. The Victorian building that was on this site,' he answered as quickly. Gascoyne thought he caught a faint gleam of triumph in the watchful eyes. *Can't catch me that way.* 'I suppose you know she worked at an archive of old building plans and drawings?'

'Of course,' Jenrich said. 'And you're interested in that stuff, are you?'

'Why not?' he said, as if it were a question rather than a throw-away comment.

Of course, there was no answer to that. 'Did you make plans to see her at the weekend?' she asked instead.

'No,' he replied.

'You were interested in the Victorian house she owned with her brother. She was planning to show it to you.'

'She'd talked about the house,' he said. 'I was interested. There was no plan for me to visit it.'

'Why not?'

'We weren't on that sort of footing. She was very reserved. She wouldn't have invited a comparative stranger to her house.'

'She told her brother a visit was in the offing.'

'She didn't say that to me,' he said firmly. 'And I'd never met her brother.'

Gascoyne said, 'Excuse me, but you don't seem to be curious as to why we're asking about Ms Chadacre.'

Shalcross turned his face to him, his gaze level and aware. 'I have a news feed on my phone. Her name was released on Thursday. I know she's dead.'

'You don't seem very upset,' Jenrich put in.

'I've seen a lot of death. I've learned not to show it.' He

took a breath. 'Of course I'm upset about Prue. It's offensive you assume to know what I'm feeling.'

'What *did* you feel for Ms Chadacre?' Gascoyne asked.

'None of your business.'

Gascoyne looked straight into his eyes. 'I don't believe you're so naive as to think that, Mr Shalcross. There are some things about your behaviour towards Ms Chadacre that need explaining. If it was all above-board, you can satisfy us here and now. Otherwise, we will have to ask you to come to the station for a more serious talk.'

Suddenly, he smiled, and the effect was shocking. It lit his face, making him look almost unbearably handsome, inviting response. It was a smile that pulled an answering smile up from the soles of your boots and Gascoyne had to consciously resist, while remembering Val Farringdon saying he could charm the birds from the trees.

'Come on, now, officers,' Shalcross said, 'let's drop the officialese. If you think I murdered her, say so, and let's have it out.'

'Did you?'

'Of course not. I'd never harm her. Poor little Prue,' he added quietly. 'It was a rotten thing to do.'

Jenrich took over. Gascoyne could tell from her voice that she didn't like him and thought he was faking. 'If you meant her no harm,' she said in a hard voice, 'why did you give her a false name, an accommodation address, and a burner phone number?'

'I didn't give them to her, I gave them to the Archive. And are any of those things illegal?'

'Depends on your intentions. They certainly need explaining, when the subject turns up brutally murdered,' she snapped back. 'It sounds like stalker behaviour.'

Gascoyne thought something registered with him, like a slap – not enough to hurt, but enough for him to notice. The smile faded just a little, but he said nothing.

'Why the false name?' Jenrich persisted.

'I've never liked my name. Tony Scrimgeour was my best friend. I always thought that was a much nicer name.'

Jenrich curled her lip. 'You expect me to believe that?'

'I don't expect anything. You asked, I answered. It's up to you what you believe.'

'Why did you give a false address?'

'I like my privacy. I don't give away personal data without a good reason.'

'Dating a woman is a pretty good reason.'

'I wasn't dating her.'

'That's not what she told her brother. She was definitely under the impression that you were interested in her. And so were her work colleagues.'

'I can't be responsible for other people's misconceptions.'

'Is this something you do a lot? Get to know vulnerable women, play on their emotions, get them to trust you, then lure them somewhere and kill them? How many other victims have you had?'

'You surely don't expect me to answer such a ridiculous question. Especially without a caution.'

Gascoyne took over, seeing Jenrich was angry. 'Can you account for your whereabouts last weekend, sir?'

Shalcross nodded, as though pleased by the 'sir'. 'I was wondering when it would occur to you to ask that. I was out of town, as a matter of fact.'

'Convenient,' Jenrich muttered.

Gascoyne poised his pen. 'If you would just give me the details, sir.'

'Certainly. I went for a fishing weekend. I stayed with a friend who has a house on the River Tavy near Tavistock. I went down on Friday night and stayed until Tuesday. There were six of us. We fished all day and drank all night. A good time was had by all.'

Gascoyne gave him a grave look. 'You know that we will have to check this out, sir.'

'I would expect nothing less. I will give you the address, and the names of all five, and they will tell you that I was with some or all of them all the time.'

'It seems you went to a lot of trouble to give yourself an alibi,' Jenrich said.

'I'm getting tired of this,' Shalcross said, with a hint of impatience. 'If you have something to accuse me of, charge me. Otherwise, please leave.'

'We will, sir,' Gascoyne said soothingly. 'But the names first.' He took down the details dictated by Shalcross, and then got in a quick further question.

'I was told you were working freelance now, or had your own company.'

'Who told you that?'

'Val Farringdon. He said you were with an agency but you left a couple of years ago.' Shalcross made no response – and of course it wasn't strictly a question. 'Can you explain how you can freelance and have no internet presence? I've tried searching for you online and come up with nothing. How can clients find out about you if you don't even have a website?'

'Personal recommendation,' Shalcross said; and then deigned to expand. 'The clients I work for are so high-powered, they would not care to trawl the internet and hire a stranger. They need to know who they're dealing with. They need the security of a recommendation from someone they trust.'

'I see. And who are you working for at the moment?'

Was there the breath of a hesitation. 'I am between clients at the moment. That was how I could take a fishing holiday.'

'Who was your last client, then?' Jenrich demanded.

'I can't tell you that,' he said smoothly. 'It would breach client confidentiality.'

'What if I insist?' said Jenrich.

'I don't think you have that authority, Detective Sergeant,' he said. He was not smiling now. There was a palpable tension about him. If it hadn't been so cold in the room, Gascoyne thought he would have been sweating. 'It will need a special warrant, given the danger it might put my clients in.'

And then they were ushered firmly to the door. Jenrich gave him one more dark look that said, *we'll be back*, and then they were outside.

'The alibi'll check out,' Gascoyne said resignedly.

'Maybe not,' said Jenrich. 'When they're that cocky, they're often bluffing. And he's not innocent. I can smell it on him.'

'The false name and address he gave at the Archive don't look good,' Gascoyne agreed. 'But if he's alibied for the weekend, what can we get him for?'

'Alibis are made to be broken.'

They stepped out of the shadow of the buildings into the heat. It felt thick and felty, hard to breathe. 'Suppose he runs?' Gascoyne said.

'He won't run. He's too full of himself. He thinks he's safe. He wants to hang around and watch us fail.'

'You didn't like him, did you?' Gascoyne hazarded.

'What's to like? Mr Smooth Bastard.' She made an irritated movement of her head. 'What was he up to with the vic? Was he after her money? How did he hope to get hold of it? Or was he just trying to mess her up? But that doesn't make sense. There must have been easier women to prey on – it sounds like he's been weeks even getting this far. I don't get it. I *know* he's guilty of something. Maybe him and the brother were in on it together.'

'But in on *what*?' Gascoyne asked with dissatisfaction.

She shook her head. They got back in the car.

'He was too cocky,' Jenrich muttered, starting the engine. 'I don't like a suspect when he doesn't even bother to deny stuff.'

The mugginess had even penetrated the station, and everyone was struggling not to feel listless. Philip Armstrong, on the other hand, seemed more normal than at any time since he had come in. Regular food, and perhaps the removal of all responsibility, had done him good. He seemed calm when he faced Slider for the fourth time.

Slider, on the other hand, felt sticky, grubby, and weary. He hated to feel he wasn't getting anywhere – the sad dead woman weighed on him, with her lonely life and pointless, heartless death. He hated suspecting her brother, who was so childlike in many ways, who he was coming rather to like. And he hated the imposition of a time limit, which hampered him like a tangle of fishing net. Of course, there always was a time limit on a murder enquiry, but it was naturally imposed by the cooling of trails, the erosion of physical clues, the fading and corruption of memories. An arbitrary time limit set for political reasons was something else.

He tried priming Armstrong with a simple factual question. 'When you came back from Poole, on the train, what station did you come in to? What station in London?'

'Waterloo,' he said simply. He didn't have to think about it, which was good.

'And then you got on the tube, did you?'

'Northern line to Tottenham Court Road and Central line to Shepherd's Bush.' He said it like a chant.

'Do you know what time it was when you got to Shepherd's Bush?'

He frowned. 'I don't . . . look at the time much. It was still morning. Not lunchtime yet.'

'And that was Sunday morning, was it?' Slider slipped it in casually.

'*Monday* morning,' he corrected without hesitation.

Slider had hoped to catch him off guard, but either he was telling the truth, or he had thought about it enough to make the response automatic. Monday morning let him off the hook and put them back at square one. But they still had all that checking to do.

'Did you go straight to the house from the station? Straight home?' He nodded. 'And what happened then?'

Now Armstrong looked uneasy. He shifted in his seat. 'What d'you mean?'

'What did you see when you got to the house?'

'There was a policeman there. Guarding the door.' He fidgeted, shifting his weight on the chair from buttock to buttock, moving his hands about on the table top. 'I knew what that meant.'

'What did it mean?'

'There was a policeman on the door like that when Mummy died. Standing there, so no one could go in or out. And blue-and-white tape. That means death.'

'Is that what you thought?'

'Not thought. I *know*.' He rubbed a hand back and forth

over his lips, and then tucked both hands under his thighs and hunched his shoulders. Defence posture. 'I-know-I-know-I-know.'

'Did you speak to the policeman? Ask him what was happening?'

He stared at the table, his shoulders almost touching his ears now. 'I was afraid,' he said in a tiny voice.

'Afraid of what?'

'I thought if I spoke to him, he'd make me go inside and look. I didn't want to look. Not again.'

'Look at what?'

'You know.' His chin on his chest, he stared at the table. 'I couldn't remember. It all went blank. I couldn't remember where I'd been.'

'But you remember now?'

He looked at Slider as if he didn't know what the question meant. 'I had to run away. Because maybe . . . I did something.'

'Did something? Like what?'

'I don't know. I forget things. I was scared. So I went away.'

'Where did you go?'

He shook his head. His hands came out and he put them on the table, moving his forefingers about as if drawing something two-handed. 'I don't know,' he said. 'Don't remember. Here and there. Up and down. In and out. Got to hide so they can't see me. They must never find me. He said don't look, but I looked. I'm a bad person.'

'Where did you sleep, after you ran away?'

He shook his head. 'Don't remember. In the park. Under the bridge. I don't know.' He looked up, inviting understanding. 'I walked about. I couldn't go home.'

'What made you come here in the end, to the police station?'

He was silent a long time, so that Slider thought he wouldn't answer. Then he said in a small, clear voice, 'I went back to the house and the policeman was still there. And Kate didn't answer her phone. So I knew she was dead. I didn't know where else to go.' He looked up at Slider. 'I don't know what to do without Kate. She looks after me, always. She nearly died once before. I was really scared then.'

'When was that, Philip?'

He screwed up his eyes. 'Long time ago. She got fat, then she got thin. A boy at school said that meant a baby, but Mummy said there was no baby. Only I think there was and it died. Katy made awful noises, I thought she would die, so I hid, and I heard Mummy downstairs doing something. She said we must never talk about it, never-never-never.' It was all said in the childish, chanting voice. Then suddenly he sat up straight and spoke normally. 'Can I go now? I'd like to go home.'

There was no need to keep him while they checked his alibi, especially as that might take a long time. As long as he stayed put, so they could bring him in again if it didn't check out. 'Can you look after yourself at home?' he asked.

'Of course,' he said. 'There's stuff there. And I always do. I'm not helpless, you know.'

'If we let you go home, you must stay there,' Slider said. 'You mustn't go off wandering again until we say you can. No trips. You must be at home every night and sleep there. Do you understand?'

'I suppose so. I don't want to go away, anyway,' he said.

Slider wondered how he would cope in the house knowing his sister was dead. Was he a suicide risk? But he had gone on living there after his mother's death. The alternative might be more traumatizing for him, to be put into protective care. He would have to discuss it with Porson and Labouchere.

'I've had a long talk with him,' said Labouchere, 'and I agree the best thing for him is to be in familiar surroundings. I don't see him as a suicide risk.'

Dale Markby spoke up. 'I don't see that you have any choice but to release him. You aren't any longer seriously regarding him as a suspect, are you?'

'Until his alibi checks out, he's not out of the woods,' Porson said, giving her a Look.

The thought sat unspoken amongst them like a large cat. If a person was unstable, there was no knowing in what direction that instability might take them. You couldn't rule out the possibility that he'd killed his sister, and you couldn't rely on his memory about where he was and when. How could you be sure he knew Monday from Sunday? On the other hand, how could you be sure he wasn't together enough to be cunning, to lie?

'My concern is as much for your client's welfare as yours is,' Slider said. 'Where would be the best place for him, consistent with his being available for further questioning should it be necessary?'

The decision was made, and they released him to his own home. Mr Carpenter would be glad, Slider thought.

SIXTEEN
Whose Soirée Now?

The storm came in the night. Though dog-weary, Slider had slept only a couple of hours and woke to the stifling velvet of darkness. He got up and went to the open window in the hope of a breath of cooler air, and heard the first big drops strike the patio below like balls of fat. Then a little air – the wind that runs before the rain – brushed his face and moved the curtains. He smelled the iron scent of water. Here it comes, he thought. And it came, in a vertical torrent. He stood relishing it, hearing it pounding on the concrete, rushing along the gutters and gurgling in the downpipes, the very sound of coolness, until Joanna appeared behind him, and said, 'Don't just stand there. There are windows open all over the house.'

'I'll check the children,' he said. He thought George would be awake, but he was sprawled on his front, and only stirred his limbs to a new position, like a sleepy starfish in a gentle current, as Slider closed his window. The baby was sleeping, her two fists resting against her flushed cheeks.

Slider went down to the kitchen for a drink of water, and as soon as he turned on the light, there was a distinctive crash from the cat flap and Jumper scooted in, did his amazing turbulence-free braking in the middle of the room, then stalked over to Slider to weave beguilingly round his ankles.

'Not a chance,' Slider said. 'It's not morning yet.' He finished his water, turned out the light, and heard the cat flap smack again as Jumper went back out to enjoy the night from the shelter of the back door overhang.

He went back to the open window, and Joanna joined him there, slipping her arm round his waist. He laid his over her shoulder and they stood awhile. 'I love the smell of the rain,' he said.

'I don't have your nose,' she said. 'But I know what you mean.'

'I miss the way the world smelled in my childhood,' he said. 'Damp grass, trees, nettles in the ditch. That was just the background smell, always there – like the wash a water-colourist puts on the paper before he starts. Then individual smells on top. Hawthorn. Cows. Apple blossom. Freshly-tarred gateposts. Sharp spikes of manure. The smell of the road after rain.' He paused, and she waited in sympathetic silence. 'Is it just getting older, or are there really not so many smells any more?'

'A bit of both. We live in the city now, don't forget.' She breathed deeply. The rain was slacking off, no longer prestissimo, just allegro now. 'For me it's the sea. I miss the smell of the sea.'

He nodded. 'It's the smell of home that gets you, right here.' He tapped his chest. 'And you can never go home.'

The air was cooling rapidly. When they got back into bed, it was just worth pulling up the single sheet which was all they'd been able to bear lately – immediately prior to the storm, not even that.

Joanna rolled towards him. 'Seems a shame to waste the opportunity, now we're both awake.'

It had been too hot to make love recently. 'I'll lock the door,' he said.

Atherton leaned against the kitchen door frame, holding the baby, a tea towel draped strategically over the shoulder of his Breton blue silk shirt. He was watching Joanna and Bill pottering about; the baby was watching him.

'You can probably put her down now,' Joanna said. 'She's stopped grizzling.'

'I'm fine,' he said. 'I like the way she gazes at me. I'm so fascinating.'

'Getting into practice for when she's a grown woman,' Joanna said. 'You'll expect full devotion then.'

'By the time she's a grown woman I'll have retired from the lists,' Atherton said.

'You? Never.'

George appeared beside him. 'Can I have another drink of water?'

'May I have,' Joanna corrected him automatically.

George thought about that. 'Why?'

'It's polite.'

'Why?' George could keep that up for hours.

'"Y" is the fourth of July,' Joanna said. 'Give me your glass. Does Grandad want anything?'

'I'll ask,' George said, and scuttled off importantly.

'He loves doing errands, doesn't he?' Atherton commented.

'He's at that age,' Slider said. 'We're making the most of it, before it wears off.'

'We're planning on sending him down t'pit next week,' Joanna said. 'It was that or up the chimney, but the mine pays more.'

Atherton smiled, shaking his head. 'You're a shining example of a happy family, aren't you? It's quite sickening.'

She opened the oven door, to shake the tray of roast potatoes. 'I'm just glad it's cool enough for a proper roast again. I'm sick of salad. How was your date?'

'Please, not in front of Zoe.'

She straightened up, narrowing her eyes at him. 'Oh dear, does that mean sexual intercourse took place? Don't you realize that sleeping with someone on the first date ruins the chances of a serious relationship?'

'I've always relied on it,' Atherton said modestly.

George came back. 'Grandad says he'd like a beer. Can I take it to him?' Then he looked up at Atherton. 'Will you come and play with us? We're playing Mau-Mau and it's better with three.'

Atherton looked at Joanna. 'She *is* starting to wriggle.'

'You can put her down on the carpet in the sitting room for a crawl,' Joanna said. 'Just watch what she puts in her mouth. Lunch will be ready anyway in fifteen minutes.'

It was a bit longer than fifteen for Slider, because he got a phone call from the factory. He waved to Joanna to carry on serving, because she had a rehearsal to get to. When eventually he joined them at the table, she and Atherton were talking seriously about music, but they broke off and Atherton raised an eyebrow at him.

'So far, Shalcross's alibi is checking out,' he said.

The initial telephone interviews with the host and the four other guests of the fishing weekend had produced ready corroboration that it had taken place and that Shalcross had been there the whole time.

'They had a leisurely breakfast on the Sunday, from about half past eight to half past nine,' Slider went on. 'Then they all went out together in a Land Rover to a local lake. So, given that it's a good four hours' drive to London, the TOD would have had to be a lot before ten a.m. for him to have done it and got back for breakfast.' He used the initials for time of death rather than excite George's curiosity. 'Unless they're all lying.'

'Which is perfectly possible,' said Atherton.

'Well, the local police still have to look for some corroborating evidence. They're going to interview the nearest neighbours and the fishing fraternity, and apparently that lake is privately owned and there's a barrier and a man checking permits at weekends in summer. But it looks as though Shalcross is covered.'

'Which is suspicious enough in itself,' Atherton said. 'Too convenient, don't you think, that he just happens to have a cast-iron alibi for that weekend of all weekends?'

'That's illogical,' Joanna said. 'By that rule, every person who can prove they were elsewhere is guilty.'

'Every person didn't know the victim,' Atherton pointed out. 'I wish we could check his fingerprints against the spare set at the house.'

'We haven't enough evidence against him for that,' Slider said.

'I thought you said they were the brother's?' Joanna complained.

'There were two lots. But of course, it could have been absolutely anyone – a gardener, an odd-job man, even a friend. We don't know for sure that she didn't have any friends – that's just the opinion of her co-workers. It doesn't have to have been the M-person.'

'I know the M word,' George announced, chasing a piece of beef round the plate with a recalcitrant fork. 'It means Murder.'

'Not always,' Slider's father intervened. 'It can stand for Malteser.'

George looked round, hopefully. 'I like Maltesers.'

'What else starts with "M"?' Mr Slider asked.

'Mars Bars. Milky Way.'

'It doesn't have to be chocolate,' Lydia said, keeping the game going with George so the others could go on talking. 'What about things you wear, beginning with "M"?'

'The thing is,' Atherton said, 'I can't believe Shalcross wasn't up to *something*. He suddenly appears, gives false information to get a reading ticket, makes friends with Chadacre, despite her being the most unlikely material for a flirtation, then suddenly absents himself just after the deed.'

'Just before the deed, actually,' Slider reminded him.

'But it all reeks of suspicion.'

'Yes, but suspicion of what?' Slider asked restlessly. 'What could he possibly want with Prue Chadacre? She had money – and if he'd married her and secured his right to it, it would be a different matter. But as it is . . .'

'Maybe that's what he intended, but it all went pear-shaped,' Joanna said. He shook his head, not buying it. 'What about the brother,' she went on. 'They're checking his alibi?'

'The Poole police are. But that's going to be harder. And it might be that it can never be fully established.'

'Which leaves him as a suspect, and no way to prove anything,' Joanna said. 'Isn't there any other evidence?'

'We're looking at local traffic cameras, but it's a slow job, especially when you're not looking for anything or anyone in particular,' said Slider. 'Whoever did it must have arrived on foot or by car, but with no camera covering the actual gate, it's a matter of elimination, which could take weeks.'

'Oh dear,' said Joanna. 'And you'll be miserable until you've sorted it out. Like a hare with a straw bed.'

With alibi checking in others' hands, and Armstrong released, it was a Sunday off for Slider – though he had taken the file home with him to beguile the evening hours without Joanna, after the children were asleep. Not, of course, that his mind would stop mulling it all over anyway. His mother, after pouring the boiling water onto the leaves, had always put the teapot back on the warm stove 'to draw'. He might overtly be doing Sunday things and family things, but in his mind the case would be drawing.

When Joanna arrived back, still a bit 'up' from the performance, he made her a gin and tonic and sat and listened while she got it out of her system, musician talk and gossip and jokes. He knew how much she missed it when she wasn't playing; understood the richness it brought to life, like his own job in many ways, except that hers didn't have the downsides his did. All the same, he would miss it if he had to give it up.

She wound down eventually, and turned instead to Atherton's amours, which had always interested her. She was fond of him, quite apart from knowing how important their partnership was to her husband.

'I worry that he won't ever find someone he's willing to settle for,' she said when the latest dates had been analysed.

'Maybe he doesn't need to,' Slider said. 'There are men who never marry and are perfectly happy that way.'

'But do you think he's perfectly happy?'

He shook his head. 'You can't ask me to do girl-talk. Especially not about my work colleague.' Then he thought of the thing Atherton had said, about him having taken the only perfect woman. It had bothered him in a vague, subconscious way. 'Do you ever think you might have been better off with Atherton than with me?' he asked awkwardly.

Her eyebrows went up. 'Why on earth would I?' she said with gratifying astonishment.

'Listening to you two talking at lunch. He knows about music, he's always loved it. I only know what I've learned since meeting you. And I could never talk about it the way he does.'

She smiled at him. 'I'll let you in on a secret. Musicians hear music in a very different way from non-musicians. We think about it differently. It affects entirely different parts of the brain. Jim's knowledgeable, but he's still only a music-lover, not a player. He doesn't know it from the inside. He can't talk about it in my particular way.'

He was pleased. 'So it's not better talking to him than talking to me?'

'What a loaded question! Not about music, not about anything. And I don't fancy him, either,' she said, going to the heart of it.

The storm had cleared the humidity, and broken the heat-wave. It was still warm, but only in an English sort of way – slightly apologetic. The sky looked washed, with giant, remote clouds passing across it like the large important thoughts of someone daydreaming.

Porson was in early, and summoned Slider for an update. He looked as if he hadn't slept for a fortnight or two. He listened in grim silence as Slider caught him up on the alibi situation.

'So we've got nothing,' he concluded.

'Alibis take time to prove or disprove,' Slider said. 'It's not reasonable to set a time limit on it.'

'It might not be reasonable, but it's politics. The budget's being squeezed all the time.' He raised bloodshot eyes to Slider's, and said, as if he was slightly ashamed of saying it, 'It *could* have been accidental death.'

'Could have been, but wasn't, sir,' Slider said. The aware-ness passed between them that Slider could stick to his guns purely because Porson stood between him and the shit currently heading for the fan. It was Porson's job to do so; and he could if he wished pass on as much shit as he could scrape off; but operational freedom diminished the closer you got to the source. Carpenter was that much closer to the Home Office. He *had* to enforce the budget cuts – sorry, restraints – that Porson deplored and Slider resisted, and he got paid a lot better than both to be a bastard and be hated. Meanwhile, into the cracks in between, fell crime and the department's ability to pursue it, to the detriment of society. Ladies and gents, *that's* entertainment.

Porson sighed. 'I suppose I'll have to take the bull by the teeth and talk to Hammersmith, get you some time. But if these alibis check out and you've got no other leads, that'll be it. What lines have you still got to follow?' His face grew greyer as Slider gave him the list, stretching it till it twanged. At the end, he waved Slider away with his fingers and an exasperated plosion of breath that said *I should have joined the fire brigade*.

Slider trudged away, thinking, *bull by the teeth?* There was always a reason for Porson's odd locutions. He'd tracked it down by the time he reached his office: a portmanteau of bull by the horns, and bit between the teeth. 'So that's all right, then,' he said aloud.

'Nothing from Poole yet, boss,' Swilley said, coming to his door. She was wearing a skirt suit, and he managed with a noble effort not to look at her legs. CID females mostly wore trouser suits for comfort and convenience, but he had noticed that, since Jenrich came, Swilley had worn skirts more often. He hadn't quite decided if those things were connected. 'Tavistock confirms that the cottage was occupied by a group of men that weekend, but that's as far as they've got.'

'Keep chasing them,' Slider said. 'We're against the clock here.'

Swilley gave him a look that said *we're always against the clock*, but went on, 'There is something. I've been looking at the photographs of the garden party sent over from the Archive. Chadacre only appears in one of them.'

She laid one in front of him, and pointed. There was a figure in the background, over to one side, almost out of the frame. Recognizably their victim, though. She had a champagne glass in her hand and seemed to be studying her shoes. No one else was near her or looking at her.

'Sad,' said Slider.

'I think she might be at the back of one of the other shots, too far away to be sure, and still standing on her own. But what I wanted to show you was this.'

Another photo, a scattering of smartly dressed people standing in little groups, talking, glasses in hand; sun shining, green grass underfoot, a suggestion of flowering shrubs in the

background. A delightful scene, you might say: the educated
middle classes at play.

Swilley's finger came down. 'There,' she said. 'Isn't that
our old friend Magnus Armstrong?'

Slider frowned, tilted the picture to angle the light, and said,
'I think you're right.'

'And that blonde next to him, I think that's his wife – Edith,
Lord Somebody's daughter.'

'Now that's interesting,' said Slider.

'Yes, boss, I thought so. Says in the notes that he told you
he hadn't seen his daughter for twenty years.'

'He did indeed. And here they are at the same garden
party. Can it be a coincidence? Could he not have known she
was there?'

Swilley smiled inwardly at his caution. 'There were a lot
of people there,' she allowed him. 'And she was a shrinking
violet. But all the same . . .'

'Yes,' he said. 'All the same. I'll ring Pandora Whatsername.'

'Oh! Yes, the Armstrongs were there. Edith – we know her as
Edith Earnshaw, of course – she uses her maiden name
at work – she's a friend of my husband, David. You know that
he's the Environment Minister?'

'Yes,' said Slider. He had come across David Ormsby-Cecil
when looking up Pandora, but actually, he had heard the
name on the news once or twice before that.

'Well, Edith is a SPAD at the DEIS, and these days green
strategy is a large part of their brief, so she and David bump
into each other quite a lot. And actually, of course, she comes
from one of the old political families, as does David, so they
all know the same people. I think her father was second cousin
to David's mother, or something like that.'

'I see. And Magnus Armstrong?'

'Oh, well, everyone knows him, of course – his charitable
activities take him everywhere and he turns up at all the major
events – dinners, awards, openings. But recently we've been
seeing more of him, along with Edith, of course, because he's
going to stand for Parliament at the next election, and naturally
Edith wants David to give him advice and guidance and so

on. The seat he's lined up for is safe-ish, but when you haven't grown up on the political circuit like David, it can all be a bit bewildering, and there are definitely dos and don'ts, besides all the back-office stuff you have to get to grips with. But he has a first-rate organizational brain, so I'm sure he'll . . .' She broke off. 'Oh!'

'Yes?' Slider prompted.

'I've just remembered. I told you someone had asked about Prue Chadacre at the last garden party but I couldn't remember who. It was him – Magnus Armstrong.'

A warm feeling, like port-and-brandy, uncoiled in Slider's stomach. 'Can you remember exactly what was said?'

'Probably not, after all this time,' she said doubtfully. 'Let me think. We were chatting together, the four of us, the Armstrongs and David and I – about the election, I think – and Magnus touched my arm and pointed and said, "Who is that woman over there?" And I looked and said, "You mean in the beige suit, standing on her own?" And he said yes, and I said, "That's one of our secretaries, Prue Chadacre." And I think I said, "Do you know her?" And he said, "No. I just thought she looked familiar." And that was all. No further reference was made so naturally I forgot all about it.'

'I see,' said Slider. 'Thank you. That's very helpful. You didn't see him approach her or talk to her at any point?'

'No, or I should have said so.'

'And he didn't mention any reason he was asking about her?'

'No, it was the most casual of questions – he didn't seem particularly interested in her, or in my answer. I didn't attach any importance to it. I'd even forgotten it was him who asked about her until just now.' She paused, then added, in a disturbed tone, 'You're not thinking . . .?'

'Not at all. Of course not. We're just at the stage of asking questions at the moment, and most of them won't lead anywhere, but they still have to be asked.'

'You haven't any idea, then, who killed poor Prue?'

'That's what we're working flat out to find out.'

*   *   *

'Standing for Parliament?' Atherton said. 'That's interesting.'

'He's come a long way from the building site,' Lœssop said. 'Millionaire, philanthropist, and now MP?'

'I suppose he's got as much money as he can stand, and now he wants social status,' said Jenrich.

'It accounts for his marrying Edith Earnshaw,' Atherton went on. 'Aristocratic, political thoroughbred, inside track, all the knowledge and contacts.'

'Maybe he fell in love with her,' Swilley objected, on general principle. She regarded it as her life's mission to bring Atherton down a peg. 'She's good-looking enough.'

'And younger than wife number two,' Jenrich put in. 'He wouldn't want to be seen with last year's model, would he?'

Atherton ignored all that. 'What seat's he standing for?' he asked Slider.

'She didn't say.'

'And you didn't ask?'

'Does it matter?'

'I don't know until I know. It might.'

'So he actually asked who she was,' said Swilley. 'And he told you he hadn't seen her for twenty years. That's naughty.'

'Maybe he'd forgotten,' said LaSalle. 'Anyway, he was told she was Prue Chadacre, not Kate Armstrong.'

'And you don't think he'd have noticed the name Chadacre? Quite an unusual surname. And Prudence was her second name. Bit of a coincidence, a person might think.'

Atherton had been searching for the seat. 'Datchet and Dorney Reach,' he announced. 'That's practically Windsor. So an aristocratic wife wouldn't do him any harm at all.'

'Practically derry-gerr.' McLaren nodded.

Atherton stared at him. 'Did you just say *de rigeur*?'

'Why shouldn't I? I bet I been to Windsor more times than you.'

'To the racecourse, maybe.'

'That's what I was talking about,' said McLaren blankly.

Atherton shook his head, like one shaking water out of his ears. Slider rescued him. 'I think another little chat with Mr Armstrong is in order. Without leaping to wild conclusions, it does seem that he has a question to answer.'

SEVENTEEN
Magnus Cum Laude

This time they were kept waiting in the PA's room, looking through the open door at Armstrong's empty office while she rattled away at her keyboard with an air of disassociating herself from the problem of them. He came breezing in through the door at last looking like a cross between an Oxford chancellor, a senior diplomat and a member of the Royal Family, exquisitely suited, coiffed to swooning point, with that added edge of distinction that said not just money, but money with *taste*. He had a phone clapped to his ear, was talking in short bursts; he waved them into his office ahead of him while speaking, broke off his telephone conversation to give his PA a rapid-fire instruction to phone someone about something, followed them in and concluded the remote exchange brusquely as he sat down behind his desk.

'Sorry about that,' he said. 'Busy morning.' He hung out a polished smile. 'What can I do for you officers?' Then he appeared to remember and took a reef in it. 'Oh! Have you come to tell me you've discovered who killed poor Kate?'

'I'm afraid that is still an ongoing investigation,' Slider said.

'But you are making progress?'

'These things take time. And unfortunately, sometimes people are not quite straightforward in their answers when we first speak to them, which means that we have to call on them a second time.'

He crinkled his eyes genially. 'Oh dear! Do I come into that category? What have I not made clear?'

'You told us that you hadn't seen your daughter for twenty years.'

'That's right.'

'Not since the divorce.'

'Correct.'

'But on the twenty-fifth of May you attended a garden party at the house of David Ormsby-Cecil, at which she was also a guest.'

'I remember the garden party. David is a dear friend of my wife. There were a lot of guests. Why should I be expected to notice one among so many?'

'You pointed her out to Mrs Ormsby-Cecil and asked who she was.'

His expression didn't change. 'Yes, I can see your problem. You think I ought to have recognized her. But she was a gawky teenager when I last saw her, and people change a lot over twenty years. I must say if I'd passed her in the street I wouldn't have given her a second glance. I thought the woman looked faintly familiar, that's all. It was only because we were all standing around at leisure and she happened to be in my line of sight for a length of time that the familiarity impinged on me, and I quite idly asked Pandora who she was.'

'Yet you didn't mention this incident when we last spoke to you.'

'It was hardly an incident,' he said in wounded tones. 'When I said I hadn't seen her, the implication was, had I seen her to interact with her in some way. I assure you I knew no more about her life after that party than before it. I attached no importance to it, and it simply didn't come to my mind when you asked about her.'

'Really?' Atherton put in. 'We are specifically asking you about your daughter and you don't remember that you suddenly and unexpectedly saw her quite recently after a long gap?'

He looked slightly annoyed. 'What are you accusing me of? It didn't occur to me, what else can I say? I wasn't even sure it *was* her. I'm still not. The name Pandora gave me was not Kate Armstrong.'

'Indeed, it was Prue Chadacre,' said Atherton. 'But Chadacre, your wife's maiden name, is an unusual surname, and your daughter was christened Kate Prudence.'

'Obviously I noticed the coincidence,' he said impatiently. 'It could still have been just that: a coincidence.'

Slider took it back and spoke neutrally to smooth his ruffled feathers. 'Did you go and speak to her during the party?'

'No,' said Armstrong.

'Or seek her out afterwards? You now had a means to get in contact with her.'

'Why should I do that? Look, if it wasn't a coincidence, if it *was* my daughter, she had taken the trouble to change her name. And she had obviously never told Pandora she was related to me. Combined with the fact that I'd heard nothing from or about her in all that time, it suggested she wanted nothing to do with me – and believe me, when a person makes a lot of money very publicly, as I have, people generally *do* want to have to do with you. And they know exactly where to find you. So it could hardly be accidental. If she *wanted* to stay away from me, why should I break in on her privacy? That would have been cruel. She was entitled to live her own life whatever way she chose. And I assure you I have plenty of problems on my own plate without seeking out more.'

'I see,' Slider said. 'Well, that certainly clears that up.'

'Good. Is there anything else I can help you with?' he asked, half getting up in a gesture of dismissal.

'Since you ask, I'm sure you won't mind detailing your movements on the weekend before last – the thirteenth and fourteenth.'

He frowned. 'Why on earth do you want—?'

'It's just routine, sir, to eliminate people. It often helps to know exactly where everyone was, even if we don't think they were directly involved.'

Armstrong sighed. 'I suppose, if it helps to keep you from turning up here every few days . . . I can't keep having my working days disrupted. Let me see. Oh yes, we were in the Cotswolds, at my place at Adlestrop. I spent Saturday with my boys. I took them shooting on a neighbour's estate.'

'Shooting?' Atherton said quickly. It wasn't the season.

He smiled. 'Just pigeons, but it helps get the eye in. After lunch we lounged about in the garden and chatted. Amyas is going up to Oxford in October, and Freddie's just done his mocks, so they appreciate some downtime. We had an early supper, then I drove them to Oxford to get the train back to

London. They were going to a party. On Sunday I played golf at the Royal Kingham, with Chris Zammit, Sir Steven Rogers and Lord Wokingham.'

Atherton dutifully took down the names of an assistant commissioner of the Metropolitan Police, the permanent secretary to the Foreign Office, and the chairman of a multi-national Footsie-100 company.

'I'm sorry,' Armstrong said with a mock rueful face, 'that sounds like name-dropping, but . . .' He made a little spreading gesture with his hands: *what can I say?* 'We teed off at ten, and had lunch afterwards at the clubhouse. In the afternoon I did some paperwork at home, and in the evening we had people in for a small dinner party: neighbours, friends of Edith's – my wife. She knows everyone. We drove back to London on Monday morning.' He looked at them with a bright, enquiring eye. 'Is that all in order? Anything else you want to know?'

'That will be all for now, sir. Thank you very much,' said Slider.

'I don't like it,' said Atherton when they were outside.

'You just don't like him. Anyone with better suits than you.'

'True.'

'His explanation about Prue is reasonable. Kind even,' said Slider. 'And his alibi is perfect.'

'Pluperfect. Can't we decide that's suspicious in itself?'

'Don't start that again.'

'Not fair. I want to hate him.'

'Someone's got to keep an open mind. Why would he want to kill his own daughter? That would be horrible,' Slider said, getting into the car.

Atherton slid in beside him. 'Well, it can't be for her money,' he allowed. 'But where does that leave us? Actually, why would *anyone* want to kill her? Unless it was a random thing, someone came to the door, forced her back when she opened it, chased her into the kitchen and whacked her.'

'And then staged the trip-and-fall scenario?'

'That does tend to suggest it was a bit less than random.'

'There must have been *something* about her. Something in her life,' Slider said broodingly. 'I wonder – could it be something about the child she had?'

'Philip said it died.'

'But he might not really know. Details would likely have been kept from him. If she had it adopted, say, and it was long enough ago, it could be an adult by now. That opens up a whole new field of complications, emotions and possible resentments.'

'And some new suspects. Worth looking into, perhaps,' Atherton said cautiously.

'We've got nothing else,' Slider said.

'We still haven't *not* got Shalcross,' Atherton said firmly.

'Eh?'

'You know what I mean. I pin my hopes on him. He's *got* to have something to do with it all. And he's a ruthless killer if ever I saw one. If we can bust his alibi . . .'

'I shall cheer you all the way,' Slider finished the sentence.

Slider met Porson in the corridor and told him of the Armstrong interview. 'It's going to be tricky checking those alibis,' he concluded.

Porson raised an eyebrow. 'Must you? You don't have any evidence against him, do you?'

'No, sir. But you know the old saying: there's many a man walking the Embankment through not clearing trumps,' Slider said.

Maybe he did and maybe he didn't, but Porson wasn't letting on. 'Hmph,' he said neutrally. 'Better leave Zammit to me. It'll need tact to ask an assistant commissioner what he was doing of a Sunday.'

'Surely he'll want to help an investigation?' Slider suggested.

'Suppose he's got a mistress and Armstrong was *his* alibi?'

'I'll leave you to it,' Slider said hastily, and escaped.

The five fishing-party colleagues had all verbally confirmed that Shalcross had been with them that whole weekend. Now the team were checking up on the five, while the Tavistock police did the local enquiries.

It was all coming in depressingly solid. The five men seemed to be respectable, solvent, and holders of decent jobs. Worse, the host of the party and actual owner of the cottage in Tavy St James, a John Hannaford, had been born in the village and was well-known and well-liked locally, and though he had lived 'away' for a long time, had bought the cottage eight years ago and since then had frequently had parties of friends down, who were free-spending and no trouble, so they had favour with the locals.

Late on Monday Slider had a call from an Inspector Challacombe, who had a pleasing West Country burr to his voice, and told him that he had made enquiries of the chap on the gate to Spenser Lake – name of Bill Dodridge. Dodridge agreed that Mr Hannaford had come through in his old Land Rover with five friends on Sunday morning. The men looked familiar, though he didn't know the names of any of them. He knew Mr Hannaford by name because he was the permit holder.

'I showed him the photo you sent through,' said Challacombe, 'and he was quite sure that was the man sitting next to Mr Hannaford, the other four being in the back seat. He had Mr Hannaford's old black lab sitting on his lap and was stroking its ears. Dodridge said he made a joke about it slobbering, the old dog – something about being a good job he had waterproof trousers on. So it looks like your man was there.'

'Did he say what time they went through?' Slider asked.

'Better'n that, he's got it logged,' said Challacombe. 'The permit number, the name – Mr Hannaford and five guests – and the time, nine forty-seven a.m. And they were logged out at three fifty-nine p.m., Mr Hannaford and five guests. They do that in case anyone gets lost. There's been times when these parties have a bit too much to drink and don't notice that someone's wandered off. Had a young chap drown in that lake four years ago. Though that was wintertime. It was the cold that did for him, on top of the drink. Anyroad, you can take it your chap was there all right. I've known Bill Dodridge twenty years or more, and he's honest as the day.'

All the same, Slider thought, the most honest man could find himself, through no fault of his own, in need of a bit of money and, being offered a roll of folding, could yield to temptation.

'If there's any other corroboration, you'll let me know?' he said.

'Certainly,' said Challacombe. 'There's a girl goes in and cooks and cleans for Mr Hannaford, she may have seen 'em on the Sunday. I'll get a statement from her when we get hold of her. But I'd say you can take it as gold your man was there Sunday morning.'

'Damn,' said Slider when he rang off.

Atherton was disappointed, but resigned. 'So that leaves us with Philip, who was always the most likely suspect. With a distinctly wonky alibi.'

'No news on that yet,' Slider said. 'But why . . .?'

'That's the beauty of a sibling – you hardly need a motive,' Atherton said. 'Families generate enough passions to go round. Added to which he's somewhat loosely wired up. Anything could have gone *ping* at a critical moment. And he's got all the access he needs.'

'But making it look like an accident,' Slider began.

'That's what particularly inclines me,' Atherton said. 'He's bright enough to think of it, and unworldly enough to think we'd fall for it.'

'Hm. You could be right, I suppose. I just hope you aren't.'

It was a long time before the door was opened. Slider thought perhaps it wouldn't be. But eventually there was a shuffling sound and a shadow over the stained-glass panel, and the door slowly opened to halfway, one eye of the thin face looked through the gap. Slider allowed himself to be inspected, while giving a mild, reassuring smile – not too little, so as to look threatening, and not too much so as to look manically well-intentioned and therefore threatening.

'Oh, it's you,' Philip said at last, letting the door open a bit more. 'Did you want something?'

'Just to talk to you. Is that all right?'

He seemed to think about it. 'Would you like a cup of tea?' he asked at last, politely.

'That would be nice,' said Slider.

Philip turned and walked away, left towards the kitchen. Slider followed, closing the door quietly behind him. There was a smell of toast on the air. The evening sun, slanting in, illuminated the dust disturbed by their passage. In the kitchen, a saucepan was on the stove, a plate on the work surface beside it, with two pieces of toast propped against each other like a little tent. Now Slider's expert nose caught the aroma of baked beans.

'I'm sorry, I don't mean to disturb your supper,' he said.

Philip had gone to switch on the kettle, which had evidently already boiled, because it began to hiss at once.

'It's all right,' he said. 'I was going to make tea for myself anyway.' He opened a cupboard to reach down a mug.

'Shall I do that while you see to your beans?' Slider offered.

The eyebrows drew down. 'I can do it,' he said sharply. 'I manage all right. I can look after myself. I do, all the time, except when I'm here and Kate comes.'

Slider saw that the heat was not on under the beans so there was no imminent incendiary problem. He stood back and leaned against the wall beside the door and let him get on with it. Carefully, but with practised movements, he prepared two mugs of tea. He offered one to Slider, then took the other and sat down at the table. The beans were forgotten, or politely postponed, Slider didn't know which. With a may I? gesture, he sat down opposite him. Philip was staring at nothing, elbows on the table, holding his mug halfway to his mouth. His eyes looked shadowed, and his hair was wild, but he had evidently shaved that morning, and the T-shirt he was wearing above cotton trousers looked clean. So he was not entirely falling to pieces, which was a relief to Slider. In the recesses of his subconscious, it was as much to make sure Philip was all right as to ask a question that he had called in on the way home.

'How are you feeling?' he asked.

'I'm all right,' Philip answered, without looking at him. He seemed relaxed at Slider's presence, but uninterested in him. Perhaps he had become accustomed to ignoring much of what went on around him – not a bad skill in a crowded world. Slider waited, sipping his tea, and eventually Philip said, 'I miss Kate. I wish she'd come back.'

'You know that she can't, don't you?' Slider said gently.

'I know that, I know she's dead,' he said angrily. 'I'm not stupid!'

It sounded as if he had often had to refute that. 'I know you're not,' Slider said.

'Just sometimes I don't remember things. Sometimes there are big . . .' He paused so long that Slider had begun mentally filling in the sentence. Clouds in the sky? Monsters in the wardrobe? Giant squid in the bath?

'. . . gaps,' Philip concluded.

'I understand,' Slider said.

Philip looked at him sharply. 'You want to ask me more questions, don't you?'

'Do you mind?'

Philip shrugged. 'S'pose not.'

'I was thinking, you see, about when Kate had the baby.'

He looked up, as though relieved it was not about recent events. His shoulders went down noticeably. 'It was a long time ago.'

'Do you know how long?'

'I don't . . . I can't think time very well. I don't . . .'

There seemed no end to that sentence.

'Never mind. It was while your mother was alive, so you were quite young.'

'Yes,' he said, seeming relieved that the question had been resolved by someone else.

'Did Kate go to hospital to have the baby?'

He shook his head. 'She never went to hospital. She was never ill.'

'But ladies generally go to hospital to have babies.'

'I wasn't supposed to know about the baby. When I asked Mummy she was upset that I'd guessed. At first she said there wasn't a baby. Then she said it died, and I must never tell anyone about it. Never never mention it. But Kate's dead and

Mummy's dead and it doesn't matter now, does it? Nothing matters any more.'

'So she had the baby at home, did she?'

'I never saw it. I wasn't supposed to know. Only afterwards I wasn't allowed to see Kate for ages, and I asked Mummy and she said it had died and Kate was sad and never to talk about it.'

'You told me you thought the baby didn't die. Why did you think that?' He looked blank. 'I was wondering, you see,' Slider said unemphatically, 'if it didn't die, maybe it was adopted.' Still blank. 'Given to some other people to bring up.' Philip had been staring at the table, now he looked at Slider quizzically, as if the question didn't make sense. Slider tried again. 'Did someone come to the house and take the baby away? Or did your mother take it out of the house? Can you remember?'

'Mummy never went out.'

'Perhaps while you were at school?'

'I didn't go to school.' He shut his eyes, screwing them tight in the effort to remember. 'It was summer holidays. I stayed outside, in the garden. I made a camp in the corner. Mummy didn't go out. She had to look after Kate.'

'So what do you think happened to the baby?'

'I don't know,' he said, not distressed but indifferent.

It was hopeless. He had wondered if there was a memory of the baby being adopted; but there was no relying on a memory so vague and so fractured. He finished his tea and stood up. 'I won't disturb you any more,' he said. 'You'll want your supper.'

Philip was staring out of the window now. 'I think she hid it,' he said dreamily. 'Grandma had a cat once. It had a kitten and the kitten died and it hid it under a bush in the garden. Jukes found it in the end.'

'Jukes?'

'He was the gardener then. The cat kept going back to it and licking it. I suppose it thought it might wake up. Jukes said it was coming to pieces with all the licking.'

That was enough of that, Slider thought. 'Thank you for

the tea, Philip,' he said. 'I'll see myself out. You should get on with your supper.'

But Philip followed him out of the kitchen and down the passage to the hall. The stately emptiness of it reminded him of something else he had wanted to know. Perhaps it was a good question to leave Philip with, to take his mind away from Kate. Or the kitten.

'I believe there used to be a lift in the house – is that right?' Philip frowned slightly, but did not confirm or deny. 'I was wondering where it was – there isn't any sign of it now. The obvious place would be here in the hall, next to the staircase. Or was it in the kitchen area?'

'It doesn't work any more,' Philip said. 'Grandma used to go up in it, when her legs got bad. But after she died, Daddy said it wasn't safe. He had the machine taken out.'

'So where was it?' Slider asked.

Philip put his hand against the stretch of blank wall between the foot of the stairs and the start of the passage to the kitchen. 'Mummy had the door nailed shut. Then she had it wallpapered so you couldn't tell.'

'Oh, I see. Well, thank you for talking to me. I'll go now.'

He was half through the front door when Philip said, 'I won't run away. But I'd like to go fishing. When can I go fishing?'

'In a little while – soon. I'll let you know. You must stay put for now.'

'I know,' he said resignedly, and shut the door quite sharply on Slider's heels.

EIGHTEEN
Alibi of Birdland

On Tuesday, the weather had definitely changed. The sky was still blue, but of a watery, inconstant shade, and the clouds had an April look about them. They scudded across on a sharp breeze with their shoulders up, as if saying, *I might rain, or I might not. I haven't decided.* The long heatwave had veered off towards the continent at last, where they were used to such things, and Londoners could go back, with secret relief, to clothes that covered their legs and arms.

Slider had a telephone call from DCI Phil Warzynski of the Poole police. He had known Phil when he worked at Notting Hill and they had been drawn together by a common loathing of Warzynski's superior.

'I've found the bloke that took your suspect out on his boat on Sunday the fourteenth,' Warzynski said, when they had exchanged commonplaces. 'I've taken down a statement from him, which I'll send over to you, but I've asked him to give you a bell and tell you his story first-hand. Then you can ask any questions that occur to you.'

'That's kind of you, Phil.'

'That's all right. I know what it's like dealing with this sort of thing through a third party.'

'Is he pukka?'

'Straight as the Mile End Road. He's OK. He's going to ring in half an hour.'

And a Mr Oliver Garston from Upton did duly ring. It was an educated voice, but with a slight Dorset broadening of the vowels, and sounded as if it belonged to a man comfortably in his forties. Slider instinctively imagined cord trousers and a check shirt.

'I've made a full statement to the police,' he said, 'but

there's a Chief Inspector Warzynski who suggested that you might like to hear it first-hand.'

'It's kind of you to take the trouble,' Slider said.

'No trouble – it's just a phone call,' Garston protested. 'It's about the young man I took out on my boat on Sunday the fourteenth.'

'Yes – carry on.'

'Well, I have a twenty-four-foot cutter that I keep in Poole Harbour – the *Frieda Brown*. She's an ex-Cornish crabber, clinker built?' His voice had taken an upward tilt.

'I'm afraid I don't know much about boats,' Slider answered it.

'OK. Well, she's just for pleasure, running about, a bit of fishing, that sort of thing. I like to take her out at weekends. I work in Bournemouth during the week. I'm a chartered accountant.'

Respectable, Slider thought. 'So on Sunday July the four-teenth?' he prompted.

'Right. I got down to the quay about half past five in the morning and started to get her ready. The tide was going out, slack water'd be about a quarter to seven. It was fine, a bit chilly, with a moderate breeze. I was going to take her out around Studland, maybe as far as Swanage. Anyway, I was busy around the deck when a man came up, just wandering along the quay. He looked quite a young man, quite boyish, until he got close, then I could see he must have been in his thirties. He was a bit dishevelled and had a rucksack on his back. He looked as if he'd been camping out. But he also had a fishing-rod bag with him, and he looked nice enough, so when he started asking me about *Frieda*, I got chatting with him. Turned out he was at a loose end, and I never mind a bit of company, so I asked if he wanted to come out with me.'

'Did he tell you his name?'

'We just did Christian names. His was Philip.'

'That's right. Go on.'

'Well, he seemed quite handy about the boat, helped me get ready, and we pushed off around ten past six. Turned out he was dead keen on birds, and you know Poole Harbour is the premium place in the country for bird watching. So I took him round to all the best places for birds, and we never did get out of the harbour, not that it mattered. Chucked the anchor out once or twice and did a bit of fishing but didn't catch anything – the wind wasn't setting right for fish. Didn't matter. He seemed as happy as a lark just being out and looking at the birds. Nice to be with someone who enjoyed the simple things so much. But I did notice after a bit that there was something . . . well, not quite right about him. Nothing major,' he added hastily, 'but sometimes he sort of went off, you know – like blanked out. And sometimes the things he said were a bit skew-whiff. But he seemed a nice, harmless bloke, and he was obviously having a great time. Knew a lot about birds, got very excited when we saw an avocet – they're quite rare. Anyway, we had a nice little potter about, till I started wanting my lunch and headed back, and we finally tied up not long after two. He thanked me nicely and shook my hand, and off he went, and that was that.'

'Did he say where he was going?'

'Said he was going to London to see his sister, but that was all. We didn't really talk much, except about the birds and the fishing. Of course, I thought no more about it until the next Sunday when I'd just come in from a tool about in *Frieda*, and was having a pint at the Jolly Sailor, and the landlord happened to mention that the police had been asking questions about a man, and it sounded like my bloke. So I thought about it, and this morning I popped into the police station and here we are.'

'Why did you wait so long?' Slider asked.

'Oh, well, you know – things to do. I didn't think there'd be anyone there on a Sunday, and Monday's always a heavy day for me at work. But I told my senior last night that I'd be late in this morning, and went and did my duty. I hope I haven't caused any trouble? I mean, I didn't hear about it until Sunday, a whole week afterwards, so I didn't think another day would make that much difference. What's he done, anyway?'

'Nothing, it seems,' said Slider. 'If it's the same man.'

'Oh it is – they showed me his photo, and it was him all right. Well, I'm glad he's OK. He seemed like such a nice, harmless chap. I wouldn't want to have got him into trouble.'

'You did the right thing, Mr Garston. And thank you for giving me your account first-hand.'

'No trouble. Oh – one other thing. At one point when we were bird watching, he got out a sketch pad and pencil from his rucksack and did a drawing of some redshanks wading in the shallows. I'm no artist, but it looked jolly good to me. He said he liked drawing – drawing and fishing. And birds, it seemed. Really nice chap.'

'Yes, so it seems,' said Slider.

Porson had his back to the door, standing at his window, hands in his pockets, jingling something, probably keys. In these credit card days men didn't often have coins in their pockets to jingle.

'You sent for me, sir?'

Porson turned. 'Yes. I've just had a very uncomfortable conversation with Mr Zammit.'

'I'm sorry, sir,' Slider murmured.

Porson scowled. 'What are *you* apologizing for? You've got your job to do irregardless, and so've I.'

'I hope Mr Zammit knows that,' Slider ventured.

Porson didn't answer. Those not precisely on the tines of life generally had different imperatives and he knew it as well as Slider. 'He wasn't best pleased at being asked,' he admitted at length. 'But it's no skin off my teeth. My back's broad. And I got your answer, that's the important thing. Mr Zammit did play golf with Armstrong and the other two named. Just not on the fourteenth of July. It was on the twenty-sixth of May.'

Slider felt his lips tighten with anger. 'He thought we wouldn't check. The arrogant—'

'Now, hold your horses. It could be a simple mis-remembering. Busy man, full diary. I dare say he hobnobs with nobs every day.' Porson paused a flicker, as if unsure that sentence had come out right. 'No need to go jumping off half-cocked.'

'If he doubted his memory he could have checked with his PA. He gave me the information straight out, without hesitation.'

'Doesn't mean he's our man. Maybe he was doing something else he doesn't want known about.'

'Such as?'

'That's irrevelant. I'm just saying, you've got no reason to suspect him, have you? No evidence against him?'

'None,' Slider admitted. And, in fairness, added, 'He might just think it's none of our damn business where he was on Sunday.'

'There you go!' Porson said encouragingly. 'Your super-rich business mongols, they live in a different world.'

'But I'd still like to know where he was,' Slider said. 'Just to eliminate him,' he added, seeing Porson's scowl making a comeback.

'Check with the golf club,' Porson said after thought. 'He might have been out with a different batch of nobs and just got confused.'

'And if he wasn't playing golf?'

Porson sighed. 'Mr Zammit's had a word with Mr Carpenter, and he's had a word with me. You can't go bothering Armstrong again about this, until and unless you've got some evidence to warrant it. You know and I know people lie to the police all the time, doesn't make 'em villains. What else have you got?'

'The alibis of Shalcross and Philip Armstrong both look good for Sunday. They were both out in boats, by coincidence, and too far from London to have got back within the time scale. Unless the murder took place a lot earlier or a lot later than Doc Cameron thinks.'

'How much later?'

'Eight hours minimum. More like ten or twelve realistically.'

'Hmph. Well, it's not impossible—'

'Just a bit improbable.'

'We're going to have to let this one go, Bill,' Porson said. Slider flinched. His boss never used his Christian name. It was a bit like the doctor shaping up to give you Bad News. 'You've got no evidence against anyone. Tidy up and file it. If anything comes in at a later date, you can always go back to it.'

Can, Slider thought going back to his room, but how often

did they? Failure would sit on his shoulder like something from Night's Plutonian Shore, to remind him in quiet moments of Kate Armstrong/Prue Chadacre. What rhymed with Kate? Wait, fate, and later date. He didn't want any of those repeated in his ear. Chadacre didn't bear thinking about.

Jenrich appeared at his open door and tapped the frame politely. 'Boss, you said I could look into Armstrong's second wife's death.'

'I did,' Slider said.

'Well, they were living in Surrey, big house just outside Ripley. Looks as though he sold it when he married wife number three, started again in Gloucestershire. Anyway, Amelia Lovell, number two, died in a tragic accident, as we know. Turns out she drove her car into a flooded gravel pit and drowned. It's called Silent Water, quite near their house. A lot of divers use it, and one of them found the car next day, on the bottom, with her still in it. Apparently she'd been depressed and taking anti-depressants, and it was reckoned she'd got drowsy behind the wheel and drove off the road. There was a bit of broken fence there, between the road and the pit. Narrow road and quite a sharp bend. I've talked to an Inspector Chilworth who was on the case at the time. Apparently someone suggested it might be suicide, given she was depressed, but the chief constable of Surrey intervened to protect the feelings of the grieving widower and his two teenage sons, and made sure it went down as accidental death, and there was no further investigation. Inspector Chilworth said Armstrong and the chief constable were golf buddies, along with some other high-ups, and nobody wanted to make a fuss.'

'Did Chilworth think there was anything suspicious in it?'

'No, boss,' Jenrich said reluctantly. 'But wife number one drowns in her bath after taking tranquillizers, and wife number two drowns in a quarry after taking tranquillizers. Are we seeing a pattern here?' Slider shook his head. 'Not only that,' Jenrich urged, 'but in each case he went on to marry a richer wife. Isn't that suspicious?'

'It'd be more suspicious if he married a poorer wife,' Slider said. 'But in fairness, I see what you mean. However, a man can be unlucky.'

Jenrich could not help rolling her eyes at this hideous objectivity.

Gascoyne appeared behind her. 'Guv, I've been on to the Royal Kingham, the golf club. They've looked at the records. Armstrong didn't play that day, and nor did any of the other three.'

'Well, that's no more than we expected,' said Slider. 'I'd like to know where he *was*.'

'Not only that,' Gascoyne went on, 'but I've done a bit of a search on his wife, and it turns out that she was in Glasgow with her minister that weekend, some sort of trade talks. She wasn't at home having a dinner party with her husband. So his whole alibi for Sunday was a crock.'

Slider sighed. 'He really thought we were too incompetent or too cowed to check it. It's depressing, really. But I have to point out again that we haven't a single shred of evidence against him.'

'Apart from the lying.'

'If all liars were murderers there wouldn't be a person still standing. Gascoyne, find out what cars he had access to. I'm pretty sure the local constabulary will know. Give them to McLaren. Let's see if we can get a ping on them anywhere useful on the Sunday. If he did go to London, he'll have driven.'

'Right, guv.' Gascoyne disappeared.

'And Jenrich, see what else you can find out about Armstrong, beyond the Wiki page. Delve deep – but make it quick. We've got to shelve this tonight if we don't get some evidence. But try to remember that because you don't like him, it doesn't make him a monster. And a man would have to be a monster to kill his own daughter like that.'

'Yes, boss,' Jenrich said, with an eye that said monster was the default setting of a man. From there, the only way was up.

'Pity we can't get in touch with the sons,' Atherton mused. 'I wonder . . .'

'Don't wonder,' Slider said. 'How would that fit in with the injunction not to bother Mr Armstrong any more? Besides, by his account, the boys left on Saturday night.'

'Yes, but I was thinking, he might not have been in Adlestrop at all that weekend. And if he was elsewhere, there's no point in trying to trace his car between Gloucestershire and Shepherd's Bush, is there?'

'Wherever he started from, we know where he ended up, if he's our man. But I'd be happier if there was a breath of a motive to hold on to.'

'You can't hold on to a breath.'

'I shan't be holding my breath until you come up with something, that's for sure.'

'*Touché.*'

'Go and do something useful. Yes, Norma?'

Swilley had appeared silently at Atherton's shoulder. 'I've got something interesting, boss. D'you want to come and look?'

Up on Swilley's screen was something from a newspaper archive – from the typeface, Slider guessed it was the *Telegraph*. It was dated May the previous year and showed Magnus Armstrong stepping out of what was unmistakably The Dorchester, the liveried doorman just on the edge of the photo touching his topper. Armstrong was in evening dress, looking pleased and very handsome, and on his arm was the slender figure of wife Edith, in a long slither of grey sequins like some kind of super-fish, diamonds at her neck and ears. The caption was 'Philanthropist of the Year – Magnus Armstrong takes Benevolent Society award'. Presumably he was just quitting the award dinner.

'Pretty good going,' Atherton said, reading over Slider's shoulder. 'People like Bill Gates and George Soros win that. And it's not always just chucking around the moolah that gets you shortlisted: they usually take other things into account as well, like whether you actually *do* anything, apart from signing the cheque.'

'I wonder how much money they waste on the dinner at the Dorch,' LaSalle said conversationally. 'Got to be tens of thousands. Wouldn't you think if it's philanthropy they're interested in, they'd save it and donate it to the good cause as well?'

'You can't ask a multi-millionaire to take his trophy over a sandwich at Joe's Caff,' Lœssop said. 'You've got to give them a bit of a show.'

'And the Benevolent Society gets publicity from the awards dinner,' said Gascoyne. 'The press cover it more than if there was no dinner.'

'Where *is* the trophy, anyway?' McLaren said, dropping crumbs from his sausage roll on the keyboard as he leaned in to peer. 'Why's he not carrying it?'

'Rich blokes like him don't carry things,' LaSalle said. 'They got people to do that for them.'

'You're all imbeciles!' Swilley said impatiently. 'Who cares about the damn trophy! Don't you notice anything else? Who else is in the photo? Behind Armstrong.'

'Well, I'll be a monkey's uncle,' said Atherton in pleased tones. Someone just behind Armstrong, a tall dark man also in evening dress, was revealed because Armstrong had already gone down two of the three shallow steps towards street level. He was looking away to the right of the picture as if checking something. 'Jason Shalcross. What a coincidence. Who'd have thought he was also a philanthropist?'

'I think, in the circumstances, we can rule out coincidence,' Slider said.

'That's the least cautious thing I've heard you say all year, guv,' said Atherton. 'I always said he was involved in some way.'

'Nobody likes a man who says I told you so,' Swilley reminded him.

'What d'you reckon?' McLaren said, licking his greasy fingers. 'Bodyguard? He's got that look about him. Looking out for snipers.'

'Snipers! Do me a lemon. He's probably just checking if the car's come,' said LaSalle.

'Yeah, but he was in Afghanistan,' said McLaren. 'He's prepared for the worst.'

'Well, let's see he gets it,' said Slider. 'Print me that out, and bring him in.'

NINETEEN
Meagre and Hollow, but Crisp

I n the time it took to get Shalcross to Shepherd's Bush, Swilley and Gascoyne had found three more photos of Armstrong with Shalcross in the background.

'And even better than that, boss,' Swilley said, bringing him the prints, 'I've got the phone records at last. And the victim got a phone call on the Saturday morning – the last one she got, in fact – from the number Jason Shalcross gave when he took out his reader's ticket. His burner phone.'

Atherton looked triumphant. 'Making the appointment to see her on Sunday morning! Now we've got him! I always knew it was him.'

'Steady down,' Slider said. 'It's suggestive, I grant you, but there are plenty of other reasons he could have rung her. And his alibi is as solid as the Rock of Gibraltar.'

'Alibis are made for breaking,' said Atherton. 'And the ten a.m. time of death isn't solid. He could have gone to London in the early hours, killed her, and got back to Devon for the fishing party.'

'He'd have to have killed her at about midnight to do that,' Slider said. 'And what reason could he give her for meeting him at the house in the middle of the night?'

'Maybe she stayed the night there—'

'And let him in, fully dressed in day clothes?'

'That's trickier. Give me a minute,' Atherton said.

Slider shook his head. 'I don't know what we can do with this phone call, but it's further evidence that Shalcross is mixed up in it somehow. We'll have to try to get him to tell us how.'

Against the background of the standard police station interview room, Shalcross looked more like a soldier than ever, and more out of place: too big, too strong, too self-assured. Where were the squirmy fidgetings, the swivelling eyes, the smell of sweat and trainers? Shalcross, clean-shaved, hair expensively cropped, in well-cut sports jacket, knife-crease trousers and highly polished shoes, emitted only the faintest whiff of cologne, and he sat very upright, still, alert. He didn't even bother with any of the usual questions or protests – why am I here, why are you bothering me again, I haven't done anything, I want a solicitor. He just waited.

Slider opened the batting. 'I wanted to talk to you about your relationship with Magnus Armstrong.'

'Who?'

'Oh, don't go down that route,' Slider said kindly. He laid out the prints. 'Astonishing how often you turned up at the same events, isn't it?'

'Coincidence,' Shalcross said grimly.

'Hmm. What a wide range of interests you share. Philanthropist of the Year awards. Opening of a new Barnardo's home. Climate change conference. The BAFTA dinner.' Shalcross was stony. 'Oh, come on! Look at yourself, watching his back, looking around for threats. You couldn't be more obvious if you had dark glasses and a plastic caterpillar behind your ear. Armstrong was the mysterious client you cast off just before his daughter was murdered.'

Shalcross didn't move, but lines seemed to come into his face. His grimness became a little sick.

Slider continued. 'If I take a look at your bank accounts – and believe me, I can get a warrant for that – I'm going to find some pretty big regular payments from him to you, aren't I? I hope he paid you enough to make it worth it.'

Now he spoke. 'I had nothing to do with her death. I would never—' He stopped abruptly.

'You befriended her, out of the blue, just after he'd seen her again for the first time in twenty years. And you dropped him as a client just before she was murdered. That looks pretty suspicious.'

'*Before*. Just *before*,' Shalcross said. 'I had no idea—'

'*No* idea?'

Shalcross didn't answer, but he looked a fraction less

composed. Slider waited until the silence bristled, then said, 'Somehow, I don't think you are an entirely bad man. Why don't you tell me all about it?'

Shalcross considered for a few moments, his eyes on the far wall. Then he said, 'I was going to tell you anyway. I was planning to come in and tell you. It's been weighing on me. But I want a solicitor,' he added sharply. 'I don't want anything I say being twisted.'

The interview resumed with the notable figure of solicitor Oscar Faversham – very smart, very posh, and very fat – beside Shalcross. Faversham was a cut-glass, top-price lawyer, and Slider reckoned Shalcross must have a healthy bank balance to afford him. Faversham certainly had one. He was wealthy enough to wear bespoke suiting that turned his avoirdupois into a display case for it; but beside tall, lean Shalcross he seemed almost circular. Together they looked like the number ten in agreeable menswear.

'To make it clear to all concerned,' Faversham pronounced in his exquisite, well-nourished voice, 'my client is not under arrest. He is voluntarily answering questions in order to help you with your investigation.'

'It is so understood. We are very grateful to him,' said Slider graciously. Two could play at that game. 'So, Mr Shalcross, how did you come to be employed by Magnus Armstrong?'

'I'm self-employed. He was my client,' Shalcross corrected him.

'Noted,' said Slider. 'How did that relationship come about?'

'Through Forward Security. They use a lot of ex-military.'

'You were employed by them?'

'They're an agency – like an employment agency. They find the jobs and take a fee. We were all self-employed. The owner of Forward, Guy Pembroke, is ex-military – EOD, like me – so he understands us and our needs. He's also very well-connected: the sort of people who want personal security at the highest level know him and trust him.'

'I can see that would be important.'

Shalcross gave him the merest nod of acknowledgement. 'He introduced me to Magnus Armstrong.'

'Armstrong wanted a bodyguard?'

Shalcross almost winced. 'Tailored Comprehensive Personal Security,' he corrected. 'We're not bald muscle-men in badly-fitting suits.'

'Quite,' said Slider. 'So you protect them from being mugged. Or burgled. Or kidnapped?'

'We offer close protection in all situations. We are also expert in covert surveillance devices and explosive ordnance – we check their premises and transports for bugs and bombs,' he translated with faint irritation before Slider could ask. 'We carry out intelligence-led forward strategy overviews – decide how safe it is for them to go anywhere.'

'And why would Armstrong want these services? Was he under threat?'

Shalcross looked merely surprised by the question. 'He's a high-profile, high-net-worth VIP – he's famous and rich,' he added the Janet-and-John bit. 'Those people are always a target.'

'And I suppose it makes them feel good to have a body-guard always hovering around them.'

Shalcross shrugged. 'Make fun if you like. Mine is a highly-skilled profession. I'm here voluntarily, remember.'

'Very well,' said Slider. 'You were performing all these personal security functions for the very prominent Magnus Armstrong. How did Prue Chadacre come into it?'

This was a question with which he was not happy. Nothing in the world could make him fidget, but he lowered his eyes for a moment, and his lips tightened. 'I never liked it,' he said at last. 'I protested against it when he asked me. But . . . there didn't seem any actual harm in it.'

'It doesn't seem to come under the heading of personal protection.'

He hesitated. 'I was paid to take care of him in the round. That sometimes requires you to be flexible. And there could have been security implications. It was basically an intelligence operation, and gathering intelligence was part of my brief.'

He paused, and added in a lower voice, 'I didn't think it wrong to do a favour for a very generous client.'

The money, Slider concluded, had been very good. 'What did he ask you to do, exactly? All the details please.'

'He told me that he'd been estranged from his children by his first wife ever since the divorce. He had no idea even where they were living. But by chance he had found out where his daughter was working. Only she'd changed her name. He was afraid that meant she was still hostile towards him.'

'Sounds feasible.'

'So he asked me to . . . to arrange to bump into her. Get to know her. Befriend her. He . . .' Was there a slight blush over those chiselled cheekbones? 'He said it should be easy for me, I was good-looking, any woman would welcome my attentions.'

Slider kept his countenance. 'And what was the purpose of this exercise?'

'He wanted to know if she was all right, if she needed help of any kind – financial or emotional. He thought she might feel awkward about approaching him for help, given the circumstances, so if she was in trouble, he would have to make the first move. But he didn't want to intrude on her privacy if it wasn't necessary.'

'Very laudable.'

Shalcross inspected his face for irony. 'That's how it seemed – otherwise I wouldn't have agreed. Look, when you do close personal security you're with the client so much of the time, you live their life with them, it's more than just a job. And everything that affects them becomes your business. If his daughter was hostile towards him, she could have been a threat. It wasn't wrong to investigate that threat.' Slider said nothing. He didn't need to. Shalcross was intelligent enough to recognize a weak justification when he heard one – even his own. He went on, trying to sound businesslike. 'It was easy enough to get to meet her. She was working at a place—'

'Yes, I know about the Archive.'

'Right. Well, members of the public can apply for a reader's ticket, and she was the one that processed them, so there was the opportunity. I took out a ticket, and visited regularly. She seemed very shy, or perhaps reserved is the right word – abnormally so. Getting her to talk at all was hard work, but . . . well, I found myself feeling a bit sorry for her. I felt she needed a friend. The fact that I was being paid to be that friend was something I didn't like, I never liked,' he added with a stern look, as if Slider had made the objection himself. 'But I felt I was doing more good than harm.'

'You gave a false name, false address, burner phone number,' Slider mentioned. Faversham stirred and looked at his client, but Shalcross gave him a tiny shrug in return.

'Mr Armstrong's orders. He didn't want her to be able to trace me back to him to begin with, in case it spoiled things. He provided me with the phone.'

'To begin with? He was meaning to meet her himself in the end, was he?'

'He didn't precisely say so, but that's what I understood. That once he knew how she felt about things, he could approach her himself and be reconciled.'

'Yes, noble sentiments. How far was your friendship supposed to go?'

'I beg your pardon?'

'The accommodation address – the flat in Soho. The . . . er . . . regular occupant said you told her she might have to clear out if you brought someone back. Taking Miss Chadacre to your – or rather, Tony Scrimgeour's – place and seducing her was part of the deal, was it? Were you going to be paid extra for servicing her?'

Shalcross shoved the chair back so violently as he stood up that it fell over. 'How dare you say that? I never laid a finger on her! I'm leaving – I don't have to stay here and be insulted.'

'My client has been extraordinarily co-operative,' Faversham said urbanely. 'May I suggest you moderate your language.'

'Please sit down, Mr Shalcross,' Slider said calmly. 'You may have entered into this arrangement with the best of intentions, but Mr Armstrong certainly anticipated a more intimate relationship developing, or he wouldn't have insisted you had a premises to take her to.'

Shalcross righted his chair, but hesitated before he sat down again. His anger, Slider saw, was a good sixty per cent guilt. He had known, all right, that getting her to fall for him was part of the plan – how else was he to get her to confide? – and that, these days, romantic relationships between men and women generally got physical at an early stage. Prue Chadacre being so inhibited as to make sexual congress highly unlikely was something he couldn't have known when he accepted the gig.

'She wasn't like that,' he said at last. 'I never met anyone so . . . shut off. Just getting her to speak to me – let alone look at me while she did. I felt sorry for her – I did! OK, it was maybe not the best thing to agree to do it in the first place, but after a bit I felt I was doing a good thing for her, getting her to open up a bit to another human being. I felt she was happier for it.'

'So what changed your mind? Why did you suddenly drop Armstrong as a client – and, by extension, stop seeing his daughter?'

'He . . .' Shalcross paused, staring at the wall, hunting for the right words. 'He was getting impatient with my limited progress. He wanted me to get more out of her more quickly. I told him it was very delicate, that she was very reserved, that I had to take things slowly. It was then that I started to feel his concern was not really for her after all, but for himself. I pressed him on his motives. And finally he said that he wanted to know what she felt about him, and what she was likely to say about him if asked.'

'What did that mean?'

'That's what I asked him. He said, suppose she was approached by the press to talk about him, what would she be likely to say? Would she say anything that would harm his reputation in any way? Naturally I asked what he was talking about. Did she know something to his detriment, and if so, he had better tell me what it was. He told me to mind my own business. I told him it *was* my business and if he'd done something dodgy I needed to know about it. He lost his temper and told me to do as I was bloody well told and not ask so many questions, and that he paid me plenty to keep my mouth shut and obey orders. Then I lost my temper and told him I was not an employee, or a dog, and I quit.' He relapsed into silence, evidently going over the last stormy exchange in his memory.

Slider waited.

He resumed. 'When I thought about it afterwards, at home, I started to feel uneasy. I didn't like what I was suspecting. I thought of how introverted and damaged Prue seemed. I did a bit of research on the internet, and discovered that Mr Armstrong's first wife – Prue's mother – had died in, well, peculiar circumstances. She'd drowned in her bath, maybe having taken too many tranquillizers. I didn't like it. It sounded a bit like suicide to me. What if she'd killed herself because her husband had been a brute? You read about situations like that – the man knocks the woman about and she's too afraid of him to run away, so suicide seems the only option. And then I thought, what if Prue had witnessed something – seen him hitting her mother, heard the rows? I felt I'd been on the brink of getting mixed up in something – something I was better off out of.'

He paused again. Slider said, 'The fishing weekend – how did that happen just at that time?'

'My pal John has these get-togethers now and then. I've known him since schooldays, he's a mate. He'd been asking me to come to one for ages but I hadn't been able to find the time. But that weekend it was just what I wanted, to get out of London, get away from the whole mess, have time to think quietly about everything. New surroundings, clean air. And I hadn't had a proper break in two years. Close personal security is very high-octane. I needed some downtime. So I rang him up and he said come, so I went.'

'And were you intending to see Prue again?'

'That was one of the things I had to think about – how to disentangle myself from her without hurting her feelings too much. I think she'd begun to get fond of me. On the other hand, it felt all wrong to go on seeing her in the circumstances – like spying on her. And if she found out my connection with her father, she'd feel horribly used.' He looked straight at Slider. 'I thought a clean break was probably the best option. When I got back to London, I had a couple of days grace because she didn't work on Tuesdays and Wednesdays. And before I had to decide anything, I found out she was dead.'

'What were your thoughts when you heard?'

'I hardly think my client's speculations are material,' Faversham said.

'I'm wondering,' Slider said, 'why he didn't come forward before, seeing that he'd had close personal contact with the victim.'

'You don't have to answer that question,' Faversham told Shalcross comfortably.

But he did. 'At first I was just shocked. I was . . . fond of her, in a way. Then I thought about things – the timing – and I started to be uneasy. I didn't like the fact that I was wondering if Mr Armstrong'd had something to do with it. You can't easily suspect someone you know, can you? I couldn't believe he'd do something so . . . so extreme. But on the other hand, there was the coincidence. It was so quickly after I'd refused to go on seeing her on his behalf . . . I started to feel guilty. But I hadn't done anything wrong. And in any case, I told myself it couldn't possibly have been him – a man in his position. So I decided the best thing was to keep schtum, sit on my hands, wait and see what developed. When your lot turned up at my flat, it was the worst shock of my life. All I could think to do was to stonewall. I thought you knew something. I was damn glad then that I had an alibi. But since then, I've been thinking and thinking, and I'd decided to come in and tell you everything – only you got to me first. But I still want it understood – I only came to explain about my befriending Prue. I'm not trying to incriminate Mr Armstrong. I don't believe – I *can't* believe – he had anything to do with it.'

Slider allowed him a brief pause, before saying, 'You've said that you thought a clean break with Ms Chadacre was best. So why did you ring her on the Saturday? The day before she was killed.'

He looked puzzled. 'I didn't. I was in Tavy St James on Saturday.'

'Phones do work from a distance, Mr Shalcross. And tele-phone logs show that she was rung on Saturday morning from the number you gave her as yours, the number of the burner phone that supported your Tony Scrimgeour persona.'

'But I gave that back to Mr Armstrong when I quit. It was his property – he'd provided me with it, so I couldn't keep it, even if I wanted to. Which I didn't.' He had answered promptly and easily, which had the ring of truth about it. Slider, adjusting his own ideas, waited, watching Shalcross's face as he went through the thoughts that were now arising. They were not happy thoughts.

'You are an ex-soldier,' Slider said at last, quietly. 'Though your specialism was saving lives through bomb disposal, you were trained to kill. Did it not cross your mind that if you hadn't left when you did, your next assignment from Mr Armstrong might have been even less to your liking.'

Faversham said, 'You don't need to answer that. Really, inspector, I'm surprised at you.'

'I withdraw the question,' Slider said.

But Shalcross had given him a burning look, and Slider knew that, despite his solicitor's protests, it *had* crossed his mind.

'It might be the tunnel at the end of the trees, but don't get too excited,' said Porson. 'You still haven't got a sniff of evidence against Armstrong.'

'The phone call—' Slider began heatedly.

'You've only got Shalcross's word for it that he gave the phone back. And he would say that, wouldn't he?'

'Sir,' said Atherton, 'there's the motive. Armstrong's standing for Parliament, and there'll be all sorts of probings into his background. He'll have to be squeaky clean to stand for a place like Datchet and Dorney Reach. Armstrong wanted to know what Prue might say to the press about him. What if there were suspicions about his wife's death, and his daughter could finger him?'

'*What if?*' Porson objected. 'All you've got is wild susposition. And motive isn't evidence, in any case.'

'But we can look for evidence now, can't we?' Slider said. 'If only we could get his fingerprints for comparison with those in the house.'

'You can't get fingerprints without arresting him. And let me make it clear, you can't even *interview* him again, let alone arrest him. Everyone from Mr Zammit down has got eyes-on now. Words have been had. Armstrong's not just as rich as Creases, he's a public figure and a philanthropist. Little orphan babies. Sick kids. Lost kittens for all I know. He's a saint in the making. You won't get any thanks for throwing nasturtiums at him.'

'But we can investigate him without speaking to him,' Slider said, half statement, half question.

'Be my guest,' Porson said. 'But make it snappy. This case is no longer a priority.'

'Homicide not a priority?' Slider said.

'No one's agitating to get it solved. But the media's all over this county lines operation in the White City, you know that. Hammersmith is being pressed on it by the Home Office. And Number Ten wants action on diversity and hate crime and we've got to get out some positive figures to show up.'

Slider must have showed his feelings about that in his expression, because Porson made an exasperated snort, like a horse ejecting a fly from its nostril. 'It's no good kicking against the pricks,' he snapped. 'Do your job. Leave the politics to the politicos.'

'In other words, to the aforementioned pricks,' Atherton murmured when Porson was out of earshot.

Slider turned away. 'No use beefing. Let's get on with it.'

'Why do we do this job?' Atherton complained, trailing after him. 'It's a misery wrapped in an enema.'

TWENTY

As God Is My Witness,
I'll Never Be Humphrey Again

'Armstrong's motors, guv,' McLaren said, bringing
Slider a mug of tea. Slider took it from him and put
it down on the only clear corner of his desk. The
mug was slightly sticky. Slider rubbed his fingers together
and looked enquiring. 'There's doughnuts,' McLaren interpreted the look correctly. 'I was going to bring you one when
I had a free hand.' His other hand was occupied with a sheet
of paper.

'In your own time,' Slider suggested. 'The cars?'

'Yeah, guv, you were right. The local boys know all about
it, for security reasons. He's got a chauffeur-driven Bentley
Flying Spur, and a BMW series 8 coupe for driving himself.
His wife's got a Range Rover for knocking about in the country-
side and a Porsche Cayenne for nice outings, that the eldest
son also drives when they're at home. Also the Kensington
boys say there's a Mini in the garage of the Kensington house
for everyone to use round London. I got all the indexes here.'

'There must be a security camera on the Adlestrop house,'
Slider mused. 'With police monitoring, I'm guessing.'

'Yeah, guv, but they won't release the tape without
Armstrong's say-so—'

'And we can't ask him,' Slider concluded. He just hoped
the local boys weren't so dedicated to their celebrity resident
that they would tip him off about McLaren's enquiries.
'Well, he'd hardly use the chauffeur-driven if he did go
secretly into London that morning.'

'No, they did say wifey'd taken that. The chauffeur drove
her up to Glasgow Friday and was bringing her back Monday.'

'So that gives you the BMW and the Porsche to look for.'

'And the Mini.'

'Leave that till third. He must have driven himself from Gloucestershire, and I can't see him bothering to change cars.'

'Right,' said McLaren. 'I'll start with the Beamer, then. He'd most likely take his own motor. Now I know what I'm looking for, it'll be easier.' He sounded quite chipper, and Slider realized again how dispiriting it was to trawl endless tapes for something suspicious when you didn't know what it was.

'Send Jenrich in, will you,' Slider said.

'She's out, guv.'

'Where?'

'Dunno, guv. She didn't say.' A detective sergeant had an enviable degree of freedom. 'She was looking up Armstrong's history before, that's all I know.'

And Atherton was talking to Armstrong's election agent. 'All right. Ask Swilley to come in,' Slider said.

'Right, guv. And I won't forget that doughnut.'

Peter Trabbett lived in a 1970s-built semi in Ruislip, with a tiny neat front garden, modestly gay with red geraniums and white alyssum. A crazy-paved path led from the oddly rustic wooden gate to the gimcrack porch – nothing more than a slab of concrete supported by two metal poles, but there was a sharp shower going on as Jenrich arrived and she was glad enough of its shelter. She rang the bell. It chimed Westminster inside, a shadow appeared behind the reedlite front door, and it opened to reveal a man in his late seventies. He was slim-built, about five foot eight, wearing grey trousers, dark-blue velvet slippers, an open-neck shirt, and a grey cardigan, buttoned up, with bulging pockets. His hair was no more than a fond memory, a short-cropped skirting-board around the sides and a few silver strands over the top. His face was fair and indoor-pale, with a large nose supporting old-fashioned brown-framed glasses. But behind the lenses the eyes were sharp and enquiring, and a pumice-stone knob of chin spoke of a certain firmness of character.

Jenrich introduced herself and showed her brief, and said, 'The secretary of Christopher Wren School told me that you used to teach there in the seventies.'

'For my sins, yes. What's this about?'

'She thought you might remember some of the boys who attended back then.'

'I remember all of them,' Trabbett said. 'It's a teacher's greatest weapon during his career, and the cross he has to bear in retirement. Which one of the little beasts were you interested in?'

'Magnus Armstrong.'

Trabbett's eyebrows went up, and he smiled a peculiar smile. 'You'd better come in,' he said.

When they were seated in the tiny front room (three-piece suite, television, electric fire in the low, tiled fireplace, whose top supported an electric clock and five pewter beer mugs all stuffed with papers, biros and other detritus) Jenrich said, 'Armstrong's Wikipedia page, and all his official biographies, state that he went to Christopher Wren School, but the school records have no trace of him. But Mrs Kravitz said she thought she had heard you talking about Armstrong at one of the reunions. So she thought you might be able to tell me something about him.'

'May I ask why you're interested in him?'

'It's an ongoing case. I can't really tell you any details,' Jenrich said. 'Actually, I probably shouldn't be here asking you at all. But I can tell you it's very important. There are some anomalies that I'd like to clear up, so that we can put his file aside and get on with other things.'

Vague and woolly as that was, he seemed satisfied with it. 'Anomalies, yes,' he said. 'I can imagine that. Well, I can tell you straight away that Magnus Armstrong did *not* attend Christopher Wren – because that's not his real name.'

Jenrich felt a glow of relief, and smiled encouragingly. 'Go on,' she said. 'Tell me. Everything you remember about him.'

'All right. He would have joined the school in the early seventies – seventy-one or seventy-two?'

'According to Wiki, he was born in 1961,' said Jenrich. 'Unless that's a lie as well.'

'No, that would be about right. I didn't have him in the first year, but I noticed him – we all did – because he got bullied so much. He was a skinny kid, badly dressed, mostly unwashed, and the other kids took it out on him. Add to that, it got out that his mother was unmarried, and didn't know, or wouldn't tell, who the father was.'

'So, not the son of George Armstrong, motor mechanic, and his wife Margaret, of Dunraven Road?'

'Nope. His mother was Denise Slack, and of course the kids got hold of that name and had fun with it. They were unforgiving times, back then. Illegitimacy was not a shrug of the shoulders like it is now. It was a shameful thing to be a bastard.'

'So his real name was Slack?'

'That's right. Humphrey Slack. God knows what made that poor woman give him a name like Humphrey, but he suffered for that, too. Kids are cruel little beasts, they'll latch on to anything unusual. And it wasn't Dunraven Road. The Slacks lived in one of those tall terraced houses in Adelaide Grove – you know, three floors and a semi-basement. They had the basement, and pretty dark and damp they were in those days. I never saw the Slacks' home, but I knew someone else who lived in one. A window at the front onto the area and a window at the back onto the supporting wall of the garden, which belonged to upstairs. In between, two rooms, a kitchen and lavatory. No bathroom. Any washing got done at the sink, so it was no wonder Slack was a bit smelly. I don't know what his mother did for a living – naturally the boys said she was a prostitute – but there wasn't much money. His clothes were always worn out and not very clean. But he was bright. Whoever his father was, he donated some brains to the mix.'

'What did you teach?' Jenrich asked.

'Maths – and he had a mathematical brain. He was really quick. He was good at practical things generally – woodwork, metalwork and so on. If he'd shone at games it might have been the saving of him – boys always respect other boys who are sporty – but he had no interest in them. Still, as he went up through the school, he got taller and put on a bit of heft, so the bullying dropped a notch, and it was more sniggering and whispering. Still upsetting, of course. He was an outsider, and he was always going to be.'

'You felt sorry for him?' Jenrich asked.

Trabbett shrugged. 'You have to take life as it comes. You

have to harden yourself. It wouldn't have helped him to coddle him. He had to learn to look after himself. Which he certainly did.'

'What d'you mean?'

'As soon as he was able to, he got himself a Saturday and evening job, working at a builders yard in Ellerslie Road. I don't know if he did other jobs as well, or found some other way to get hold of money, but at any rate, by the time he was in the fourth form, he'd moved his mother and himself to a maisonette in Percy Road, just two rooms and kitchen but it had a bathroom, so it was a big step up. He got hold of a bicycle somehow, because I saw him biking into school, and I suppose that gave him access to other jobs, during the holidays, for instance. He was doing the right things for himself. He was clean, his clothes weren't in holes, and he was doing all right academically.'

'Did he have many friends?'

'I don't recollect he had any. He was always a loner. Bullied kids generally don't make friends. Either they go under, or they find a way to survive, but either way they do it alone.' He paused to blow his nose. 'It was a shame, really, that he couldn't go into the sixth form, because I think he had academic promise. But according to his form teacher – I talked about it with him – there was no money at home, and he had to get a job. He had good O Levels and went straight in at sixteen to a local building firm—'

'Larson's,' Jenrich supplied.

'I'd forgotten the name. Larson's, you're right. Anyway, he left school and that was it as far as I was concerned. He was out of my orbit. But a few years later I saw a photo in the local rag that I recognized. It was a wedding photo. There was Humphrey Slack outside a church, grinning like a dog, with this girl on his arm; carnation in his buttonhole, girl all in white and looking as if she was about to be sick – you know the sort of thing.'

Jenrich nodded.

'Only the caption underneath didn't say Humphrey Slack, it said Magnus Armstrong. My curiosity was piqued, and I phoned up the rag and asked if they'd got it wrong. No, they said, it was definitely Magnus Armstrong, he was a well-known local businessman, he was marrying the daughter and eventual heiress of Chadacres, and even I'd heard of them. You saw their boards on building sites all over the Bush. So poor little Slack had done all right for himself.' He chuckled. 'I even rang up Larson's – my wife had taught one of their daughters – she was a teacher, too – so I had a sort of "in" with them – and got them talking about him, and they were all over him, what a brilliant chap he was, so valuable to the firm, and how disappointed they were that he was leaving them. But the upshot was he had joined them at sixteen under the name Magnus Armstrong – they'd never known him as anything else. So it seemed he set to work to reinvent himself as soon as he left school. I thought, good for you! And I've followed his career at a distance ever since. Or, well, I did until a few years back. When my wife died. 2011 it was. That sort of took the stuffing out of me and I lost interest in a lot of things.' He stared at the floor for a moment, then roused himself and smiled. 'I often think about the name he chose – Magnus Armstrong. Magnus – the big man. Armstrong – the powerful man. The runty kid who was bullied. He picked a good 'un. I often wondered whether it was subconscious, or deliberate. I'd love to ask him.' He blew his nose again. 'Either way, I don't blame him for dumping the Humphrey Slack handle – not very propitious, and it must have had rotten memories for him, given his early experiences. He pulled himself up by his bootstraps, and you've got to admire that.'

'Yes,' said Jenrich, who didn't want to admire him at all. She thought of two dead wives and now a dead daughter. How unlucky could a lucky man be? She remembered Slider saying that coincidence was God's way of telling you to pay attention. If it turned out that Magnus Armstrong was entirely innocent, she'd be very disappointed.

'It's an interesting aspect of this case,' said Atherton, 'that nobody's got the right name. Prue Chadacre wasn't Prue Chadacre. Tony Scrimgeour wasn't Tony Scrimgeour. And now Magnus Armstrong isn't Magnus Armstrong.'

Jenrich gave him a withering look. 'Everything about him is bogus. His whole life is a lie.'

'I don't know that you can say that,' Slider said mildly. 'He had a poor start and improved his lot by his own efforts. That's admirable, surely.'

'Magnus Armstrong,' Atherton mused with a smile. 'It hadn't occurred to me before, but it's quite telling for a false name. Like calling yourself Butch Muscleman.'

'Is it legal?' Slider asked.

'Oh, it was all done officially, by deed poll. I checked the Enrolment Books of the Supreme Court of Judicature,' said Jenrich.

'Enrolled as well? Most people don't bother. Then it's completely pukka,' said Atherton.

'Except that it's false.' Jenrich wasn't ready to let it go.

'Maybe that's what he wanted to find out – whether Prue knew about his real name and was likely to spill it,' said Gascoyne.

'But she wasn't even born when he changed his name, and I doubt he'd ever tell anyone once it was done,' said Slider. 'And I don't think, given how far he's come, having a wonky name at birth would derail him now.'

'Being called Humphrey Slack wouldn't be enough to get him deselected as a candidate,' Atherton agreed. 'There are MPs with far sillier names than that.'

'No, if she knew anything to his detriment, it would have to be something more serious,' Slider said. 'And, let's never forget, we don't have any evidence against him for the murder.'

'Except lying about his alibi,' Atherton reminded him. 'We could get him on wasting police time.'

Slider shook his head. 'Tempting thought. But unfortunately, like the man who was best mates with a sewage worker, he has friends in high places.'

It was going-home time. Atherton walked down the stairs with Slider. 'As soon as we get something on Armstrong, we will pursue him, won't we?'

'With forks and hope,' Slider said. 'At the moment, the only line we've got to follow is the car. Anyway, put it on the back burner until tomorrow. Date tonight?'

'I can't, I'm afraid. I'm going out with a woman.'

'Don't get smart with me, detective sergeant. Who is it this time? The underwear model?'

'Not tonight. Different one. She's a fitness trainer.'

'Joanna worries about you. Also, she worries about all the hearts you may be breaking.'

'Oh, I think they all know the rules of the game.'

'You may think so, but they're not like us, you know. No man can know what it is to feel like a woman.'

'That's not true. I feel like a woman every night,' said Atherton.

Wednesday was gloomy. A summer rain was falling from a soft, all-grey sky that said *I can keep this up all day*. The damp street had broken out in umbrellas, as though with mushrooms. Under pressure from above, Slider was trying to collate something on Operation Foxglove – hoping to keep his mind off Prue Chadacre and not succeeding very well – when McLaren appeared at the door with a cheerful grin and a fried egg sandwich.

'I've got it, guv,' he said triumphantly.

'Acid indigestion, I shouldn't wonder,' Slider murmured.

'Eh? No, guv – it was the Beamer, just like I said. The ANPR picked him up, A40, M40, then A40 again.'

'That only shows him heading into London.'

'Right, guv. But once I knew which way he come, I looked at the traffic cameras. There's one at the lights at Savoy Circus, catches him turning right off the A40 down Old Oak Road. And then the camera on the lights at the junction of Askew Road and Uxbridge Road show him turning left out of Old Oak onto Uxbridge. Which is yards from Dunkirk House. And that was at ten fourteen.'

'Good work,' Slider said. 'What a pity there's no camera actually covering the gate to the house.'

'But we know he was in the area at the right time, and he's got no other reason to be there,' McLaren urged.

'I know. But you know that's not enough for the Crown

Prosecution Service. If only we had an eyewitness . . . I think we'll have to put out another appeal. Somebody might have been going past – on foot, in a car, on a bus – and noticed him going in.'

'Want me to get on with that?' McLaren offered.

'Yes, please.' McLaren backed away as Atherton took his place, just having got in. 'You look – terrible. Bad night?'

'Never again,' Atherton said in hollow tones.

'What, never date again? This is a big moment.'

'No, just never date any woman that flexible again,' Atherton said. 'Gymnasts, ballet dancers, contortionists – none need apply. I'm wrecked. She had more positions than a government minister.'

'You're just not as young as you were,' Slider reminded him. 'Now, to get your mind off your libido . . .' He told him about the BMW.

'The time's right,' Atherton noted. 'Add the phone call on Saturday – presumably to set it up – and it looks as though he did visit her that morning.'

'You know we need more than that.'

Atherton knew. He mused. 'We've been asking all along what Prue Chadacre had that was worth killing her for. What did she have that anyone could want? The only answer we've come up with is: her silence.'

Slider sighed. 'You may be right. And the only person left who knows anything is Philip Armstrong. Much as I'm reluctant to disturb him, I'm afraid I shall have to talk to him again.'

TWENTY-ONE
You Can't Have Your Kate and Edith Too

They took Philip to the soft room, and he looked around with careful attention. 'I've been in here before. Is this still the police station?'

'It is. This is just a room where we talk to people who want to help us.'

He frowned. 'Did I do something? I don't remember.'

'No, you didn't do anything. You're not under arrest. You can leave at any time. We just want to talk to you. We think you can help us understand some things. You said you didn't mind talking to us, do you remember?'

'I suppose so.'

'You remember me, don't you?'

'Of course I do,' he said sharply. 'I'm not an idiot.'

'I know that. And you remember Ms Labouchere? Are you happy to have her sit in with us?'

He shrugged, still looking around him. 'You don't have one of those mirrors in here. But you do have cameras. I can see three of them. You've tried to make it look like somebody's sitting room, but it's not really, with the cameras in it. But I like the pictures of flowers. That's a primrose, that's a celandine, that's a dog rose, that's a foxglove.'

'Would you like to sit down?' Slider said, hoping to deflect him from his lists. He took a while to select from the sofas and chairs, and finally perched himself at one end of a sofa. He was looking thinner, still dishevelled, not quite so clean; there were shadows under his eyes.

'Have you had anything to eat today?' Slider asked, suddenly worried.

He shrugged. 'Don't remember.'

'Are you hungry now? Would you like something? A sandwich, maybe.'

'A sandwich. Yes. I'd like that.'

'Ham? Cheese?'

'Yes, please,' he said.

Slider nodded to Swilley, who went to the door to relay the order. Philip was murmuring something under his breath – it sounded like a list of sandwich fillings. But he didn't seem uneasy – it appeared to be more habit than nervousness. Slider called his attention. 'Philip, you do understand you're here voluntarily. You're not afraid, are you? Or worried?'

'No,' he said. 'I'm thirsty, though.'

'A cup of tea's coming, with your sandwich. Are you managing all right at home?'

'I can look after myself.'

'You're remembering to eat?' He shrugged. 'Have you got enough money?'

'I can get money out of the bank. Kate puts it in for me. I can always get more if I want.'

Slider made a mental note to contact the solicitor and make sure that some interim arrangement was in place until probate could be arranged. He wasn't sure if anyone would have thought of that.

'That's all right then,' Slider said. 'Can I talk to you now about when you were a boy? About your father and mother. Was your father kind to your mother? Were they happy together?'

Philip only shrugged, staring about the room still, his lips moving as he chanted something to himself.

'Did he ever make her cry?' Slider tried. Now he looked at Slider sharply. 'He did something to make her cry, did he?'

'I must never tell. Never, never, never.'

'I know. But it's different now. Because of Kate. It's important that you tell us. Kate would have wanted you to tell.' He glanced at Labouchere, but she didn't seem to object to this line.

'I shouldn't have looked,' he said, almost under his breath. 'But I couldn't help it. I was hiding in the cupboard and there's a hole in the door I could see through. I couldn't help seeing.'

'Why were you hiding? Were you afraid?'

'Sometimes. Sometimes it was just . . . I went there. It was my place.'

'Your safe place?'

He frowned, trying to find the words. 'Sometimes. Sometimes there was just . . . too much of everything. It was better in the cupboard. It stopped things going on and on and on and on. Where you can't stop them. I used to go in there when . . . when there was too much.'

'I understand,' Slider said. But he thought he did. *The world is too much with us; late and soon.* All that input would be harder still for a boy with a damaged processor. 'What did you see when you were in the cupboard? The thing you felt you shouldn't tell about? You can tell me now. It's all right.'

He was staring at the wall now, staring into his past. 'The door was open a bit. The bedroom door. I could see the bed. I saw him go in.' He stopped.

'Your father?' He nodded. 'What did he do? Did he hurt her?'

'He lay on top of her. She didn't like it. She didn't want him to.'

'Did she cry out?'

'He put his hand over her mouth. Afterwards, when he went away, she was crying. She always cried afterwards.'

'You saw this more than once?'

'It was wrong to look. I did a bad thing. Never look, never touch. I was a bad person.'

'It wasn't your fault,' Slider said.

He was thinking, But is this enough? Sandra May might well not have liked having sex with her husband, and forcing himself on her was not acceptable, though it was something that had gone on for centuries. These days it was considered rape, but there was a certain sort of man who believed it was his absolute right to have his wife whenever he wanted, and Armstrong was arrogant enough to fit into that category. Evidently Sandra May had never laid a formal complaint against him, which could have confirmed him in his view. So would he be likely now to believe it so bad it was worth killing to keep secret – something that probably never even registered with him as wrongdoing?

It was as well that the tea and sandwich arrived at that point. Slider let him eat and drink without interruption. He must have been hungry, because he demolished the two rounds, one ham, one cheese, in record time. When he was halfway down the cup of tea, Slider resumed.

'Where was this cupboard you hid in?'

'Next to the stairs,' he said easily, restored by the food.

Slider remembered seeing the door, in the wall just to the left of the top of the staircase. He made a connection. 'Was it part of the old lift?' he asked.

'I think so,' Philip said. 'It was just a cupboard, though. With a Hoover and an ironing board and a bucket. But it was big enough for me as well.'

'And you could see your parents' bedroom from there.' He looked blank. 'You looked through the hole in the door. And opposite you, you could see the door of your parents' bedroom.'

'Mummy and Daddy slept down the hall,' he said. 'The big room at the front.'

'You just said you could see the bedroom.'

'Kate's bedroom. I liked that it was hers because she looked after me and it made me feel safe. I used to watch her sometimes when she was in there, reading and things. But I didn't like it when Daddy came and made her cry.'

'No, of course not,' Slider said, while his thoughts went through a rapid readjustment. He had asked Philip if Armstrong had made his mother cry, but Philip had taken the word and connected it up differently in his head.

Not Sandra May. Not the wife – the daughter.

Now all sorts of thoughts were flooding through Slider's mind. It was so much worse than he had thought. It opened the door on so many speculations that he would much rather not give headroom to.

But Philip was looking better now. Having let go of that poisonous secret he seemed more connected. He looked at Slider as though he actively wanted another question.

'Were you afraid of your father?' he asked.

'We all were,' Philip said.

'Did he hit you?'

'Not hit, but his hands hurt. He'd shake you, and shout. Sometimes, when he shouted, there were little bits of spit.' He touched the corner of his own mouth. He screwed up his eyes. 'He got so angry, so angry,' he moaned.

'With you? Or with everybody?'

'Me and Kate and Mummy.' He searched for words. 'He was so big and loud. And sudden. It was awful when he shouted. You did what you were told so he wouldn't get angry. Always. You had to.'

Yes, Slider thought. Domination doesn't always require physical pain – though the menace of it is always in the background. 'You said he told you you mustn't look – what was that about?'

He shifted uneasily, pulling more unhappy memories up from the dark. 'That was . . . another time. That was Pammie. She lived next door. She used to come through the fence and play with me. In the garden.'

Slider nodded encouragingly. 'Go on.'

'One time, we were in the bushes, playing, and she said she'd show me something. Only Daddy found us. I didn't hear him coming. He was just there. I was so scared. He was angry, he dragged me out. His hands hurt my arms, he shook me and shook me and told me I must never look, never touch. He said I was a bad person and I'd come to a bad end.' He picked up his cup with a shaky hand, and swallowed the last of his tea. 'Pammie ran away. She was crying. She never came and played any more.'

He paused, and Slider let him alone, thinking that he seemed to want to talk now, and would prime himself. After a while, he said, 'It was better when he went away. He went off to marry someone else. We were all glad. Except that he came back sometimes, and you never knew when he might suddenly come. But mostly it was better. Kate and I were all right. Then she got ill, and stayed in bed for ages and I couldn't see her.'

'Was that when she had the baby?'

'Mummy said there wasn't a baby, but I think there was. I

think it died and they hid it. Kate got better after a while, but Mummy got sadder and sadder, and then she died.'

'On the day your mother died, you were the one who found her, weren't you?'

'Kate was at college. She got back later.' He looked down at his hands again, twisting them together. 'It was terrible. I didn't want to look, but I had to. I wasn't being bad.'

'I know.'

'I went into her bedroom to get something to cover her, so I wouldn't have to see. And I knew he'd been there.'

'Your father?'

'I could smell the aftershave. When he lived with us, I hated that smell. I could smell he'd been in the room.' He stopped, and started again. 'I expect Mummy was glad to die. Kate cried an awful lot, but I didn't. I thought, now he can't make her sad any more. But after that, he didn't come to the house any more anyway, so it was all right. It was just Kate and me.'

'Didn't you get any help from outside? From officials? Or . . . doctors?'

'We didn't need anyone. Kate said we were better off on our own.'

'Why did you stay at Dunkirk House? It was a big house just for the two of you.'

'Kate wanted to leave, she didn't like it, she said it reminded her too much. But I didn't want to go. It was . . .' He paused a long time, at a loss for words. 'I knew where I was there,' he said at last. He waved a vague hand around, as if indicating the world outside.

Too much of everything, Slider thought. In Dunkirk House there was always his cupboard. 'Why did you sell all the furniture?' he asked, just to satisfy his own curiosity.

'Kate said we didn't need it. I didn't mind. She didn't like it. She didn't like keeping things. She threw everything away. She moved away to a house on her own. I didn't like that. She said I must never tell anyone where she was. But she bought me a phone so I could call her, and she always, always answered. Always. Until . . .' He put his hands to his face and dragged the flesh down in that gesture Slider had seen before. 'That's how I knew,' he whispered. 'Because she always answered.'

'I'm sorry,' Slider said.

He loosened his hands, rubbed his eyes, put his hands in his lap, chewed his lip a little. Then spoke, in a low voice. 'Kate looked after me. She said she'd always look after me. And she did. But now she's dead too. Everyone's dead except me.' He looked down at his hands, then up at Slider, a clear, steady look. 'I have to take care of myself now, all the time, don't I? I have to be a man.'

'That's right,' said Slider.

He took a breath, and said resolutely, 'I can manage.'

It seemed to Slider among the braver things he'd ever heard.

'Armstrong's worked himself up the ladder, made a fortune, made a reputation, and now he's married a political thorough-bred to give him the entrée to the right circles. He's about to enter public life in a big way. He's on the verge of achieving what I suppose is a long-held ambition – and his daughter could explode like a hand grenade in the middle of it all. Not just destroy his chances of being elected, but his whole life. He'd be the most hated man in Britain for sexually abusing his daughter. And if he did have anything to do with his wife's death, he could end up in prison. The impact of a custodial sentence on a man like him, a man of immense wealth and privilege . . . No wonder he wanted Shalcross to find out what Kate might say about him. If what Philip says is true, there's a motive worth killing for.'

'If it's true,' said Porson. 'Your Philip's not a solid witness. You couldn't put him up in court. He's not the full nine bob. He doesn't know dates. He'd be easily confused. Was it his mother he saw Armstrong boffing, or his sister? Or did he imagine the whole thing? He smelled his father's aftershave? What sort of evidence is that? Defence'd take him to pieces – even if the CPS allowed him to be put up in the first place, which they wouldn't. How would it look, a man with learning difficulties being grilled in the Old Bailey?'

'Fragile people have made successful witnesses in trials before,' Slider said.

'As to the baby, he only thinks there was one. What would he know about it? He even admits his mother denied it. And in any case, all that's only motive. It's a big step from motive to action. Do I have to remind you again that you have no reason to suppose Armstrong had anything to do with the murder?'

'No, sir. But we know he was in the area at the right time, and what other reason did he have to be there? He asked questions about his daughter. He put his security man on to her, while denying to me that he'd had anything to do with her since the divorce. He lied about his alibi. He said the divorce was messy and contested when it wasn't. And I believe Philip. I just need one thing so that I can arrest Armstrong and get his fingerprints.'

'Yes, you need one thing,' Porson said impatiently. 'And you haven't got it. So get on with some authorized work before the spam really hits the frying pan.'

It took some delicate negotiations, but Philip gave his permission, and seemed quite content for the moment to stay at the station. Slider ordered a large lunch from the canteen to be brought to him in the soft room, with Swilley to watch over him and keep him happy. Then he briefed Jenrich and Gascoyne, gave them the keys and sent them off, while he retreated to his room and ostentatiously worked on the Foxglove files.

Not that he really knew what he was reading. He thought of Prue Chadacre and her horrible childhood. Presumably her mother was too afraid of her father to go to the police. Betrayed by both the people who should have defended her, it was no wonder Prue had shut herself off from people, and wanted nothing to do with anyone but Philip, especially men. But she had coped, without help, without counselling or therapists or any of the modern tools, looked after her brother and given herself a life of a sort. It seemed Armstrong had donated some of his can-do-ness to his daughter. If only he had left it at that.

It seemed like a long time before Jenrich came back, but it wasn't. She looked as though she'd had a shock.

'I've left Gascoyne there,' she said. 'We need to get a forensic team in there.'

'What did you find?' he asked.

'We pulled the wallpaper off, and there was the door, just an ordinary internal door, except that it had been nailed shut. Bit of a job getting the nails out. Inside it was just an empty space like a cupboard. I suppose they took out anything that made it look like a lift when they took out the machinery. The only tell was a hatch in the ceiling. We got a chair from the kitchen, and Gascoyne got up there with a torch, pushed the hatch up, looked around. It was like a square chimney, going up to the cupboard above. Then he made me go up and look. There was something lying on the top, just beside the hatch.' She made a face. 'I don't know how you guessed.'

'I didn't guess. I wondered.'

'The body of a baby. It was wrapped in a newspaper. Dated August 2000.'

'A skeleton?'

'No. It's mummified. I'm not sure if that's not worse. I suppose it's cold and dry in there, with an airflow, like in a chimney. I saw one before, when I was at Highgate – that was a baby as well, in a disused chimney, but it was from right back in the twenties. What made you think of it, boss?'

'He remembered so clearly his mother nailing up the door, and later papering it over. He must have sensed it was important to her to have remembered. And why would anyone nail up a useful cupboard in the hall? I just thought it was worth checking.'

'So he was right. There was a baby, and it died, and they hid it. But why?'

'To keep Armstrong from knowing. For fear of what he'd do.' Slider looked out of the window. 'It probably never occurred to them to ask for help.'

'She could have died in childbirth,' Jenrich said indignantly. 'Or something could have gone wrong during the pregnancy. This woman let her daughter have a baby with no medical attention? What sort of mother does that?'

'A frightened one.'

*   *   *

Now they could get a DNA profile – but they still couldn't attempt to match it, any more than the fingerprints, because there was no obvious connection with Armstrong, so they couldn't arrest him. It wasn't the 'one thing'. Slider sat drumming his fingers on the edge of his desk for some time after Jenrich had left to update the rest of the team. They had so many little pieces, but not the single direct link they needed. If only, he thought again, they had an eyewitness.

His fingers slowed and stopped. There was a witness, of sorts – the 'elderly lady' who had rung in the anonymous tip-off. Somebody with enough civic decency to make the call, but who didn't want to get mixed up with Authority. His mind clicked through connections, throwing up images. A heap of rubbish in the sheltered corner of the garden of Dunkirk House – rubbish of a particular kind. The garden gate, that opened on a latch, not a lock. A little old lady wearing a black coat and hat on the hottest day of the year. Maybe it was nothing. But, no, it had to be something, because someone had gone right up to the door, in order to be able to see the fallen woman at the foot of the stairs. You couldn't see *that* from the road. And there was no way on earth it could be a guess – someone had to have seen it.

He got up quickly and went downstairs.

By a piece of luck – he was due one now – D'Arblay was in the station, doing some paperwork on an arrest.

'You still keep up with Very Little Else, I gather?' Slider asked.

'Mrs Mason? I see her around,' D'Arblay answered. 'Of course, it's not the same now we're not walking the beat, but I sometimes stop when I see her and have a chat. She's a decent old bird. And she keeps her eyes open.'

'So you know where she might be?'

'She walks more or less the same route she always did. I could hazard a guess as to where she might be most times.'

'Good. I'd like to have a word with her. Would you come with me and find her? I think she'd be more comfortable if you were there. I know she likes you.'

'Is she in trouble, sir?' D'Arblay asked. 'I hope not. She's a good old girl, really.'

'No, no trouble. Will you come?'

He gestured to his desk. 'Would it be all right if I finished this first? While it's fresh in my mind. I need half an hour.'

'Of course. Don't want to get you into trouble. I'll go and have a word with your skipper, and get permission to abduct you.'

O'Flaherty was the duty sergeant. 'Course you can take him, darlin',' he said. 'What's it about?'

'I don't want to say too much, in case I'm making a fool of myself,' Slider said. 'Easier to shrug off a wild goose chase—'

'If you haven't promised everyone a big goose dinner, I know,' said O'Flaherty. 'Is it this Dunkirk House case?'

'You never heard me say that. I'm supposed to have shelved it. Mr Carpenter has other priorities.'

O'Flaherty grinned. 'What was he thinking, telling my Billy-boy to give up? Doesn't he know a bulldog when he has one?'

'I'm on the brink of giving up. If this goose turns out to be—'

'A turkey?'

'You can still eat turkey. I was going to say a marsh-light.'

'Sure, don't take it to heart,' O'Flaherty comforted him. 'There'll be another murder along before you can spit. You'll never be out of a job.'

'How's Mary?'

'On the pig's back. The last little one's leaving home, so she'll only have me to cook for in future. You should come to dinner some time – she'd like that.'

'I have fond memories of her cooking,' Slider said. 'That steak-and-kidney pudding she does . . .'

O'Flaherty slapped his girth. 'What d'you think made me the man I am? Will I go and hurry D'Arblay along? It's Little Else you're looking for, I take it?'

'How did you know that? Don't say a little bird told you.'

'Deduction. Ah, t'wasn't that hard.'

'You should be a detective, Fergus.'

'Join the CID? Sure I couldn't take the pressure,' O'Flaherty said with an innocent look.

TWENTY-TWO
Telling Right from Ron

I t was a warm day, and though cloudy, didn't look like rain. Slider took an unmarked department car, but let D'Arblay drive, since he knew where to be looking. He drove in silence for a while, but then said, 'You think she might be the person who phoned it in, sir?'

'It has crossed my mind.'

'Any particular reason?' he asked diffidently.

'They said it was an elderly lady. And she was standing outside on the street, watching.'

'Yes, I remember.'

'And she gave me a nod. It might have meant nothing, but there again . . . Why was it rung in anonymously? And on a payphone, when everyone these days has a mobile? Must be someone just on the edge of, or just outside, society, was what I thought.'

'But why would she have gone up to the door in the first place?'

'That's what I want to find out.'

They found her just past the Seven Stars, sitting on the wall of Ravenscourt Park and blinking in the warmth like a dusty cat. Slider told D'Arblay to drive past a little way so they could approach her on foot and not frighten her. He had armed himself beforehand with a packet of biscuits cadged from the canteen – not custard creams, her favourite, but something rather oaty and wholesome, as was the way of public catering these days. Still, he hoped they'd be acceptable.

She watched them approaching through squinted eyes, turning her head a little but not otherwise moving.

'Hello, Mrs Mason,' D'Arblay said. His politeness to all people was one of his strengths.

'Mr D'Arblay,' she responded with a gracious inclination of the head. 'Nice day, ain't it?'

'Not too hot, just right,' he responded. 'How are you today?'

'Can't complain.'

'You remember Mr Slider, I expect.'

'Course I do. Nothing wrong with me memory.' She looked up at Slider. 'I see you coming outter Dunkirk House. You on that?'

'I am,' said Slider. 'That's what I wanted to talk to you about. Would you mind?'

She smacked her lips. 'Thirsty sort of a day, ain't it? I could go a cuppa tea.'

Slider glanced at D'Arblay, who said, 'There's Ali Baba's, just down the road. Only a step away.'

'Ali Baba's?' Slider queried.

'It's a café. It's run by a bloke called Ali, and it's next door to the barber's shop.'

'Impeccable reasoning. Let's go.'

It was actually called the Star Café, after the pub, the Seven Stars, that had stood on the corner and given the area its name; but the writing over the door was so faded and peeled it probably needed its popular designation for identification. It was a very basic tea-and-sandwich bar, with just three tables inside, probably surviving mostly on takeaways for office workers. Very Little Else sat upright and queenly at the table by the window, enjoying the attention of two nice men, while D'Arblay, helmet off, went up to the counter and bought three cups of tea. When she had ceremoniously sugared and stirred her tea and taken a sip, she put the cup down and squared herself for questioning.

'When I saw you outside Dunkirk House that Monday, you nodded to me,' he began, 'and I thought to myself that perhaps you knew something I ought to know. Was it you who rang in the nine-nine-nine call about the dead lady?'

It was a horrible moment, as he waited to hear if he'd made a fool of himself. But she gave a tight, pleased smile, and said, 'Took you long enough to come and arst me, din't it?'

'So it was you?' She nodded. 'Will you tell me about it? How did you happen to see that poor woman's body?'

'Oh, t'weren't me. I never see her at all. It was Ronnie Roscoe found her. He ast me what to do, and I told him the pleece gotter be told. But he said he coon't do it. So I done it for him. As a friend.'

'Ronnie Roscoe?' Slider queried.

'Rancid Ron,' D'Arblay murmured to him.

Elsie looked displeased. 'Don't call him that,' she said. 'It ain't respeckful. And s'not his fault. He's got a Medical Condition.' The capital letters were quite clear.

Rancid Ron was one of the street people they had failed to get off the street. He had some kind of metabolic imbalance that gave him a strange odour – not hugely unpleasant, but noticeable, a bit like paraffin mixed with over-ripe fruit. It made him unwilling to be near people, or to go indoors. On the whole he was no trouble, except in the way rough sleepers are trouble, in making the Bush look untidy, begging, and the occasional bit of petty theft. As long as he didn't nick anything more than the odd bit of food or clothing he was on fairly safe ground because nobody wanted him inside the police station, so he was unlikely to be arrested. Business proprietors didn't want him putting off their customers, so he was occasionally given small amounts of money to go away; or, if he lingered outside a café, he might get a stale sandwich or squashed cake in payment for his immediate absence. In this way he eked out a living.

'So where is Mr Roscoe sleeping these days, Mrs Mason?' D'Arblay asked, being respeckful, in spades.

'That's jest it, innit,' she said. 'He was sleeping in the garden of Dunkirk House. That's how come.' She nodded significantly. *That's how come he knew about the dead woman*, Slider translated it. 'He come to me all of a dither. Well, when he seen it, the dead body, he run away, dint he? S'only nacheral. But, see, he had it on his conscience. Suppose nobody found her, the pore soul, on account of the house was empty, far as he knew. I was sitting on a wall the end o' Galloway Road Mundy morning when he come up to me. He told me about

it, and when I said he should go to the pleece, he said not
likely, they woont listen to me. And no more you lot would've,'
she added sternly.

'I'm afraid that's probably true,' said Slider.

'No probly about it! So I said I'd call nine-nine-nine for
him. Which I did. Had to walk all the way down to the
Westfields, cause there's no telephone boxes any more. They
all get vandalized. But they got these scurity guards in
Westfields, keep the vandals off.'

'You say you didn't see the body yourself. So you rang it
in without checking what he said was true?' Slider asked.

She was stern again. 'I known Mr Roscoe years and
years. He's straight. If he says that's what he saw, that's good
enough for me. Anyway, he was right, wunt he? You found a
body all right.'

'We did,' said Slider. 'Can you tell me exactly what he said
he saw?'

She frowned a moment in thought. 'You'd be better orf
hearing it from him, if it comes to it. I mightn't get all the
details right.'

'Would he talk to me?'

'He won't come into the pleece station. But if you talk to
him *out*side – if I tell him it's all right.' She looked from Slider
to D'Arblay. 'You might give him a few bob, to help him out.'

'Where's he sleeping now?' D'Arblay asked.

She looked prim. 'I'm not telling you that, case you feel
obliged to move him on.' She made the most of the word.
'But I know where to find him.'

'Will you take us there now?' Slider asked.

She nodded. 'S'only just down the road.'

It was in fact in Ravenscourt Park, where Rancid Ron was
sitting on a park bench. The park had a thick and extensive
shrubbery where once the body of a young woman called
Chatty Cornfeld had been found, and Slider wondered if that's
where Ron was sleeping since he left Dunkirk House. It would
not be safe in the way Dunkirk House had been – there he
had been able to accumulate the cardboard and newspaper
layers that made sleeping out comfortable. In the park, he

could leave nothing substantial, and was always in danger of being ejected by park keepers. He looked startled as they approached, and was halfway to his feet, when Elsie told them to stay where they were and approached him alone.

They made a curious couple as she stood talking to him, evidently having both to justify herself and persuade him to co-operate. Ron wore an old two-piece suit of dark cloth over a series of sweaters of different hues and with different neck-lines – despite the warmth of the day, it was easier to wear them than to carry them. What with Elsie in her coat and hat, Slider wondered if street people's metabolism altered so that they did not react any more to external temperature. It would certainly be a useful evolutionary adaptation. Ron wore very dirty and dilapidated trainers, and carried a modest single bag, one of the hemp shopping carriers the supermarkets had introduced when plastic bags had been phased out. He wasn't sure what Sainsbury's would feel about having him as a walking advertisement.

Finally, Elsie beckoned them forward. They greeted Ron gravely and politely, and though he still seemed nervous and uncertain, he nodded agreement when Slider asked if he would speak to them. He stayed sitting on the bench, with Elsie on his right side, and Slider perched at the very end of the bench on his left, ostensibly so that he could turn his body sideways to face him, but also to get as much air between them as possible. D'Arblay, with his helmet under his arm to be inconspicuous, stood behind the bench and made notes.

Ron's story was that he had been sleeping in the corner of the garden of Dunkirk House for a couple of weeks. 'I fought the 'ouse was empty,' he excused himself. 'There was shutters over the windows and I never see anyone go in or out. And I had a little peep in. You could see through the gap in the shutters in the middle, and the rooms was empty, no furnicher or nothing. So I fought it was a bit of all right.'

'I saw your little camp in the corner of the wall, behind the tree,' Slider said.

'I wasn't doing no harm to no one,' said Ronnie.

'I know,' said Slider. 'There's no trouble coming to you, Mr Roscoe. Just tell me everything you saw.'

He looked doubtful. 'Well,' he said.

Slider guessed he was not used to constructing a narrative, and helped him along. 'What day was it that you saw the dead lady in the house?'

'Sundy,' he said promptly. 'Only she wasn't dead when I saw her come in. I was lying down, and she give me a start, because I'd not seen anyone come in before. But she couldn't see me if I kep still. She walked straight up to the 'ouse and let herself in.'

'Can you describe her?'

'Youngish sort of lady. Posh. In trousers, blue trousers and a striped top.'

'Right. What did you do?'

'I stayed put.' He looked uneasy. 'See, I shoulda scarpered, but I'd got comfortable, and nothing's open that early on a Sundy, an' I thought if she didn't see me going in, she wouldn't see me going out. S'long as I kept an eye on the front door, and didn't try and leave when she was about.'

'I see. You say it was early Sunday morning. Do you know what time?' He looked despairingly at Slider – what a question! Slider abandoned it. 'Was she carrying anything, the lady?'

'Just a hambag.'

'No shopping bag or carrier bag?' He shook his head. Interesting, Slider thought – so she wasn't going in to stock up for Philip. That made it more likely she was there by appointment, to meet someone.

'What happened next?'

'I musta fallen asleep,' Ronnie said apologetically, 'cause I woke up when the gate opened, and the sun was up a lot more. And this bloke come in.'

'Bloke?'

'Gentleman, I should say, cos he was well posh. He had this suit on, in this sort of thin material . . .'

'Linen?' Slider helped him out.

'Could be linen,' Ronnie said doubtfully. 'It was, like, camel-coloured and dead posh. And I noticed his shoes.' Well, if he was lying down, they'd be on his level, Slider thought. 'Proper gent's shoes, brown, and all shiny. You could tell he was well rich.'

'Was he carrying anything?'

'Yeah, he had a newspaper, like folded, under his arm. And he goes up to the door and rings the bell, and the woman comes and lets him in. So I'm thinking about getting up and going. Only I don't move so fast these days, and I fought, what if he's only in there a minute and comes out and catches me? It's one thing to face up to a posh woman, but a posh bloke . . . And he was tall, a big bugger.' He shook his head. 'So I dint move. And after a bit I hear 'em having a row.'

'Inside the house?'

'Course. There was lots of shouting. Well, it was him shouting, really. I couldn't hear her. Then it all goes silent. Then after a bit he comes out again.'

'Was he carrying anything?'

'Yeah, that was the funny bit, he had a bag under 'is arm, looked like the woman's hambag. But I coulda bin mistaken. And the newspaper, still folded. Cos he'd got the bag under 'is arm, he was carrying that in his hand, like sort of in front of him.' He demonstrated. 'Like it had something inside it.'

'You didn't see what?' Slider asked without hope. But this was gold, pure gold.

'Nah. Never saw, only the newspaper.'

'Go on. What did he do?'

'He comes down the path towards the gate. Then he stops. He looks right at me corner. I nearly shat meself, I was that scared. I fought he'd seen me. But after a minute he walks on and out frough the gate and gone. I nearly died of relief.'

'I can imagine. Did you get a good look at this man? Would you know him again?'

'Burned on me mem'ry, after the scare he give me.'

'If I showed you some photographs, would you be able to pick him out?'

'Might do,' he said warily. 'But—'

'So what did you do next?' Slider asked, to deflect him from his caveats.

'I just kept quiet for a bit, scared he'd come back. But then I started finking about the shouting and the hambag. You wouldn't expect a posh bloke like that nicking a lady's bag.

I dunno really why I went and looked in. I crep up to the door, and there's a sort o' porthole fing you can see frough.'

'I know.'

'And I see her lying at the bottom of the stairs, like she's fell down 'em. That was enough for me. I hooked it.'

'You didn't think you should have sent for help for her?'

Ron looked at him in dumb misery. 'I can't get mixed up with the likes of them. I'm sorry now for the lady, but there's them and then there's us, and it never does you no good to cross the line. Maybe I shoulda . . .?' He looked at Slider helplessly, begging for understanding.

'Go on,' he said. 'It wasn't until the next day you asked Mrs Mason for help?'

'I kep thinking about it and wondering. It was the hambag, see. Why'd he took her hambag? Anyway, Mundy morning I found meself going past the gate, and it was all quiet in there, and I just sorta went in. It all looked the same, me stuff was still there, and I crep up to the door and looked in. And she was still there, hadn't moved, not an inch. Then I knew she was dead. I felt really bad. I fought, what if she was just hurt and needed an amblance, and she'd died cos I ran away?'

'So what did you do?'

'I dint know what to do. I come out quick as you like, and walked away, and then I see Elsie sittin' on the wall. So I went and told her. And she said, the pleece gotta be told. I said I can't do it, and she said she'd do it for me. Only, I said, I'd got no money for phone calls, and she said you don't need no money for nine-nine-nine. She said she'd go up the Westfields, that's a 'ell of a long way, but she's a good walker. Not like me. Not with these feet. I'm a martyr to me feet. So off she went. And I made meself scarce.'

'You didn't want to stick around and see what happened?'

'Not likely. I never want to see that place again.' He raised beaten eyes to Slider. 'Did she die cos of me? If I'd done summink, would she 'a made it?'

In mercy alone, he had to say, 'No, I'm pretty sure she was dead already when you first saw her.'

'Lord God A'mighty,' he murmured.

Elsie slapped his hand sharply. 'Don't blaspheme!'

It was the measure of these people's aversion to Authority that Elsie had walked right past Shepherd's Bush police station in her long trek to Westfields in search of a payphone. But though she was now living respectably in a hostel, and though she actually liked D'Arblay and presumably trusted him, it would not have occurred to her to go in and up to the desk and speak to the duty officer. That was *them*, and *us* knew to keep well clear.

It was going to be tricky getting Ronnie to come in and look at photos, but it had to be done right, he had to identify the man he had seen by picking him out from a decent number of faces, if it was going to stick.

And it had to be done now, because Ron was already scared, and if allowed to depart from Slider's presence might disappear all too well.

'I'd like you to come with me to the station, and see if you can pick out the man you saw from some pictures,' he said.

Ronnie shrank into himself like a salted snail. 'Not down the nick,' he whispered, half protest, half plea. 'I couldn't.'

'You're not in any trouble, Mr Roscoe,' Slider said. 'You're just going to help us catch a very bad man and bring justice to that poor lady.'

'You reckon he murdered her?' Ronnie asked fearfully. 'I don't wanna get mixed up with no murder.'

'I know you don't, and I don't blame you, but it's the right thing to do,' Slider said firmly. 'You want to do the right thing, don't you?'

Not in these trousers, might well have been Ronnie's reply. But Slider was The Man, and Elsie was nodding away encouragingly to him like a plastic dog in a car's rear window, and he sighed and muttered, 'S'pose so.'

Of course, no one was going to thank Slider for bringing Rancid Ron into the station, where his distinctive odour would take days to dissipate. But a glance at his watch told Slider that the relief would have changed and it would be Sergeant Paxman on duty, so he felt a bit better about it. He felt one should always seize any opportunity that presented itself of discommoding Sergeant Paxman.

TWENTY-THREE
The Devil's Leavings

'Y ou look tired,' Joanna said when he finally got home.
'Politics,' he said. 'Always knackering.'
'Like a G & T?'
'Is the Pope a Catholic?'

Shoes off, sustaining beverage in hand, he caught her up on the day's occurrences.

'That's terrible! Awful!' she said about Philip's testimony. 'Can it really be true?'

'It may be true. Or some of it. It's impossible to tell how reliable his memories are. What's more important is that Rancid Ron picked out Armstrong from a gallery of faces without hesitation.'

She wrinkled her nose. 'Rancid Ron?'

'He has a strange body odour. And yes,' he sighed, 'that's the difficult point. Obviously it's not going to be easy to sell him as a reliable witness, although there's no reason to suppose there's anything wrong with his mind. But the CPS is naturally prejudiced in favour of people you don't need to keep upwind of. Likewise, Philip – a qualified psychiatrist could probably get to the bottom of what he really remembers and what may be fantasy. But again, the CPS won't like it. But all I want,' he went on sturdily, 'is permission to arrest Armstrong so I can get his fingerprints. Once we've matched those to the ones inside the house, we've got him.'

'So . . . why can't you arrest him?'

'Because he's a VIP and knows everybody.'

'One law for the rich and one for the poor?'

'Don't look at me. I've never held with that.'

'I know you haven't. I remember in a previous case when you were warned off, you said you'd bloody well question anyone you liked.'

'And I'd arrest anyone I felt I should,' Slider agreed, 'but these things are not any longer entirely up to me. I have to run it past Porson and he has to run it past Carpenter, and Carpenter's as limp as a dead eel and won't do anything without permission from further up. So as soon as I got Rancid to ID Armstrong there started to be frantic phone calls and urgent conversations, and they were still going on when I left. My real fear is that the more people know about this, the more likely it is that someone will leak and Armstrong will get the tip-off. I really, really want to turn up and arrest him when he's not expecting it.'

'So you think he did it?'

Slider thought a long moment. 'Yes,' he said, and lapsed into silence.

She looked at him sympathetically. 'Do you want to be distracted?'

He heaved himself back to the now. 'God, yes. What have you been up to today?'

'Practised. Phoned around. Got a gig.'

He scrutinized her false insouciance. 'Something big?'

She grinned. 'Yeah! *Films in Concert* at the Albert Hall.'

'Sounds like a Sid Saxon Extravaganza.'

'You nailed it. They show popular blockbusters – excerpts from – on a big screen and a live orchestra plays the scores to accompany.'

'I'm always bothered by that phrase, live orchestra. Makes you wonder how often they use orchestras of zombies.'

'Oy! This is my story.'

'Sorry. How did this remarkable gig fall into your lap?'

'Fall is about right. I'd rung a few people and nothing doing, then I thought I hadn't tried Geraldine Ruddock for a while – Sid's assistant. And I just struck lucky. She'd had someone cancel, was about to ring round for a replacement, and I saved her the trouble.'

'Terrific. Congratulations.'

'It could be very good,' she said. 'I rang up Peter White afterwards for a bunny, because I had an idea he was on it, and he was. Loads of brass in these things, natch. And he said there's a whole lot of these "films in concert" gigs coming up in the autumn – a Harry Potter evening, a Star Wars evening and so on – and there's a good chance that now I've done one, I'll get called again. Peter said he'd put in the good word with Gerry Ruddock for me – you know Peter, he's a bit of an operator and he knows everyone, so it might make the difference.'

'We really will have to get an au pair, won't we?' he said jokingly. 'If you're going to get regular work . . .' She looked so happy. And, well, they always managed somehow. 'I'm really pleased for you,' he said.

'Honestly?'

'Honestly.'

'You're a nice person, Bill Slider.'

'I used to get hit if I wasn't,' he said modestly.

He went in to work in some trepidation, afraid he'd be told there was no way he was going to be allowed to arrest Magnus the Great. When he looked in at Porson's door on his way past, his boss was on the phone, listening hard, with a scowl gathering on his brow like a category three storm. He waved Slider impatiently away.

In his own room, however, there was good news. The fresh appeal for witnesses had had one good result – not the solid gold of someone seeing Armstrong entering the property, but at least a good quality solid silver. It was an off-duty traffic warden, on his way back from church, who had noticed a BMW series 8 coupe parked on a double yellow on Uxbridge Road. All his wardenly instincts had naturally been aroused, but being off-duty he couldn't write a ticket. He had, however, taken a note of the number, because in his experience, rich people who didn't care about parking restrictions were often serial offenders, and he hoped to catch the bastard, excuse my French, some other time, when he *was* on duty.

The registration number was Armstrong's, and the time was just after half past ten.

'That's good,' Atherton said happily. 'Catching him on the traffic camera turning into Uxbridge Road was one thing. But parking there's another matter. He can't explain that away. Pity the bloke didn't actually see him.'

'But it's a good solid witness – respectable,' Slider said.

'You can take it to the bank.'

'Better than that, I'll take this straight to Porson.'

He caught Porson just putting the phone down. He looked weary. 'It's a go,' he said.

'Really?'

'Two assistant commissioners were for and two against, so they chucked it upstairs to the deputy commissioner.'

'It went that far?' Slider said nervously.

Porson gave him a look. 'That's what I like about you, Slider. Always behind the door when they're giving out shit. Well, it turns out, lucky for you, the DC doesn't like Armstrong – had a run-in with him over something or other – and he refused to let it go any higher, and he tells the ACs there's no fear or favour in the Met and everybody's got to answer for their actions, no matter how rich they are. So the upshoot is, you can go and squeeze him. But you've got to ask nicely first, will he volunteer his fingerprints and DNA. If not, you can nick him.'

'Oh glory be,' Slider said.

Porson looked sour. 'You got a funny idea of pleasure,' he remarked.

Armstrong came sailing in like a flotilla, large enough and splendid on his own in a beautiful lightweight suit and colourful Hermes tie, but with other vessels bobbing in his wake: an almost-as-splendid solicitor, his PA, and a very sleek young man he introduced as his assistant, without mentioning what he assisted with. Buffing up his ego probably, Slider thought. He had gone downstairs to meet him, alerted in time to be there waiting for him. That was what you called tact.

'Now, what is all this nonsense?' Armstrong demanded, but genially. 'Your attentions to me are beginning to border on persecution, Inspector.' He smiled as he said it, but with teeth. 'I've only come because my great friend the commissioner asked me to co-operate with your investigation into my daughter's death.'

'And naturally, you would want to co-operate anyway,' Slider suggested, filing away the new lie with interest. 'My great

friend the commissioner' indeed! Armstrong didn't know that
he knew the question had not gone that high. And given
Armstrong's previous record, he'd have taken a moderate bet
they were not even acquainted.

'Of course,' Armstrong allowed graciously. 'Poor Kate. But
somebody quite senior in the Met told me the other day that
it was thought to be an accident after all. That you have no
evidence of foul play.'

'Who would that be, sir?'

'I had better not tell you,' he said coyly. 'Let's just say, he's
pretty senior. Really *very* senior, if you follow me. Now, I'm
a busy man. What did you want of me this time?'

This time was a nice touch.

'Something very simple, sir, which will only take a very
few minutes of your valuable time,' Slider said, who could do
genial as well as the next man when he had to. So much oil
was being applied on both sides you could have greased a
fair-sized liner's turbines and have enough left over for
chips. 'We would like you to give us your fingerprints and a
sample of your DNA. For elimination purposes.'

The sun went in. 'Out of the question!' Armstrong snapped.
'Have you dragged me all the way here for that? You've
wasted your time, and mine too.'

He was about to spin on his heel, but Slider caught the
solicitor's eye, and he looked thoughtful. He detained
Armstrong with a beautifully-manicured hand and whispered
into his ear.

Armstrong barely listened. 'I don't care what it looks like.
I will not be treated like a common criminal. If my word isn't
enough for these . . . clowns, that's their look-out. I've told
Inspector Slider all I am prepared to tell him, and that's the
end of the matter.'

'I'm afraid it isn't, quite,' Slider said. 'I have asked you to
volunteer your fingerprints and DNA. If you persist in refusing,
I will have to arrest you. And then, you understand, I don't
need your permission. You will be obliged to give them.'

'Arrest me!' Armstrong said scornfully. 'What fantasy is
this? Arrest me for what? For not playing your silly little
games?'

'Arrest you on suspicion of murder.'

Armstrong started a bark of mocking laughter, but it didn't quite come off. The solicitor gave Slider a very sharp look, which he returned steadily, and it evidently gave him pause. He must have reckoned Slider wouldn't come this far without some ammunition in his locker.

'Perhaps it would be better to co-operate,' he began.

Armstrong, however, was angry. 'Shut your mouth! Whose side are you on? I've co-operated all I'm going to. He wouldn't dare arrest me – he's a nobody. I'm leaving now, and I shall have serious words with the commissioner about this whole business.'

But Atherton stepped in from one side and PC Renker from the other, blocking his exit.

Slider had some serious words of his own. 'Magnus Armstrong, I arrest you on suspicion of the murder of Kate Armstrong, otherwise known as Prudence Chadacre. You do not have to say anything but it may harm your defence if you do not mention when questioned something that you later rely on in court. Anything you do say may be given in evidence.'

'You'll regret this,' Armstrong snarled. 'Oh, I promise you, you'll regret this.'

'Just doing my job, sir,' Slider said, calculating it would annoy him most of all the possible responses.

So they got his fingerprints, hand prints, and a buccal swab, and while Armstrong was having a lengthy confab with his solicitor, McLaren took the fingerprints to compare them with those found in the house, and the hand prints to compare them for size with the bruises on the victim's arms. The DNA would of course take longer to process, but could later be compared with that of the mummified baby. Meanwhile, a team was despatched to take possession of the Beamer.

When at last it came to interviewing Armstrong, he had stopped blustering in favour of quiet seething, but the simple sight of Slider broke through whatever control the solicitor had managed to instil, because his first words, before they'd even got the tape running, were: 'You'll be sorry for this! I'll see you broken!'

The solicitor murmured something to him, and as soon as they were settled, said, 'I think you must present my client at once with whatever evidence you have.'

'He hasn't got any!' Armstrong said.

'Shall we begin,' Slider said, 'with what you were doing on the morning of Sunday the fourteenth of July?'

'I've already told you,' Armstrong snapped. 'I was playing golf at the Royal with Chris Zammit, Steven Rogers and Lord Wokingham.'

'Except that you weren't. All three have denied they were with you that morning, and the golf club says you were not there at all. You lied, Mr Armstrong.'

The accusation didn't seem to bother him. 'I don't have to tell you anything,' he replied. 'Why should I account to you for my movements?'

'I'll account to you for them, then. Your BMW coupe travelled from your home to Shepherd's Bush and was parked in Uxbridge Road a few yards from Dunkirk House, at ten thirty a.m.'

'It must have been stolen,' Armstrong said. His solicitor whispered something to him. Sullenly, he said, 'All right, no comment.'

'You told me that you haven't had any contact with your daughter since the divorce, twenty or so years ago. Is that correct?'

'Up until I saw her at that tedious garden party in May, yes. I wasn't even sure it was her.'

'And how often have you seen her since that party?'

'Never. I don't know anything about her.'

'You've never been to Dunkirk House?'

'Not since I left there after the divorce.'

'Then how do you account for the fact that your finger-prints were found on the front door and in several places in the kitchen?'

'They must have been there from when I used to live there.'

'You don't need to answer any questions,' the solicitor reminded him.

'These were fresh fingerprints,' Slider said. 'And we know from the blood spatters that it was in the kitchen that Kate

Armstrong met her death. You were there, Mr Armstrong. You wanted to know if she would keep silent about your murky past. When she wouldn't give you the assurances you wanted, you lost your temper. You grabbed her by the upper arms and shook her – bruises on her arms match the size and span of your fingers. And then, realizing she could never be trusted not to betray you, you killed her with a violent blow to the head.'

'Fantasy. Absolute rubbish. I mean, no comment,' he remembered.

'The thing that gets me,' Slider said conversationally, 'is that you were so arrogant, you didn't even bother to wipe off your fingerprints. You arranged your daughter's body to look as if she had fallen downstairs, and cut a slit in the carpet at the top to look as if she had tripped. But it was plain from the nature of the wound on her head that she could not have got it falling downstairs. But you were so pleased with your own cleverness, you thought that your feeble ploy would have us put her death down to a tragic accident.'

Armstrong looked a little put out, but said nothing.

'Of course,' Slider went on, 'you must have felt sure of yourself, because the death of your first and your second wife had both been put down to accident.'

The solicitor was surprised. 'What has this to do with the present case?'

'We have a witness to the fact that you were inside the house on the day your first wife died, though you claimed at the time not to have seen her for weeks.'

'What witness?' Armstrong scoffed. 'That's rubbish. There was no one there.'

If highly-paid solicitors were accustomed to smiting their brows, he would have smote then. 'You only need to say "no comment",' he reminded Armstrong, who gave an irritable shrug, as though shaking off a fly.

'You know there was no one there, because you were there? Thank you,' said Slider. 'And the investigation into your second wife's accidental death was short-circuited because you had friends in the local constabulary.'

'That is an improper suggestion, Chief Inspector,' the solicitor said.

'We will be asking for a full investigation into that incident, and I think we will find some interesting correlations. Both wives died of drowning, after ingesting tranquillizers. In both cases Mr Armstrong had an alibi which I think we will find does not hold up, any more than his alibi for the fourteenth of July holds up. It's an interesting fact that people who get away with murder like to repeat their effects.'

'This is gross speculation,' said the solicitor. 'Unless you have evidence to substantiate these allegations, I must ask you to withdraw them.'

'As I said, we shall be re-opening the inquiry into the second Mrs Armstrong's death. And there was a witness to Mr Armstrong's presence in the house when his first wife died. This is all what you might call a background to the principle charge, Mr Armstrong, of the heartless murder of your own daughter.'

'You've got nothing on me,' Armstrong sneered.

'We have an eyewitness to your arrival and departure from the house during the time that she died. We have your fingerprints inside the house. And I'm sure that we will find a spanner in your BMW's tool kit that matches the wound on Kate's head. You took it in with you, Mr Armstrong, which proves you went there with the intention to kill. You carried it in concealed in a folded newspaper, carried it away after-wards in the same way, and you took her handbag away with you. Why did you do that?'

Armstrong opened his mouth, shut it, then said, 'No comment.' His face was red, and it wasn't only anger now. The solicitor was looking worried. The detail, probably, had disturbed him.

'I suspect it was to delay identification of her – though as far as you knew, no one was going to come and find her anyway. And also to make sure there was nothing that could incriminate you – like a note, or a message on her phone. You called her to make the appointment to meet on the burner phone you had got back from Jason Shalcross – you were cunning enough to know a call from your own phone would be traced.'

'If Jason made the appointment, it must have been Jason that killed her,' Armstrong said. 'Ask him – don't ask me.'

'Jason Shalcross has an alibi, one that, unlike yours, checks out at every point. And he had no motive for killing her – unlike you. Isn't that right, Mr Armstrong? Kate could tell the world things about you that would finish you. Things it was worth killing her to keep from coming out.'

'I don't know what you're talking about,' Armstrong said, but he looked sick.

'Did she have suspicions about her mother's death? She could certainly bear witness to your coercive behaviour towards her. And then there was the matter of your sexual abuse of Kate herself.'

'It's a lie! If she said that, it's a lie!'

'She's dead, Mr Armstrong. She can't tell anyone. But there was a witness.'

'How could there be?' Armstrong cried.

'You don't have to say anything,' the solicitor reminded him. 'Please stick to "no comment". And, Chief Inspector, I hope you can back up these wild allegations.' He was looking a bit sick, too. He obviously had not expected any of this. Slider felt almost sorry for him, walking blindfold into this shit storm.

'As I said, there was a witness. In fact, two witnesses – a living one, and a silent one. You sexually abused your daughter, Mr Armstrong, and she had a baby. The baby died, but its mummified corpse has been recovered, and we now have your DNA to match to it. That's the silent witness.'

Armstrong looked stunned. 'Kate had a baby?' he said. 'No. You're making it up.'

'For God's sake,' Slider said, sickened, 'would I make up something like that?'

'But . . . I didn't know,' Armstrong cried. 'When? When was that?'

'In August 2000,' Slider said, and watched him calculate dates in his head. 'It was while Sandra May was still alive.'

'I didn't know anything about it. She never told me. They never told me. I didn't know.'

'Whether you knew or not hardly matters,' Slider said. 'What your daughter could tell about you was enough either way. She was in a position to ruin your life, and you took action to eliminate her. It didn't matter to you that you had already ruined hers.'

Armstrong cracked. 'You don't know what it's like, battened on by all these women! I came from nothing, I had to fight my way up, every inch of the way, to get to where I am – and you don't need me to tell you that's right at the top! Nobody helped me. I didn't have any bloody silver spoon in my mouth, I can tell you! I did it alone, with my own brains and guts and determination, against all the odds, and I wouldn't let anything stop me. But these women do nothing but pull you down. Always crying and whining and nagging and clinging, always trying to hold you back. Useless parasites, the lot of them! You can't let them stop you, you can't allow—' He stopped abruptly.

'It's quite evident that you didn't allow them to stop you,' Slider said politely.

Armstrong looked at him with less arrogance than before, but with a hardness undiminished. '*You*'ll never stop me,' he said. 'You're nobody. A chief inspector? It's an insult! I could buy and sell you. You can't make any of this rubbish stick. I haven't come all this way to let a tuppenny-ha'penny hick copper like you get in my way.'

'The only thing I don't know,' Slider said, as if he hadn't spoken, 'is what you said to her on the phone that Saturday to make her agree to meet you on the Sunday.'

'She was never hard to persuade. Weak-minded like all these females. A bit of sweet talking – an apology – she'd be falling over herself to be reconciled. To be Daddy's Little Girl again. Women! Not a spine between them – they make me sick!'

'Mr Armstrong, I have to insist—' the solicitor began.

'Oh can it, Gordon,' Armstrong snapped. 'I'm not worried, if you are. They've got nothing on me. He's bluffing. He talks about a witness, but there isn't one. How could there be?'

'How could there be a witness to your abuse of Kate, you mean? Oddly enough, there was. I'm interested that in all our dealings, you've only ever spoken about your daughter. You've never mentioned your son.'

'Philip?' He seemed genuinely surprised. 'The boy's

mentally deficient. He was always subnormal, but he got worse after I left his mother. I suppose without a man's influence there was nothing to stop him deteriorating. I believe he ended up in a home – I'm pretty sure they must have put him somewhere after Sandra May died. I don't suppose he's even still alive.' He looked at Slider for a moment, and then a sly smile slithered across his lips. 'Oh, don't tell me!' he said with glee. 'He's not dead, then? This is your wonderful witness, is it, a delusional, half-witted boy? You trawled the homes and hostels and dragged the poor creature out to shore up your fantasies. Really, Inspector, that's low even for the police.'

'You show remarkably little compassion for Philip, considering he's your own flesh and blood,' Slider remarked.

'Is he? Is he? Well, I wouldn't be too sure,' Armstrong smirked. 'He didn't get addled wits from my side, I can tell you that. And who knows what Sandra May got up to? She was practically half-witted herself, and you know those types never have any self-control. That sloppy imbecile boy was nothing to do with me. She should have been sterilized, that's what. I tell you—'

'Mr Armstrong!' The solicitor seemed properly shocked. 'I think you've said enough. I do advise you most strongly to limit your answers to "no comment". You are doing yourself no favours.'

'It's all right,' Slider said. 'We have quite enough to be going on with. We have solid evidence on the murder of Kate Armstrong, and we will be investigating the deaths of the two previous Mrs Armstrongs. You thought you were untouchable, didn't you, Mr Armstrong, with your money and your friends in high places? But you'll find they're just as eager not to have their names tainted as you were when you killed your daughter. They'll abandon you so fast it'll make your head spin.'

'You're a fool if you think this is all over,' said Armstrong. 'Money talks, my friend. As for heads spinning, I'll be out of here so fast yours will revolve like a wind turbine. Now, Gordon, do your stuff. I've had enough of this noddy. I want to go home.'

Before the solicitor could speak, the door opened, and Mr Porson came in from the pokey. His eye skipped contemptuously over Armstrong to Slider, and he nodded. 'Book him,' he said.

'When men grow virtuous in their old age,' Slider muttered as he and Atherton trod up the stairs.

'Come again?' Atherton said, roused from his own dark thoughts.

'Swift,' Slider explained. 'I don't think I've ever handled a more unpleasant villain. And when I first found out about his origins, I wanted to admire him.'

'Yes, it can't have been easy to begin life as Humphrey Slack,' Atherton said.

'And he certainly went a very long way,' Slider went on. 'But he seemed to think the world was there for him to plunder. The lives he wrecked on the way – without compunction. Not a word of regret or compassion for anyone. He didn't even have the decency to try to cover his tracks properly.'

'He didn't even have the decency to be worried when we nabbed him,' Atherton added. 'Do you really think we can bring it home, guv? We've got some good evidence, but some is a bit dodgy.'

'We can make as good a case as we have for anything we've investigated,' Slider said. 'Now he's arrested, we can investigate without our hands tied. I'm confident we'll find more. The question is, as always—'

'Whether the CPS will go for it,' Atherton finished for him. 'All those charitable donations and good works. They might decide it's not in the public interest. There could even be political interference – I dare say he's made substantial donations to all the parties.'

'If he doesn't go down,' Slider said, 'you have to wonder what will happen if the lovely Edith outlives her purpose. Or if his sons turn out less manly than he thinks appropriate.'

'What if he gets into Parliament? Doesn't bear thinking about.'

Slider shook his head. 'That at least won't happen. Even if it never goes to trial, enough people will know about it. His career in that direction is over, at least.'

He thought about Kate, or Prudence, to give her her preferred name. Had she suspected something about her mother's death? Had Philip discussed it with her? At all events, she had been afraid enough of her father to hide herself away, to change her name, to retreat from the world as much as she could – avoiding having her photograph taken, avoiding talking to anyone, going anywhere, making friends. She had torn up and disposed of the evidence of her life even as she lived it, trying to leave no mark on the world, no sign of her existence. And it had worked, until a freak conjunction of chances had delivered her up to her father's attention.

And the worst irony was that he probably had not given her a single thought in all that time. His arrogance continually whitewashed his conscience, and his massive self-assurance had made it possible for him to entirely forget her, until seeing her again at the garden party caused him to remember what she knew, and realize that she might possibly be a threat. When Jason Shalcross had failed to find out what he wanted, he had impatiently taken the business into his own hands. If you want something done right, do it yourself.

Slider could imagine the telephone call, the charm and humility, the regret and the yearning, the wheedling request: 'I just want to see you, to apologize properly. I know it was unforgivable, but I need your forgiveness.' And then her weakness and meekness – combined, he suspected, with an exasperating stubbornness she got from him. And then, the lost temper, the shaking, the ferocious blow . . .

But no, he was forgetting – he had taken the blunt instrument with him. There would still have been the anger, but it would have been calculated, the little bit of self-justification saved for later, for the dark of night (*I lost my temper, I couldn't help it*), before it was all put away and forgotten. He had gone there knowing she could never entirely be trusted to be silent. Unless she was permanently silenced by him.

He hoped they could bring this one home. There were too many people who would haunt him if they didn't.

* * *

Slider and Atherton turned into the CID room, and the assembled troops broke into applause. Word of the interview had raced like heath fire ahead of them.

'Drinks tonight at the Boscombe?' somebody called. It was the custom to celebrate at the local when a case broke.

Slider smiled his appreciation and went through to his own room, started absently shuffling papers together. He felt hollow, like a scooped-out rind. He was emotionally drained by Armstrong's sheer awfulness.

Atherton followed him. 'Are we doing drinks tonight?' he asked.

'You'll have to host them,' Slider said. 'Or we can do it tomorrow. Sorry, I'm too beat. I'm going home to my wife and children.'